Intersections

Short Stories from

the Frederick Writers' Salon

ISBN: 1983982148
ISBN-13: 978-1983982149

DEDICATION

To our readers. As always.

CONTENTS

The Color of Love and Olive Trees – *Fabulist fiction*   9
by D. M. Domosea

Only Together – *Science fiction romance*   21
by Dr. Dale A. Grove

The Consolation of Voices – *Anthropomorphic fiction*   29
by Tisdale Flannery

Follow the Sound – *Young adult*   42
by Amanda Linehan

Occupational Karma – *Paranormal fantasy*   54
by A. Francis Raymond

Set in Stone – *Urban fantasy romance*   63
by Charmaine Weston

The Ocean – *Contemporary fiction*   76
by Edwin Stanfield

Ted and the Time Plumbers – *Science fiction*   96
by J. J. Maxwell

Paxton – *Contemporary fiction*   140
by James Allnutt

Trouble with Mountain Faeries – *Fantasy*   148
by Anna O'Keefe

Mr. McGrady's Haunted Driving School –   165
Speculative fiction
by Anna O'Brien

Portals – *Fabulist fiction*   178
by Suz Thackston

ACKNOWLEDGMENTS

A special thanks goes out to our artists, Kirby Evans and Claudia Tisdale, for their visions of Frederick and our stories combined, and to Josh Jones and the rest of the Frederick Writers' Salon—your critiques, revisions, and edits have polished this anthology to its true shine.

INTRODUCTION

Welcome to the second anthology produced by the Frederick Writers' Salon. In this edition, we collaborated in a way that we hope further fosters a sense of community pride in Frederick, Maryland. Among the creativity, spirit, and inclusion that Frederick proudly wears on its sleeve also lies a space for the small things that make Frederick uniquely Frederick. One of these aspects is First Saturday.

On the first Saturday of each month in downtown Frederick, shops are open late, musicians perform along the sidewalks, and art galleries reveal new exhibits. In this collection of short stories, authors created a shared universe—that of a First Saturday in May. On this particular day, the weather is pleasant until a late afternoon thunderstorm rolls through downtown. Characters in each story experience the sights and sounds along Market Street in a myriad of ways but each story is somehow connected to another. Whether it's a passing suspicion of someone seen in Baker Park or the minor chaos of a cat running through the streets, these stories weave between and through each other as a breeze might tousle your hair—sometimes barely noticed, sometimes undeniable.

As a group that comes together regularly to share our stories for critique, we felt compelled to create an anthology that captures the creative spirit of our host city. We hope you enjoy reading the stories in this anthology as much as we enjoyed writing them.

THE COLOR OF LOVE AND OLIVE TREES

BY D. M. DOMOSEA

I think Micah plans to ask me to marry him, and the prospect is already leaching the color from me.

I stuck out my tongue in the mirror last night after brushing my teeth, and I'm sure it was less meaty red than it had been that morning. He'd made several playful remarks throughout the day yesterday and teased me about our special dinner plans at Volt. Having spent a rather restless night in bed next to him, tossing and turning and knotting the sheets around my legs, yesterday turned into today, and now, that "special" dinner was tonight. I was certain he meant to propose.

In my opinion, marriage isn't necessarily a disastrous affair for those involved, but neither is it a happy and sacrosanct institution. It's just a thing you do that sucks the color from you and turns you gray. I know this to be true because my mother and father have existed in grayscale for as long as I can remember. My earliest memories of them are only vivid because of the festival of colors that always seemed to surround them. Every room they walked into, every street they strolled down, every venue they visited, thrived with color so bright it hurt your eyes. It wasn't until I was much older that I realized this was because they themselves were drab and plain.

Their skin, their hair, their eyes, all bleached to a dreary palette of leads and clays. Even the clothing they donned—shirts and pants that were bright and colorful only seconds before—drained of life, button by button, until every stitch of thread matched the washed-out hues of their bodies.

I asked my mother once why this was. She glared at my father—a hint of resentment almost igniting her eyes aflame—and said:

"Happiness and love give birth to color. But in your father's family, marriage saps joy away. Remember that, my darling, colorful son."

I was nine at the time and didn't truly understand her. I understand what she means now.

Micah and I have been together for nearly three years and have shared this apartment for the last sixteen months. Our lives are damn near perfect together, full of brightness and color. Why ruin it with the monochrome of marriage? I *like* colors. I like them on me. I like the hearty sandalwood of my skin that speaks of Middle Eastern heritage mixed with summers on Miami beaches. I love the sandy brown of my wavy hair, spiked through with a varietal of greens that grow from my head naturally. I love the hazel of my eyes that sparkle like a honeycomb drenched in sunlight. I'm not vain, but when you are raised by parents who look like they stepped right out of a 1950s TV set, you appreciate every speck of color on you.

A zombie of the early morning variety, I plod into our kitchen and pour a cup of coffee from the pot Micah brewed earlier. He left for work at the winery an hour ago. I, of course, have the day off, as the Frederick School for the Deaf doesn't hold classes on Saturdays. I grab the *News-Post* from the counter (Micah brought it up for me—he is always doing thoughtful things like that) and settle into my usual spot at the far end of the sofa. The air of distress around me must be as thick as the coffee when I brew it, because it takes Sarah only a few minutes to start in on me.

"You're going to need another carafe of Colombian."

I don't answer and instead stare into the steaming mug wrapped in my hands. It needs a dash more cream.

"You can try to ignore me, William, but it won't change the facts."

I glance sideways at the ceramic bust sitting on the end table and take an extra loud slurp of my coffee. My sister detests noisy eating and drinking, but she doesn't have hands to cover her ears.

"Being a brat won't fix it either, so you might as well tell me. We both know you will eventually."

I sigh. She's right. When I commissioned a bust be made from her ashes five years ago, she quickly took up residence within it. It's now a personal hell for both of us—she can't leave, and I can't, in good conscience, throw her away. Once, I thought about dropping her off at the local Goodwill. The very real possibility that a kid might push her off the shelf and shatter her—or worse, that she'd end up in the smoky, wood-paneled home of an old couple who spent their nights watching *Wheel of Fortune*—kept me from doing so. Now, she serves as my private confidant, but only because she hears everything anyway, whether I want her to or not.

I take another noisy slurp, to which she makes a distinct noise of disgust, before I speak.

"I think Micah is going to propose tonight."

"I see," Sarah says. "And you don't love him."

"No, you know I love him—"

"But you're scared of losing your color."

"Yes. You saw how it was for Mom and Dad. And for you, before Victor . . ." I stop. Sarah's failed marriage remains a sore topic of conversation. They'd each started out full of life and color, just like all happy newlyweds in love. It gave me hope. Perhaps it stopped with our generation. And then, the hues of their happiness began to dull, Victor's faster than Sarah's. His color didn't return until the night he drowned her in their marble-surround garden tub. He kept that color, too, until the day they put the needle in his skin.

Her color is forever now the ivory gray of the ash-ceramic mixture. She's still upset I didn't ask to have her painted before they glazed her, but I'm not a fan of painted ceramics. I think they look cheap and amateur, like a junior high art project.

Sarah huffs. "You're right. Don't do it. It will just lead to misery." She sounds bitter. My fault, of course, for bringing up Victor.

"It doesn't always, does it? I mean, not everyone in our family turns gray when they marry, right?"

"You've seen the photos," she snaps.

I have, but then black and white photos don't reveal much on that front. Even the ones shot after Kodachrome was created have faded to yellows and browns that are inscrutable. Extended family of my generation doesn't seem to care for digital photography at all. Hardly any photos make the rounds on social media, except those of the younger, unmarried nieces and nephews. Those are lush with color. Occasionally, you get an errant gray thumb in the corner, or the muted, static-like great aunt lolling in the background that someone forgot to hustle out of the picture before taking the shot.

"That doesn't mean anything," I say.

"Then why ask me if you don't like the answer?"

I don't bother pointing out that I didn't ask her. I never ask her. She just offers her opinion, unprovoked. And only ever to me. She never speaks to Micah, and only once or twice yelled at Bilbo, Micah's labradoodle, when he got a bit too slobbery in her face. He won't go in the living room now unless Micah's with him.

I take my mug to the kitchen and dump out the dredges of my coffee, rinse it, and place it next to Micah's cup to dry. I glance at the clock on the oven. Nine hours until our dinner reservations. Nine hours to come up with an answer. Nine hours before life will change. Whether my answer was yes or no, it will change.

I amble back to the bedroom to prep myself for the day. I have a few errands to run, and then an actual run on my to-do list. Bilbo lifts his head as I walk in. He's made himself comfortable on our bed, stretched out across the jumble of sheets and comforter, waylaying any plans I have to make the bed. His tongue, a ridiculous shade of pink, hangs from his mouth, creating a drool spot on the comforter. I scratch his ears. "Fine, but you explain to Micah why the bed's a mess when he gets home."

I open the closet and riffle through my wardrobe. Not by accident, I pull out the brightest clothes and toss them onto the bed next to Bilbo, who treats me to a one-eyebrow-raised gaze. A look that says orange and green polos won't solve my problems.

A half hour and four outfit changes later, I'm dressed—maybe even clashing a little—and head straight for the front door. I pause only long enough to pick up my phone, wallet, and keys before Sarah has a chance to be snarky about my clothing choice.

Outside the building, I pick my way through packed sidewalks and head up Market Street. First Saturday in May means there's no shortage of crowds in downtown Frederick. I squeeze past a young couple shimmying to a Shakira song rendered in slow guitar. The man's eyes are a striking blue, like the Mediterranean Sea at the height of summer. The stones on the woman's necklace—an ostentatious display of color and flash—twinkle at me in a cheeky dance of their own across the woman's rich, dark skin.

A voice inside me taunts their happiness: if she were like me, and if they were married, the stones would appear as dull river rocks on matte gray ropes, limping across a pallid complexion. And the man would look upon her with eyes as wan as laundry water.

No. Stop, I tell that bitter voice. The threat of my family's curse already taints the outlook of my own future; why should I let it discolor my perception of strangers' lives? Why not find some joy in the hues of their contentment? I cannot be this jaded before I've even made a decision on marriage, can I? Before I'm even proposed to?

I glance back at the couple as I continue up Market toward Third. The man dips his dance partner, leaning her backward until her dark hair brushes the sidewalk. The multi-tiered necklace glimmers against her throat. I make myself wish them a long, vibrant life together, and I try to mean it.

I reach my destination—Lebherz Oil and Vinegar Emporium (otherwise known as LOVE, if you can believe that)—just as a sudden, but thankfully short, rainstorm hits. Once inside, my thoughts pivot from red and yellow stones to green and gold oils.

Micah is a certified olive oil snob, having spent summers in Italy on his grandfather's olive farm. He often tells stories of how he and his cousins would climb the trees to pick and then pelt each other with half-eaten green and purple fruits, and then fall asleep in the branches, cradled and rocked as they might be in their mothers' arms. I like listening to his stories and imagining him as that child, running through sunny Italian fields, climbing into the arms of trees that loved him. When I hold Micah in my arms, I wish to be one of those trees. Trees in love don't lose their color.

LOVE carries a variety of oil Micah says is the only one in Frederick that is 100% olive-based, so he won't touch any others. One of the only fights we've ever had was over my decision to bring a bottle home from a supermarket when I'd missed LOVE closing by ten minutes. He immediately poured it down the sink. We sniped at each other for over an hour before he retired to bed early, and I was left eating a dry dinner by myself on the sofa, with Sarah whispering Micah's words back to me: "Better no oil than a bad oil, William. You should know that by now."

I browse through the selection of vats filled with flavored oils and vinegars, arrayed in a culinary menagerie for sophisticated shoppers and weekend tourists to sample. I try three new ones and four of my favorites. They dribble into the little white paper cups in various shades of brown, amber, and green—all the colors of my hair. In addition to our regular selection (for after that night, I made a concerted effort to own the oil snobbery and make it "ours"), I decide on a luscious chocolate balsamic for drenched strawberries.

The cashier, a young girl with a nose ring, black-rimmed glasses too big for her face, and a slight aura of boredom with the world, lifts her eyebrow at me as I approach the counter. I think her name is Cassie, but Micah could say for certain. He knows everyone on a first-name basis. It's one of the traits that first drew me to him—his outgoing sense of social confidence.

"Small bottle of the dark chocolate balsamic and a large of our usual."

As she hops off her stool to fill my order, I glance at the book she'd been reading. It's a manga comic, splayed open, the pages screaming with action and dialogue but no color. The text is in the original script.

"I didn't know you knew Japanese," I say.

"I don't," she says, as she returns to the counter to seal and package the bottles. "Why?"

"Oh, well, how do you understand the story, then?" I nod toward the book.

She glances at me, then down at the comic and frowns. "It's in English," she says, quite irritated. She turns on the hair dryer used to shrink the wraps around the bottle necks.

I peer down at it again. The words are all boxes and strokes, windows and katanas. "No, that's Japanese," I challenge her once the droning stops.

She sets down the dryer and pulls the book to her. "I've been reading these my whole life, Mr. Zeytoon, and I think I'd know English when I see it."

"So then what's that one about?" I ask.

She can see I'm not willing to let this go. She sighs, slides the book back over and rotates it so it's facing me. She points to an imposing character with large eyes and a top hat. "That's The Copper Doctor. He's a doctor for automatons and robots. And that's his true love, Mia. She's half robot, but she used to be all robot. The Copper Doctor gave her human body parts: an arm, both legs, eyes, and her heart."

Cassie leans over the comic to squint at the half-robot, half-girl, and I get a glimpse of the book through her glasses. The pages are filled with color, and the words appear in English.

"Why did he do that?" I ask, trying to pick out some of the words through her oversized glasses.

Cassie looks up at me. "Because in their world, humans can only be with other humans, or they lose their humanity. He made her part human so they can be together, but he shouldn't have done it. Her robot half still loves him, you see, but she won't forgive him for changing her, for changing who she is. Plus, her human half is still in love with someone else."

"That's depressing," I say.

She shrugs. "He should have left her the way she was."

"And lose his humanity?" I ask.

"To be with his true love? Maybe."

I fall into silence as she wraps the bottles, places them in a bag, and runs my card. I wish I hadn't asked her about the damn thing.

"Here." She shoves them across the counter at me and hops back onto the stool. "Tell Micah I said hello." I take a few steps then glance back to find she's resumed her reading. Behind her glasses, her eyes travel across the page from left to right, left to right, like a typewriter. I think I hear her read a few words out loud in English as the shop door closes behind me, but I'm not sure.

My next stop is the Common Market for organic strawberries. My stomach starts growling so I grab lunch at the deli. I settle in with my turkey and avocado wrap—which is always amazing—and think about that comic. Some things are worth losing part of yourself over—that was the message. Is Micah worth losing my color? Or, for all intents and purposes, my humanity? Is pledged love worth being a lesser version of myself? Micah seems to think so. At least, he's willing to risk his own color to be my husband, but will he regret it? Will he resent me, as the half-human, half-robot Mia resents The Copper Doctor?

With lunch now sitting uncomfortably in my stomach, thanks to the side order of anguish I added, I head over to the housewares shop down by the mall. I've been given the task on my day off of finding a wall frame for a photo Micah had printed and enlarged to an 11x13.

I remember the day we took that photo. We were hiking on Catoctin Mountain early last summer. We came to a large clearing at a bend in the trail and were caught in a sudden sun shower that consisted of large raindrops and small ladybugs. Warm curtains of rain woven in textiles of prismatic droplets and red wings covered us. The bugs sparkled as they rained down on us, as if each one had been made with speckled rubies by a cosmic jeweler who, in a fit of pique, sent them scattering from his workbench in a spray of scarlet.

Their tiny legs tickled our faces and arms, and we laughed at the sight of each other, soaked and pimpled with the ladybug rain. The miniature storm ended as quickly as it started, and Micah herded the insects left behind on our faces to form half-hearts—his cut from the left side of his face and mine from the right—so that, when we leaned in for a selfie, our faces pressed together formed a whole heart.

I hate the idea of being the type of couple who owns a selfie stick, but on this particular occasion, it was worth it. The picture was priceless. And vibrant. The royal blue of my shirt. The red-beaded bodies of the ladybug heart on our joined faces, stretched wide with grins of utter happiness. The warm cinnamon mocha of Micah's eyes that still gives me goosebumps each time he looks at me and tells me he loves me.

I bite my lower lip and turn back to the task at hand. Picture frames. I follow the store guides to the frame and gallery section and find an entire realm of rectangles in various styles, shades, and sizes. The selection is overwhelming, but I generally know what I'm after. Something simple and elegant, perhaps in brushed nickel or glossy black. Something that gives an air of being worth more than it costs.

I make my way over to an aisle that contains the "high-end" frames and stare heavy-hearted at the scene before me. Every frame here features the same stock photo: a bride and groom rushing down a set of stone steps, the unfocused faces of family and guests lining the way. A wedding scene. In black and white. God, how I hate cosmic messages.

I pick up an 8x10 frame—cherry wood and matte glass—and study the photo. The newlyweds, models who've likely never met before the photo shoot, appear happy. The groom looks straight into the camera. A large smile creases his youthful face. The bride is caught mid-laugh, her head canted in the direction of her new husband.

"But you're colorless now, so are you really as happy as you look?" I ask the picture.

The man's smile weakens a fraction as he winks at me. Complicit and flirtatious, yet ambiguous. The woman shrugs. A small movement, just enough to acknowledge the question, but not enough to provide a clear answer.

I harrumph and place the frame back on the shelf. I suppose obfuscation is what I get for talking to housewares. I'm no longer in the mood to pick out a frame and leave the store. To be honest, there isn't any point in buying one until I know how tonight plays out.

I wish I could jump forward in time to dinner, to watch Micah pop the question. Would he do it with the wine? Wait for dessert? Would he get down on one knee? Oh god, I hope he doesn't get down on one knee. Would the other diners ignore us, or would they clap in congratulations?

The answers to these questions don't matter, because in less than five hours, only one answer to one question would. And that answer is mine to make. I just wish to hell I knew what it's going to be. I glance at the sky before climbing into my Mini Cooper. Steel-colored clouds are gathering over Frederick. Rain is on the way.

Back at the apartment, I hurry past the living room before Sarah realizes it's me and not Micah and starts in on another frustrating lecture. Bilbo is still stretched out across the bed, his pink tongue hanging out as he snoozes. I doubt he's moved at all.

I change into my running gear as quickly as I can. I have every intention of getting this run in before one drop hits the pavement. I have a half marathon coming up, and any training day I don't run is another couple of seconds added to my finish time. I tug on my sneakers—neon yellow, orange, and blue things that always make me smile when I wear them. Micah calls them loud. I call them effective.

I look around for my iPod. It's on the table next to Sarah. Damn. I steel myself for what I know is coming as I go to retrieve it.

"So you're going for a run?"

"Yes," I say as I whisk the music player off the table.

"Do you hope to find your answers out there, in the park? Among the trees and the squirrels and the clouds? Do you think they'll tell you what to say? Do you think they'll tell you if marriage will make you happy or gray? They don't even know what marriage is."

"I just need to clear my head, Sarah. Running helps." I turn from her and head for the door.

"At least you have legs to run with. At least you have a choice," she calls after me as I shut the door. Her voice—which is all she has left to her, really—is full of spite and regret. I wonder, not for the first time, if demolishing the bust would cause her pain or set her free. I'm too scared for her to try it.

I push the down button and wait, bouncing on the balls of my feet, until the carriage arrives. The elevator door pops open. Mr. Turvy is there as usual, with his shoebox crammed full of vintage postcards at his side. It's a rare occasion we find the carriage without the old man. Micah has a theory that he rides the elevator all day because he's homeless, but I'm certain he lives on the fifth floor. More than likely he's just lonely and uses the elevator as his social medium. Some residents have resorted to using the stairs to avoid him, but I don't mind the stories he tells about the postcards.

"Lobby?" he signs. It's a formality. He knows I only have two destinations—home to our third floor apartment or out of the building. Yet he still feels it polite to ask.

"Yes, thank you," I sign in return.

He smiles—an expression that is more wrinkles and folds than lips and teeth—as he presses the lobby button. Mr. Turvy adopted me as his preferred elevator audience soon after Micah and I moved in, mostly because with me, he can sign his stories rather than speak them. He does both well, but his hands speak better than most people's mouths, in my opinion, and I'd told him as much. That earned me a friend for life.

The elevator carriage begins its slow descent as he reaches into the shoebox and pulls out a careworn card. The front features a bright red, double-decker bus. He examines it for a brief second before tucking it between the second and third buttons of his western-print shirt to free his hands.

"I ever tell you about my second cousin, Phyllis?"

I shake my head.

"One of Great Britain's first female double-decker bus drivers. She'd tear up and down the north countryside, taking villagers here and there, dodging cows and sheep." He removes the card from his shirt and hands it to me, beaming with pride. "Not a single accident in her entire driving history. Until some dang Yankee chap goes crossing the road in front of her."

"How awful," I offer.

He grimaces and places the card back into its spot in the shoebox. "Ah, she was all right. Just a bit of a dent on the fender, and they let her keep her license, seeing as how the Yank was looking the wrong way and stepped right out in front of her."

"Oh," I say.

"Speaking of, be careful out there crossing the streets tonight," he signs as the elevator jerks to a stop on the ground floor.

"I'm sticking to laps in the park today, but any particular reason I should watch the roads?" The door slides open. I step halfway out, holding the door in place with my back to continue the conversation in ASL.

"My grand-niece is taking driving lessons." He makes a terrified face then chuckles. "But seriously, I don't know whereabouts they're driving, but it could very well be downtown. I'm sure it's fine, but . . ."

"Who's she taking lessons with? Greg's?"

"No, some small, private company. Not much about them online. A bit mysterious."

"Small means more attention to the students. She'll probably be the better for it. See you in an hour or so, unless the rain comes hard." I unblock the doors and give him a short wave.

"I'll be out for the evening, but you kids have fun tonight. I hear it's going to be magical." The door slides shut on Mr. Turvy as he signs the last few letters. The gleeful expression on his face conveyed most of the meaning in the word.

Damn, again. Micah must have said something to him. No telling how many people he'd talked to about his plans to propose. He was a true social butterfly, the kind who knew no strangers.

My stomach knotted. Micah. He was so sure of my answer, so sure of my love for him, that he'd already told others about it. But love isn't the problem. It's the mundanity of marriage. The doldrums of domesticity. The license gets signed. The commitment becomes a contract. And then the happiness leaves, taking your color with it. That's not magical. That's marriage, at least to me, and Micah knows. Yet it means enough to him to still ask. I say yes and drown myself in a corporeal life of ash and slate. I say no, which *will* end our relationship, and wallow in loneliness more dreary and depressing than all the gray storm clouds in the heavens. Either path feels like a death sentence.

I make my way down Patrick Street to Baker Park under a sky much darker than it had been only an hour ago. Rain is imminent. I only hope the worst of it holds off until I finish my laps. I stretch and lunge as I scope out the foot traffic I might have to dodge. The park is empty. The walking path is usually packed with dog walkers, moms with strollers, and other runners. Today, I see only one couple.

The wind plays with the woman's loose brown hair, the long strands dancing like stubborn tree limbs in a maelstrom. The man wears his hair short in a military-style cut. He points to the bell tower. The woman hesitates for a moment before making a break for it, the man following close behind. I catch the warm gold of her wedding ring from here.

I take off down the south side of the park, past the playground and the carillon, and turn into the wind. Each strike of my feet on the asphalt path echoes an exclamation in my head.

It's not fair!

It's not the end of the world!

It's a punishment! (Though I don't know who in my family line might have sinned to a degree deserving this fate.)

It's not a big deal!

Over and over, my bright neon shoes slap down, one after the other, propelling me through the park. And over and over in my head, I fight with myself. I debate. I war. And still, no clear answers come. I run faster, faster, as though I might outrun the decision waiting to be made.

As though I might outrun the entire problem altogether, but it keeps pace with me. It stays beside me, needling me, begging me for an answer.

Large drops of water splotch the path around me. The rain is here.

I stop and rage into the storm. I scream with all the power in my lungs, with all the breath I can shove from my throat.

"What do I want? What should I say?"

I call out again and again to the copse of trees along the creek, for they are the only things still here in this weather listening to my cries. The uppermost branches of the largest tree shift and move, the wind shaping them into words to answer my question.

"YOU KNOW."

I blink and wipe the rain from my eyes. The wind shifts, erasing the words.

"No, I don't. I don't know. Tell me what to do," I sob. The water on my face is no longer just rain.

Again, the wind plays in the trees, like a puppeteer manipulating a marionette, and forms the words, "YOU DO."

I break down and cry, my entire body soaked by rain and wracked with misery. I stand in the grass before the tree, my hands stretched out, beseeching. "Please. Please. Just tell me what to say tonight."

The storm answers with a crack of thunder and the sharp scent of ozone, as lightning strikes my head and races through my body. A million tiny needles prick my flesh, like a mass of ladybug legs tickling across my skin. Like the goosebumps I still get when Micah looks into my eyes and tells me he loves me. And it's then that I know.

I know.

I know, but I can't answer. My legs are now rooted to the ground. My skin is a rough, knotted bark. My arms remain stretched to the sky, covered in verdant green leaves that move like waves in a windstorm. Green and purple fruits spring from my fingertips.

I can't answer, but at last, I know.

Eleven Months Later

A young man strolls down the park path, a dog with chocolate wavy fur and a ridiculous pink tongue trotting beside him. It's the first clear day of spring. The first time he's been to the park since before last summer. He settles in the grass beneath a tree and plays with the dog. He starts with a game of keep-away, teasing the dog with an orange neon chew toy, and then throwing it several times for the dog to retrieve. After the fifth time, the dog lies down at the man's side and busies itself with tearing into the rope toy.

The man lays back and stares up at the branches, marveling at the olives that decorate the tree like glittering stones in a crown. He wonders what sort of whimsical person plants an olive tree in the middle of a public park.

"Oh William, I miss you," he says. "And I still love you, but I need to let you go now. I just wanted to come out here and say that, whatever happened, wherever you are, I miss you." He closes his eyes, eyes the color of warm, spiced mocha. He lies silent, breathing in the smell of the olive tree, inhaling the rich pungent perfume of the ripe fruit.

After several minutes, he stands up and clicks his tongue at the dog, which brings the now-soggy chew toy over to him. The man laughs and rubs the dog's head. He takes a few steps, then stops and turns back to face the tree. He thinks about summer days, cradled in branches of trees like this one. He thinks of mock battles with his cousins, with partially-bitten olives as weapons. And he thinks of the stories he'd share about those days to a man he loved. A man with hair streaked the color of olive tree leaves.

"I just wish I knew . . . if I'd been able to propose to you, the night you disappeared, would you have said yes?"

The top-most branches rustle and move, as if a breeze dances through the emerald leaves, but the air is still that day. They bend and curl and twist, until shapes appear. Shapes that are letters. Letters that form a word.

A word that says "YES."

ONLY TOGETHER

BY DR. DALE A. GROVE

Rain washed the chalk artwork clean from the sidewalks and pulled at my aching heart. I miserably stared out my top floor window into the streets of Frederick with desperation sitting beside me serving as my only companion. Raindrops slid down my windowpanes as tears streamed from my eyes.

I had failed. Not once, not twice, but numerous times to finish my love's mission: bring together two people who would bear a child that would change everything. My reflection was that of a late middle-aged man; at least that's how I appeared now. It hid my true Venitian form of fiery red hair, red eyes, and pale-white skin on a humanoid physique.

Sure, Venitians had the power to fire small flame balls from their eyes at will, but what good did that do in a diplomatic mission that could lead to the rise of the Silver Wolf? Regnus security had knocked out Venitian time travel, particularly travel that altered their technological timeline. I suppose they believed that if I could not refuel my hypersource—a hyper-dimensional device that enabled travel to alternative multiverses by unfurling higher dimensions, not to mention time travel—that this mission was doomed. Our hypersources took the form of reading glasses with small dials on either side of the main frames. By turning the dials and employing the mind link option, travel to anywhere and anywhen was possible, provided the critical energy threshold wasn't exceeded.

Regnus believed Alpha and I were of little consequence now, unable to affect their cherished technological history. Who could blame them? The odds of succeeding were now one in a million, too low to waste their precious manpower. They positioned their resources in other areas across time to ensure that no other civilization overturned them. Although Venitian representatives served in the multiverse's governing body, only Regnus officials occupied the prominent roles.

A sudden lightning strike at Carroll Creek Linear Park sent shivers down my spine, breaking my train of thought. I looked out from my FSK apartment into the distance, desperate to see any sign of hope. There in the distance stood a beautiful olive tree that I had never noticed before. It swayed and weathered the oncoming storm just as I had. Was this a harbinger of good fortune or a sign that heaven waited for me? I closed my watery eyes and decided that the olive tree brought me strength.

Alpha, my fiancée, believed in this mission. She believed in the Silver Legend so strongly that she risked it all, perishing when her hypersource failed in her final jump. My only hope of seeing her again is to complete her mission. By changing history, the amount of historical energy required to make her final jump would be diminished, and she may make it. To be honest, I still don't believe in the legend, but I do believe in my Alpha. My name is Beta.

I glanced down at my remaining hypersource energy. There was just enough power for one last time jump and to conceal my true form. I had one last chance to reunite Samantha Williams and Peter Sterling.

She was a beautiful, headstrong young woman with a passion for the arts; he was a handsome, yet socially inept, young medical doctor. The power requirements needed to separate Samantha and Peter prior to their argument were impossible now. I had worked with Peter on multiple occasions, but he was a poor listener, poor orator, and poor learner who constantly tripped over the lessons that I had provided. Hopeless. This time I decided to interact with Samantha, to reason with her, to get her to understand Peter better. If I failed, I would probably meet the same fate as my Alpha. If there was a heaven, that's where we'd meet again. At least my final failure would end my constant misery.

Sam and Peter's argument resonated through my mind, a constant pinprick that poked my memories with every breath I took.

~~~

During a Saturday night out in Frederick, Peter invited Samantha to Vini Culture where they sampled more than a few select wines. They had gone out on a dozen dates and had drawn close after spending several nights together. He made her laugh several times that evening, and she appeared to be enjoying their conversation.

"So, Sam, what's your dream? What would you do if nothing held you back?" Peter swirled his wineglass to aerate his fourth glass of Chilean red wine.

Sam played with her long brown hair between her fingers. She set her glass down with a twinkle in her eye. "I want to become a famous author like my father. I want to travel the world and write about famous works of art."

The wine affected Peter's judgment. His poor opinion of art majors came to the surface when he blurted out, "Are you kidding? There's no money in that. Do you have a fallback plan in case it doesn't work out?"

Sam shook her head. "I don't care about money. I want to do something that I love, not be tied to a job that feels like I'm putting in time."

"How will you support yourself? Nearly everyone who becomes an artist or writer lives off of relatives or the government, even if you do improve your skills. I don't want to be the sole financial provider in a long-term relationship."

The light smile on Sam's face faded as she glared at Peter. "Are you telling me that I'm not any good? Is that what you're saying?" A frown now clung to Sam's face. She had heard this same tired speech from many people before, but she certainly didn't want to hear it coming from her boyfriend.

"Of course not, Sam. It's just . . . don't put all your eggs into one basket."

Sam let out an extended sigh and wrapped a light sweater around herself.

Peter threw in, "Some role model your father was. He could have been one of the greats, but he traded it all away. He should have taught you better."

With that, Sam grabbed her wine glass and flung its contents at Peter. Sam's lips trembled as distinct lines showed across her forehead. "I'm sick and tired of other people's poor opinions of my father. He put everything aside to care for my sick mom and me. Who the hell are you to judge him?" A single tear fell from her eye as she rose. Sam grabbed her purse and umbrella.

With wine dripping from his hair, Peter shifted in his seat, realizing he had said something wrong, terribly wrong.

Sam headed for the exit as Peter gave chase.

Outside, large raindrops began to fall.

"I'm sorry, Sam. I didn't realize that this meant that much to you." Peter had no idea that he'd broached two sensitive subjects.

Sam raised her umbrella and kept going.

When Sam ignored him, Peter stood in her path.

"Out of my way!" Sam screamed in a hurt voice.

"Would it help if I told you that I love you? I said those words without thinking. I'm sorry." Rain pummeled Peter's clothing, soaking him through and through. His hair became disheveled as a passing wind whipped it into the rain, transforming Peter's appearance into that of a mere troll.

"Leave me alone. Just when I think we had a chance, you say something that hurt me to the bone." Tears scoured Sam's makeup.

Peter looked down. "I'm a jerk. I didn't mean it."

Sam paused before answering, "Don't ever call me again, asshole."

Peter stepped aside, glanced at the ground, and muttered, "I'm sorry. I don't deserve you." It wasn't enough to assuage his vicious tongue slip from earlier. Slumping forward, he placed his hands in his pockets and made his way back to Vini Culture to pay the bill. Along the way back, Peter passed a middle-aged man and did a double take as if he'd seen the man before. Beta noticed Peter's reaction, and he assumed it was a residual reality hiccup. Somehow part of a previous quantum reality had clung within Peter's memories. It didn't matter. Beta already had made his final time jump, draining his hypersource to dangerously low levels.

~~~

Samantha boarded a bus, and Beta quickly climbed on before the driver pulled away. She sat in a back seat, quietly weeping. There were hardly any passengers on the bus, so Beta changed his form to resemble, but not perfectly match, Sam's father, as he took a seat in front of her. The appearance shift drained Beta's hypersource to the critical mark as he placed his hypersource glasses into his shirt pocket. Her tears fell to the floor in rhythm with the storm. Beta's stomach clenched as he made his move. He handed a handkerchief to Sam with the words, "What's troubling you?"

Sam noticed Beta's appearance, squinted to make sure it wasn't her father, and wiped her eyes. Deciding whether she would accept the handkerchief, which was lined with a powerful pheromone extract for safety's sake, she took in a deep sigh before accepting it and answering. "My ex-boyfriend ruined everything." Sam dried her eyes and blew her nose. "Oh, sorry, do you want this back?"

Beta's eyebrow rose before turning sideways. "Keep it. I've got plenty more. If you don't mind my asking, what did he do that was so terrible? I'm a good listener if you want to vent."

Sam held the handkerchief with her right hand. "He doesn't understand me. He mocked my dreams and ridiculed my father. We were getting close until . . ." She blew her nose into the handkerchief, releasing oodles of noodles.

"I can't keep this, here." Sam handed the used handkerchief back to Beta.

Gingerly picking up the dirty handkerchief from its corners and being careful not to expose the disgust in his eyes, Beta's nose rose slightly, and his lips bent downwards as he deposited it into his coat's pocket. *I'm certainly not doing laundry tonight no matter how this turns out.*

Beta patted her hand. "People sometimes say and do the wrong things without bad intentions in their hearts. We can't all choose our words carefully, Sam." *Oh shit. Why did I say her name?*

Sam straightened. "Do I know you?"

A long sigh left Beta before he gulped. Since his next jump would undoubtedly bring on his own death, he had to decide whether he would take that jump or level with her by revealing his alien appearance. If he chose to expose his true form, Beta would spend the remainder of his life in the shadows of this world. If he dyed his hair and wore contacts, he may pass as an albino. "Please don't let my appearance scare you." Beta removed the hypersource from his shirt pocket and turned it off, revealing his white-pale skin, red eyes, and fiery red hair.

Gasping, Sam turned and stood to leave, but Beta reached out and firmly grabbed her arm. Sam struggled but couldn't free herself. She considered screaming, but something in Beta's eyes comforted her. Either that or the handkerchief's sedative effects kicked in.

"Let me finish what I have to say, and then I'll let you go. You'll never have to see me again. I promise." Beta raised his raincoat over his hair to avoid alarming the few other passengers that sat ahead of him. He would avoid looking at others on his way out and try to conceal his face.

"What are you, and why are you here?"

"I shouldn't do this. It breaks every rule to reveal ourselves, but my name is Beta. I was sent here to reunite you and Peter." *If I fail now, at least I gave it my best shot.* Beta released his grip.

"I don't understand. Why does this matter to you?" Sam rubbed her arm where Beta had held it.

"My fiancée, Alpha, believed in the Silver Legend. She thought your future child, Wolfe Sterling, was the best chance of getting the multiverse back on track again. Alpha believed it so strongly that she sacrificed herself over it. Unless you get back together with Peter in the next few hours, her life will extinguish. To be honest, I never believed in the Silver entity saga. How could an earth-bound Silver entity change the multiverse that much? Your kind is constantly warring and battling each other to the point that human extinction is nearly guaranteed over the long run. I just want to see my Alpha one last time before I pass." Air escaped from Beta's lungs. "I've said enough. I'm sorry if I've troubled you."

The bus's brakes squealed as Beta rose. The abject horror of the situation settled in upon him as shudders ran up and down his spine. *It was over. Alpha was destined to die, and there was nothing I could do about it. This world would follow in due course.*

"Wait." Sam tugged on the back of Beta's raincoat. "Why did you say my name, Beta?"

Beta shrugged as he looked to the bus's ceiling. "I'm like your Peter. No matter how hard I try, sometimes the wrong words escape from my mouth. No matter how many time jumps that I've made, I can't undo my past mistakes. I can't take back the words that I told Alpha before she perished. She'll never know how deeply I loved her." A loud squeal from the bus's brakes filled the air again. "I've said enough. You'll either give Peter a second chance or you won't. I can only promise you what the legend says: only together will you grow stronger."

"I need some time to think about this. You're asking a lot of me."

~~~

A short time later, Samantha's muscles tensed as she stood outside of Peter's apartment. She was about to knock on his door when a young woman materialized beside her, causing Samantha to step back.

"What the . . . where did you come from?"

"Your decision to give Peter a second chance has altered this world's reality stream. Everything is as it should be and will be." The young woman nodded approvingly.

"Is that you, Beta?"

"How do you know that name?" Alpha tilted her head to one side. Her version of history seemed flawed now.

"Beta is the one who talked me into this. I assumed that you took the form of a woman this time." Sam shrugged and smiled.

Alpha lightly struck the right side of her own face with an open hand. Beta's alternative reality wave had not caught up to her yet due to her hypersource's time mitigation effects. The new reality wave would not affect Alpha's timeline for a few hours more. "That idiot! He's not supposed to reveal his true form. I'm going to have to tell the council of his indiscretions." Alpha folded her arms.

"Please don't. It was his sincerity that changed my mind. He thinks that he's failed you."

Alpha paused. "Men can be so stupid sometimes."

"I agree. Let me set things straight with Peter. You should do the same with Beta."

Alpha nodded. Before she departed, she provided some advice to Sam. "Have you ever visited Toledo, Ohio? There's a lovely museum there that could use someone like you. It won't pay much, but it will be enough for you to live your dreams with Peter and Wolfe."

~~~

Peter answered his door after several loud knocks reverberated around his apartment. Residual tear lines stained his face as a smile cracked across his lips. "It's you. I thought I'd never see you again."

"Let's try this again. This time, I want you to be more supportive." Sam's arms remained interlocked.

Peter went to Sam and wrapped his arms around her body. "I'll never let you go again. Together?"

Sam undid her arms and hugged him back as she whispered, "Only together."

Neither one of them knew why the phrase affected them so deeply. It was as if they dreamt an alternative reality upon uttering it, like this destiny was meant to be.

They hugged each other until Peter's large Saint Bernard ran them over, knocking them to the carpeted floor. With his dog licking Sam's face, she burst out laughing. Deep in her heart, Sam realized that she had found her true love.

~~~

The evening's lightning storm tormented me. My ultimate failure had come. I could either wait until the world ended in a few decades when Earth's nuclear arsenals were unleashed, or I could take my life in the here and now. I found the rope that I had hidden in the closet and tied a noose. When I finished the last wrap, I realized that my heart wasn't in it. I was too much of a coward to even do this correctly. My stomach remained tied in knots as I saw a reflection of myself in the mirror. An unfamiliar, broken, middle-aged Venitian stared back.

No, stop being so weak. This was not my future. This was not how things were supposed to turn out. Anger filled my soul when I realized how foolish and selfish I had become. With a deep breath, I used my fiery, red eyes to burn away the noose. Moments later, I opened the windows to avoid setting off the smoke detector. This world needed help, even if it came in the form of me. Maybe I could find other ways to nurture this world's civilization.

Loud knocks broke my concentration. I opened the door, and Alpha stood on the other side. My heart leapt into my throat. "Alpha." I rushed to her and wrapped my arms around her. My dreams had come true as warmth filled my empty soul.

We held each other until Alpha explained what had happened. "You did it, Beta. You lowered the power threshold enough so I could make the final jump. I always said you were stronger than you thought. Thanks for saving me." Alpha hugged me again and then took a good look at me as her hug softened. She bit her lip as we separated moments before a third Venitian materialized.

"Beta, your mission was successful," the intruder said, "however, council has ruled that you must remain here to repair your timeline tampering. Additional fixes may be required. Alpha, you're free to return home whenever you wish." The security officer handed two fresh hypersource glasses to Alpha and me, nodded, and vanished after powering up his own hypersource. Our visitor had no idea of the vast reality wave that had swept through the rest of the multiverse due to the birth of the silver entities that would follow.

"You should go home, Alpha. I'm too old for you now. All I wanted to do over the past thirty years was to see you again, to feel your body pressed against mine, to regain hope. I have that and much more now."

"But you'd be alone. What kind of life is that?" Alpha reached out and put her hand on my face.

I turned from her. "It's for the best. I've broken every rule to bring you back. Please leave me."

With tears in her eyes, Alpha hugged me from behind. "I promise that I'll peek in on you. When you finish your assignment, please come home." Alpha paused. "I need to visit my family before they don't recognize me."

"I understand, more than you know." I turned, held Alpha's hand, and kissed it as she jumped home with tears streaming down her face.

I let out a long sigh and reasoned with myself that it was for the best. A small portion of my fresh hypersource's power was used to change into my familiar human façade. I sat in a comfortable chair in my humble apartment where I picked up the *Frederick News Post*. Now that I was free to make whatever changes were required, I scanned the newspaper for ways to improve the local community. I would start small. I spotted a march against cancer and circled it with a pen when suddenly, an older Alpha materialized before me. My breath escaped me.

"I can't let you go. Peter and Sam are not the only ones who will give birth to a Silver entity. Our daughter will become known as Melek, the Silver entity from Venitia." Alpha's wrinkled eyes beamed.

My heart sunk. "What did you do to yourself? I know that you believe in these legends, but you've thrown your life away. Why?"

"Since you don't believe in the legend, let me explain this another way. I want to be with the man that sacrificed his entire life to bring me back. Time spent with you means more to me than physical years. I love you, Beta. Together?"

I rushed forward and hugged my wife-to-be. "Only together."

THE CONSOLATION OF VOICES

BY TISDALE FLANNERY

The mouse tail twirled, a pelted worm dangling from the crack in the bricks. Syd watched the bait. He sat on his haunches, his own tail softly scraping cement behind the ceramic planter. He resisted the temptation to strike. If he pounced now, then quick as a knock, the mouse would pull in his tail, and Syd would have lost his chance to eat that night.

How long before the mouse grew too bold for safety? A cat can wait, but hunger is hard. Then from behind Syd came tiny foot taps, a hair brushing the metal bar of the grate—it was a second mouse, apparently unaware of the danger. The teaser in the stair opened his mouth to warn his friend. Now it was time. Syd set his hunger free. He pounced on the newcomer, a leopard on the hare, and the sweet taste of blood was in his mouth. He ate with abandon.

29

That was his mistake.

A squeak behind him made him pause in his devouring, a thread of intestine hanging from his teeth. Pain, sudden, hit his right haunch. Syd spun. The first mouse had jumped from the crack in the steps to Syd's hip, bitten him, and now clung to his fur. It lifted its head and cried out something in mousish, which Syd sometimes understood; the sense was, *Avenge, avenge the hero, Gilgamouse is fallen and lays upon the ground in seven pieces! Humbaba the Great has pierced him with curved claw, and we must avenge! Kill Humbaba!*

The mouse ran up Syd's spine. It bit him again, between the blades of his shoulders. Syd cried out. He couldn't help it; it hurt. He rolled on the rough ground. The mouse was dislodged, and Syd pinned him with his left paw. He looked into the tiny black button eye, all the rest of the mouse a quivering morsel.

Why did you do that? Syd asked.

Gilgamouse is fallen and lays upon the ground in seven pieces! Nay, in six pieces, Gilgamouse lays upon the ground. Gilgamouse lays upon the ground in six pieces, and a seventh in your belly!

Both Syd and the mouse looked over to where the half-eaten friend stained the concrete.

Make that five, said the mouse. *Gilgamouse is fallen! He lays upon the ground in five pieces, and two in your belly . . .* He went on; Syd stopped listening.

Several parts of Syd now fought for his attention. One, he was still ravenous; the half mouse he had eaten was nowhere near enough to satisfy the beast of hunger, even if it was the head. This, his hunger, rejoiced at having scored a second course. Two, he was angry. To bite an attacking cat was an understandable action from prey. From the friend of prey, it was less so, though still within the bounds of reasonable prey behavior. But to run out from a hiding place where one had been taunting a predator, to shout about vengeance, to actually leap up on his back? And then bite him? Twice? It broke all rules of sense, and Syd's feline pride demanded retribution. Three, the pain took over a large part of his thinking. A mouse does not have the courtesy to keep his teeth needle-sharp and so a mouse's bite wounds flesh and nerve, much more than the bite of a cat. This pain made it difficult to reason properly and compounded Syd's anger, almost to the point of irrationality. He watched the mouse writhe under his paw, singing on about numbers and body parts.

I should eat you, Syd said to the mouse.

The mouse raised his voice further, ready to be the noble sacrifice, the Enkidu, the true friend, whose death an act of beauty lived forever in the songs, and so on.

Syd gently applied pressure with his paw until the mouse's voice was cut off.

But I'm not going to. Do you know why?

The mouse shook its tiny head, as much as it was able.

Syd lifted his paw, gently, pulling the needles of his claws out from this mouse's body. *I am not going to eat you, or even kill you,* he said, *because it breaks the Laws.* He shook himself and sat up. The mouse, bewildered now, looked at Syd and blinked. *Go on,* said Syd, and the tiny creature trundled off into the gutter.

Syd stretched to try to ease the pain between his shoulder blades. That bite was worse than the one on his haunch; the emboldened mouse must have found energy from his first success. The pain wasn't going anywhere. The best Syd could do was apply himself to finishing his meal. He did so and walked in pain back to his Crypt.

For five months now, Syd lived on the street, by choice at first, but then because he couldn't remember how to get home. In the cold winter he'd yowled, late, hoping that the silence of the city would allow his beloved mistress to hear him. He'd cried out from the empty streets. He'd watched his breath freeze into little pointless clouds. Night after night he looked, and found nothing, and grew hungrier, until one shivering snowbank day he asked himself, what could he do to survive? What had been successful, so far, in living this life? And all that he had learned, in his five years of domestic, sheltered life, he conscripted to the needs of a bigger reality: he was on his own.

His hunger then was a silent rat in his belly, working bites from the pantry inside. His hunger was his teacher. Just as the rats of All Saints Street explained, later, the first time he trespassed into their territory, drawn down by the smells of the barbecue there. *You gotta listen to that hunger, and learn The Laws,* they'd said, lounging in the darkness of the dumpster on black plastic trash bags, picking their teeth with chicken bones. *The Cat Laws. You're new, you don't know 'em. Learn the Laws, my friend. Now get lost,* and they'd broken into a rude song about cats getting buggered when they go to the vet.

But the rats were wrong about one thing—Syd knew a few of the Laws already. A left turn into shadows on the corner of the broken sidewalk; a pause under the picnic tables, until the pause was done; a day-long stare at the One True Brick on the seventh Brick Day of the era; a polite startle at nothing in the place where a ghost once dissolved—these made the difference between eight remaining lives and none. In the case of the second mouse, an object of prey with which one has had discourse must be set free for no less than a cycle of the Moon.

And yet these were only the first level of Inanna's Laws.

Inanna, barefoot protector of the stores of grain, Goddess of abundance in love and harvest, called all cats to her service in the first days of human cities. She who became Bast, who became Aphrodite and Venus, Lakshmi, and Akna across the ocean, who blessed humanity wherever they set their hands to turn seeds to gold—she drew cats under her protection, promising to permit them to retain their titles as Lords of Wild Things while still living in the storehouses, streets, and catacombs of men. In return, they must follow her Laws. But cats dwelling in

31

houses now hardly remembered the first level, for they had forgotten their pride, relied on the protection of men, and grown soft.

It was only by his philosophical nature that Syd saved himself and dedicated himself to learning her Laws. They'd first come by patient study, of dust motes in the sunbeams. He learned them because it was his nature, a kind of play. Now he knew that what was play when safety was certain was necessity in the world of danger.

Since he had accepted life on the street, Syd applied all of his skill to learning the second level, which involved a more fundamental understanding of the world around him. For instance, water is sacred, for healing and anointing, not for the profane lapping and slopping that dogs do. Birds are wicked, and must be kept in line through rigorous hunting. Crypts are Art, the pinnacle of cat creation, but Crypts can only be created properly within an elaborate framework of rules.

A cat indoors may have many Crypts, some even without walls. Indoors, there is no requirement about how these boxes are claimed. One may truly be the coat of a guest smelling of inexplicable mystery, or the crevice between loving masters' bed pillows, and another may be the angle made by two walls and a memory. But a cat outside keeps one Crypt, only one, and if another must be found, then sacrifices must be made. Syd's Crypt was hard-won, the southwest corner of a rarely-used shed, and the only way in was to scrape through rough boards, past evil-smelling buckets and bottles, to a space behind paint cans. It kept him warm. Now, in the comfortable May pre-dawn chill, it gave him some safety.

And yet he wasn't secure in his safety. There were other Laws he had broken, simply from ignorance. This pain between his shoulders, sometime before the dawn—was it enough of a sacrifice for his transgressions? He curled up and tried to sleep. He dreamt of fire. A distant fire, at first, a chanting by humans with torches and spears; he was a panther, and the humans sought him from beneath the tree boughs. He was safe. They could not see him in the dark. But they brought with them into the jungle a Giant of men, tall and black, with oiled hair and breastplate. *Humbaba!* cried the men, and the giant was up at his level in the tree tops, looking into Syd's eye with a round black button for his own. The Giant raised his arm. The spear reflected shards of fire. It drove straight down into Syd's back. Pain arched his spine. The torch spread fire between his shoulder blades, and the dream bled into reality. Syd woke to a desiccated awareness. The mouse-bite infection festered.

~~~

There was only one thing to do. If he were with his mistress, she would take care of him; she would bring him to the healer and make him well. But he was alone. He needed to find his way to the healing waters

32

of the canal. He squeezed out from behind the paint cans. Already each step with his front paws felt tight, restricted. He pressed himself through the hole in the wall out into the alleyway. It was still dark but with a settling in the air, a feeling of satiation from the night, ready to yield.

A car went by, slowing ever so slightly as it passed him. The wind and noise reminded him of another world. *The canal*, he told himself, and turned south.

Pumpkin's basement window was closed. When Pumpkin's second-favorite masters were home, they left the basement window open for him to come and go as he pleased. That was how Syd and Pumpkin met. It was almost five years ago, when Syd was a tiny kitten and knew absolutely nothing about the outside world. His mistress left him alone for the day, and he felt hungry and scared, so he sat by the window and watched for her. An enormously fat orange cat suddenly filled the lower half of the glass. It stared at Syd with green eyes, head cocked to the side. It hissed. Syd hissed back. That was the start of a great friendship. Since then, Pumpkin showed up at irregular intervals, depending on the vagaries of the humans who occupied his basement. Pumpkin was past caring about Laws. He knew of them but found them distasteful, from long habit of pleasing humans. He was hardly a cat, but that didn't bother Syd; Syd's philosophical nature embraced the challenge of conflicting ideas in friendship. Pumpkin belonged off and on to a group of half-feral cats who, like himself, lived outside Inanna's Laws. They prowled the Third Street Cemetery and called themselves the Forsaken. Neither they nor Pumpkin could help Syd with this infection, but a little friendship—and encouragement—would have felt nice, and Syd passed the closed and darkened basement window with regret.

He was at the canal without realizing how he got there, exactly. The water reflected the starless blue of the pre-dawn sky. How was he to get that water up to the infection on his back? He wasn't sure. He couldn't dive in; he might not have the strength to climb out. He lay down on the smooth gray concrete lip and stared into the water.

A bright orange koi, grandchild of the Sun, flashed around his reflection. It bubbled then surfaced. At that moment, something came from behind Syd with a soundless wash of air, swept over him in total disregard, and seized the seraphic koi with the tongs of its beak. The eyes of the koi went wide. Its mouth gaped. The bird flapped, struggling to keep its meal. The koi was huge, perfect. The night heron was determined. It turned, mid-flight, and brought the fish to the concrete three feet away from Syd. Straps on an executioner's table, its talons held the fish flat to the ground. Yellow legs rose to a belly and breast as white as death, capped by a black-masked head.

CAWP! The night heron shouted its victory, its voice as coarse as its manners, while the koi beneath faced death with grace and courage. The heron turned its head to eye the best place from which to tear the delicate flesh. It opened its beak slightly and drew back to strike.

33

Without pause, Syd sprung past the pain in his back and bowled the heron off the koi. A great whirl of feathers and beating wings surrounded him. Syd fought off the buffeting blows and swiped with claws fully extended. The bird aimed the spear of its beak at him, which he dodged, in time to see the koi flopping, struggling for air, begging for help. The heron reared back to spear him again. The koi gasped. Syd rolled, sweeping the koi with his tail. The bird's beak struck stone. The koi flopped once more, then splashed into the water. Syd sat up, facing the heron.

It's you and me now, he said. He bared his teeth.

Nah, said the heron. *Just you*. It backed up three long steps, massaged the air with wide tapered wings, and lifted its feathered body up into the night.

The blue light before dawn seeped into all the shadows, and hosts of songbirds filled the air with their battle cries. In the canal, the koi swirled, dancing her gratitude. The beauty of her movement was Syd's reward. She saw him watching and came to the surface to bubble once more.

You are an odd one, Syd, she said.

Syd turned his head. *How do you know my name?*

The water effervesced. *All knowledge is free for the taking, when it is ripe.* She gave Syd an image of the Sun feeding the earth in all its particulars, from the lilies of the field to the multitude of waves in the ocean to the crystalline spires of skyscrapers. *But as I said, you are an odd one. You have broken a Law, simply because you love beauty.*

It was true. Law: A Cat must never interfere with the hunting of another predator, for Cats are to be the models of predatory behavior, above reproach. Syd, sick, had probably ruined his last hope of survival when he interfered with the heron's hunt.

You may die because of this, because of me, said the koi. *And so, Syd, I give you a gift.*

A gift? Could she heal him? That would be all he needed, and he would be careful to follow all Laws from here forward.

No, said the koi. *That is not mine to give.* She started to swim away. *What is mine to give, is*—she swam beneath a lily pad, which muffled her voice so he could barely hear it—*a prophecy.* Then she disappeared.

Syd waited on the concrete lip. The light grew, from blue to white. The sounds of cars multiplied, the armies of birds wore out their song, but from the waters, no prophecy came. *Perhaps I simply don't know how to listen for it*, he thought. He struggled to his feet. He never had managed to get the waters to his back. The idea of getting into the canal now filled him with terror. If he went down under the water, he would never have the strength to climb back up, and he would drown there. His body would become part of the water. He would never escape death itself. He would never reach the lands of the Anointed.

There was, however, one other place he could go for help, a place

34

that he had been to before and received wisdom. He forced himself to take the first steps east, beside the canal. Lilies and lotuses graced the surface of the water. Their shades of pink and white and yellow were little gifts unto themselves. As Syd passed the first lotus, rising on a thin brown stilt, it moved, slightly. Was the koi beneath? But no, it was not the base that was moving, just the white petals, opening. They eased outward, trembling, one by one. Syd stopped where he was. When the flower sat fully spread out upon its leaves, it stretched once, and from within, a single voice—that of the koi—sang, *Beware*.

Was that the prophecy? That was all it said: beware. Beware what? He was in danger already. The sun was bright and painful. A human voice, too close, said the word *cat*. It was time to go. The next lotus was already opening. *Beware*, came the voice from within, and across the canal, a pink-tipped white lily opened and let out its word, the same one, again. *Beware*. Behind him, a lily sang. They set him on edge and filled his mind with pictures of danger. They were all opening, now, all singing in dysrhythmia. There was nowhere to go but forward. *Beware, Syd. Beware*.

He walked this gantlet of Cassandras, this symphony of tolling, and could think of nothing but their words. Under the long bridge, the weight of cars above him, to the steps that would take him to the top of the bridge, across it, and to All Saints Street, leaving the healing waters, Syd forced himself forward. Every step said *Beware*. When he reached the steps, a yellow cluster of lilies particularly close to the concrete finished the prophecy: *Beware the voices in the storm*.

~~~

The entrance to the parking garage on East All Saints Street sheltered him with cool shadows. He needed rest. His pain and sickness raged. He tried to vomit but nothing came up; the little Gilgamouse inside him held on. *You've broken three rules now, Humbaba*, it said.

He knew, but he was too weak to answer. Coming to All Saints, invading the rats' territory, was the final rule he had broken. The rule he had broken at the canal, to save the koi, was significant, but it had only added to his first transgression, which is that when sick, a cat must spiral inward, stay hidden, and do not seek help. Too many cats, said Inanna, is as bad as too few. Yet Syd sought healing. Why? For what reason had he broken these Laws? Because he was loved. Because he once had a mistress, who called to him with joy when she opened the apartment door, who sought his company when she sat on the couch and read, who let him sit among her tubes of paint and scattered palettes, for no reason other than that she loved him. That love she gave him lived in him and made him separate from the wildness of his ancestors. Boethius, imprisoned in the baptistery at Pavia, wrote, "Who would give a law to lovers? For unto itself, love is a higher law." Love she had given him; this is the Law he had chosen and it had betrayed him.

Or had he betrayed it? Five months ago, while Syd still lived with his loving human, there was a winter night of sparkling lights and music and many guests, and the window was open to the fire escape where he was often allowed to enjoy the fresh air. The window was open, the night unseasonably warm. The guests grew louder. The warm night beckoned, and the fire escape was quiet, but something had changed. A guest, in a fit of play, had pulled down the fire stairs. Syd followed them. The stairs led down in a sequence of hops, three stories, from the attic apartment to the alley below. From the pavement, the stars around him extended into eternity; the sparkling lights inside had been nothing but the toys of children, or words on a page, and now he was surrounded by the living thing, the real world.

Did he always know this would happen? Perhaps. The night was silent now and getting colder, and Syd on the street could almost remember the kittenhood years ago when he was rejected for having the wrong spots, left mewing in the gutter until he was found and adopted. But on the night he left his human, something within Syd awoke for the first time in his five years. He was free. No walls could hold him except those within his own mind. It became his duty to break down these walls and discover all that Inanna laid out for him in the city of man.

Mostly, he discovered hunger and hardship. Gone were the safety nets. Gone the comforts, gone the luxuries. And yet, replacing them was something only wild creatures know: in the fight for survival lies purpose and direction that never belong to the tame. "The value of a thing does not lie in what one attains by it, but in what one pays for it," said another philosopher, dwelling more in the luxury of the present than Boethius but still hunting truth with the desperation of a starved man. Perhaps Syd would fail his purpose. Perhaps he would die, sick and fevered in the shadows of the parking garage. But perhaps he had not really lived before this year. While he slept, the pieces of Gilgamouse made themselves comfortable in his stomach, and the microscopic creatures of the infection claimed the territory of his blood.

Something woke him. A hand on his body. A human hand. It dug beneath him, between his body and the smooth floor, now hot from his own heat. A human voice said something he did not recognize. Syd woke fully. A face, a human face, was right there at his. Adrenaline shot through him. He didn't have control anymore; he fought until the human dropped him, and that jolt of pain on hitting the floor woke him in every cell. He shot out of the building. He almost ran into the street, but the wind of a car turned him away, and he ran, breathless, until he reached a stoop. What was he doing here? Where was he?

All Saints, said Gilgamouse, bored, from his belly. *You're trying to get help for your infection, remember?*

There were no rats around. Of course there wouldn't be; it was full day now, even past the middle of the day, and people were everywhere. Rats slept in the day. There would be no way to find them. He was hopelessly lost here, and without help. A few feet away, a pigeon landed on the grate around a tree. It flashed rippling iridescence below a coal black eye. Pigeons were said to be mad from the consumption of human trash, but Syd had never encountered one. He was mesmerized.

Pickly turbulence, it said. It strutted back and forth. *Micromanagement of barnacles*. It pecked viciously at a pebble.

Hey, Syd whispered.

The pigeon jumped. *What hoser! Fiduciary instrumentation!* It goose-legged a step forward and cocked its head. *Porphyria?*

I need... What did he need? *I need to find the rats.*

The pigeon put its head down and strutted around. Mango feet curled around the bars of the grate and reluctantly let go with each step. *Such omophoria*, it murmured, then side-stepped closer and looked straight at Syd. *All the rats are at the fairground.*

Had it actually made sense, or did Syd imagine that?

The pigeon shook out its feathers, making a Tudor ruff around its neck. *Bulbous*, it squawked at him, eyes bulging. *Interminably ameliorative.*

Syd took a deep, painful breath. *Please*, he said. *The fairground?*

Mayday! Mayday! The pigeon marched in circles, and looked coyly over its shoulder, a dancing girl in a wild west saloon. *Today is their Mayday.* It turned its body, holding its head still facing him. *May. Day.* It walked two steps closer. *Fairground.* Two more. *Fair.* One more. *Ground.* One more, and it was right up in Syd's face. *Fair?* It made the question a demand. *Fair?* A nun at the head of the classroom, smacking a ruler on her palm. Syd could do nothing but cringe. Its voice dragged nails right down the chalkboard. *FAIR?* it shrieked, and with that, it flew off.

The sun beating down on Syd made him feel sick, like a circle of bologna with green edges. *Whatcha gonna do?* asked Gilgamouse, the tiny voice echoing up his esophagus. *Are you finally going to yield to the Laws of Inanna and find a hole to crawl in and die?*

In answer, Syd struggled once more to his feet, and set out east, down All Saints toward the Patrick Street fairgrounds. From a tangle of vines on the hillside across the street, the sleepy eyes of a rat watched him go.

On the corner of All Saints and Carroll Streets, the Sky Stage rose in tumble-down glory, a fair-weather venue born from a burned out building by creative vision. What was once a warehouse for gun parts was now a stone shell full of ramps and platforms all covered in grass. Fresh air from inside the doorless entry turned Syd's head. His Rules, the formation he had put so carefully in place in his inner world, seemed to be an inchoate version of this building, burned out by the fever and flourishing with the new green of remembered affection.

Once inside, however, Syd struggled to fight the instinct to hide. Life was pain. Darkness, soft, called to him. The quiet, the isolation, the green around him reminded him that he was an animal, not from the world of men.

He needed to get to the rats. He dragged himself out of the roofless building, into the city again. Humans, seeing him now, walked in wide arcs around him. The bright sun hurt his eyes. Something ahead stood in his way and did not move. Syd kept walking toward it, more because he could not find the energy to change direction than because he was not afraid. The something in his path drew itself into a hostile posture. The human holding it tried to placate it, but its attention was fully on Syd. It growled. It snarled. It jerked its leash out of the hands of its old man. It came thundering at Syd. It was faster than he thought.

Like an electric shock from a live cable, Syd's fear picked him up and hurled him, right into Carroll Street. The cars came directly at him from two directions. They bore down upon him. The dog ran into the traffic, after him. Syd scrambled across, claws on the pavement. Wind from the cars stole his breath. The sounds of horns and shouting and screeching and barking crescendoed, and he ran.

He did not stop; his fear would not let him. He did not have control over himself. His fevered body collapsed among the trucks of the post office, their wheels a solemn rubber forest. The noxious smells of gas and rubber forced him to move again. He stumbled out to East Street, where the cars were even thicker than on Carroll, five lanes of chaotic movement and noise. There was no way to cross. In his panic, Syd had missed the canal path that led almost directly to the fairgrounds. He'd have to get back to the canal, somehow. He turned left, up East Street, believing that was the way. Past Church, up Shab Row to Second Street he made it, and by this time, he was sick enough to have forgotten where he was going. All he could hear were the calls of shadows. The philosophy was gone, the ideological aesthete that he once was, was withered. He was nothing but an animal. He needed to crawl into a hole, and yet there were none to be found; the sidewalk ended in a stone wall. He turned down Third Street because it was quieter.

He waited on the sidewalk, waited for all the cars to go away, so that he could cross the street. A human voice called out a word that sounded vaguely familiar. It repeated the sound, a fuzzy meaning in his brain. What was the word? What was its meaning? The cars were gone; it was time to cross. Several other voices joined, frantic. Halfway across the street, Syd realized that the sound they made was the sound his human made in calling him. They were gone now, behind him, and he slipped into the graveyard, where the voice of darkness beckoned.

~~~

Hello, said something that came from the body of a cat, just inside the graveyard wall.

Syd blinked. How could it look like a cat, but not be? He sniffed, delicately, still able to perform that primal behavior. The smell was wrong, a smell of darkness deeper than night. Had Syd been any less sick, he would have growled, but now he himself was also wrong. The creature's oddly-slitted pupils widened slightly as it watched him.

I am dying, Syd said.

I do not know death, said the creature with polite curiosity. *May I watch?* It affected licking a paw, but no cat with solid bones could flow so fluidly; Syd backed away, into the graveyard.

The sky had grown darker, but it was too early for night. The small white clouds that had begun the day now spawned bigger clouds, and darker ones, gravid with storm. A light wind lifted the fur on his neck, and inside something tickled Syd's throat. He tried to vomit again but did not have the strength.

I'm here for good, said Gilgamouse.

Then, voices came from the stone walls of the cemetery. Many small voices, all echoing the words of Syd's attacker, the object of his mercy, from the night before. *Kill Humbaba!* they cried in a tiny chorus. *Humbaba the Great is punished by the gods. Humbaba the Killer of Gilgamouse is forsaken of the gods, for he is a faithless breaker of rules. Slay Humbaba!*

One of the Forsaken wound a sleek body out from behind a stone angel. *Come a little closer, mousie,* he said. *I couldn't quite hear you.*

The mice obediently raised their voices. *Gilgamouse is fallen, and the monster Humbaba has come here to die! We are the instruments of the gods, and we are their vessels; we shall exact revenge upon Humbaba! We shall hasten his death! We shall compound pain with humiliation, we shall smear his name with unspeakable degradation. He is Forsaken, now, and we shall kill Humbaba!*

With that, the mice chanted, *Humbaba! Kill Humbaba!* and a few more of the Forsaken eased into the open, sensing a feast.

Who? asked a gray tabby. *Who are you here to kill?*

Humbaba the cat!

And why do you want to kill him? The tabby stretched out and put his ears up, looking Sphinx-like.

He has slain Gilgamouse! Kill Humbaba! They chanted this, repeatedly, until Syd felt the rhythm in his quickened pulse.

I'll make you a sandwich board, so you can save your breath, said a young black cat to the mice. *Then, I'll make you a sandwich.* The others yowled with laughter. They seemed content to ignore Syd, dying in the corner. Under cover of the darkening sky, however, something landed in the tree directly above him.

CAWP.

The night heron wrapped talons around the branch. Some of the Forsaken cowered a little, intimidated by the large bird. Lightning violated the sky.

Kill Humbaba!

Thunder shook spirits free of their graves. The Forsaken muttered among themselves and took shelter in the doorway of an ancient mausoleum.

CAWP!

Syd painfully turned his head to see the bird. He could only see the underside, the breast and beak, but he knew it was here for him. *You are a night creature*, he whispered. *Why are you here in the day?*

The heron pointed the spear of its beak downward, focusing red eyes at Syd. *Oh, a good storm is darkness enough*, it said. *Besides, you ruined my feast, cat.* It rubbed the black-capped head against the white feathers of its neck. It looked down at him once more. *Now I will savor your death.*

At that moment, a group of humans entered the cemetery. They called for Syd, they called him by their name for him. Desperate-sounding, plaintive as kittens, they used all their human wiles to try to draw him out of the shadows. They shook the little treat can as if it were a magic rattle. *I only ever humored you because I loved you*, thought Syd, knowing with heartbreak that humans could never hear the voices of other living things.

The sky tore open, finally, releasing the flood of waters that it had tried to hold back. Rain came down in sheets, in walls, in buckets, in waves. All of the Forsaken huddled miserably where they were, soaked despite the stone roof above them. The mice were washed out of their hiding places, out of the cemetery to Third Street and swirling down the gutter. The rain increased beyond what seemed possible. Syd was awash, himself, awash with water, and wondered even, for a moment, if he could drown on land. It was then he thought of the canal, and the prophecy of the koi.

Beware the voices in the storm.

The rain beat upon Syd's back. He was unable to move away from it. It pounded him with fists of water. It opened the infected wound of the mouse bite.

"Syd!" called the humans, walking between the markers on the other side of the cemetery.

The water hurt him. He could not move away from it. He felt that he was drowning. The rain increased, and the healing waters touched Syd's blood. He could not breathe without taking in water, but he had a flash, a lightning vision, of one last act of mercy from Inanna. Mercy, as he had shown last night to the mouse, following her Laws. The water her hand, the rain her fingers, she massaged his back with fluid hands. She touched the infection and washed it clean. She healed his flesh and she healed his blood. He sat up in the rain. His fur was soaked through and clotted by water in the hollows between his ribs. The water ran over him, into his ears, his eyes. He had never in his life been so wet as he was now, but the fever was gone. The infection was gone. The humans called, getting closer. He was once a pet, and lived in a closed box of love. *Beware the voices in the storm*, came the warning again into his thoughts, and above him, the night heron croaked.

Syd shot up the tree.

The heron never saw him coming.

Syd's jaws closed around the evil bird. The two of them fell to the ground. He landed on his shoulder but held onto the bird. He tore its throat and ate its head, separating it from the long beak with ripping claws and teeth. He shattered the skull in his jaws. The Forsaken, still under the entrance of the mausoleum, watched in awe. The rain became steady. The humans saw none of this; they gave up, with sorrow, and left. Syd finished eating the entire heron, smothering the mouse with heron flesh and forcing it down his digestive tract. Feathers littered the graveyard. The rain let up, and Syd lifted his head. He was alive. He was reborn. All around him, the world shuffled back into place, no longer threatening. The shadow-cat, the not-cat who had asked to watch him as he died, was nowhere to be seen.

One by one, the Forsaken came out of their hiding place. They laid down upon their backs and showed him their bellies.

Syd looked up to the sky. A last roll of thunder came from the east, where the storm moved on, and in it, he heard the voice of Inanna: *Welcome to the third level.*

FOLLOW THE SOUND

BY AMANDA LINEHAN

The four teens rounded the corner on foot, approaching The Weinberg Center, an historic theater, on their right. Hannah held Derrick's hand loosely, just their fingertips touching, really, and Alice and Mason walked behind them, bickering.

Hannah's gaze went to the upcoming events listed on the theater's marquee, and then shot up half a block to where Patrick Street crossed with Market Street. In an instant, she grabbed Derrick's arm and pulled him off of the sidewalk toward the theater's box office, then whisper-yelled for Alice and Mason to join them.

"What are you doing?" Mason asked, looking around the street for the cause of the interruption.

"Shhhhhh," Hannah said, still clutching Derrick's arm tightly. "I don't want them to see us."

"Who?" Derrick asked.

"Leah and Rachel," Alice said. "They've been wanting to meet up with us all day."

"You mean from AP Bio?" Derrick said.

"Yep," Hannah answered.

"Why don't you just tell them you're busy?" Mason asked, peeking around the corner of the building.

"I can't do that," Hannah said. "We're just going to have to dodge them all night."

"Why not?" Derrick asked, finally prying his arm out of Hannah's hand.

"'Cause it would just be awkward," Alice said, as if this was the most obvious thing in the world.

Derrick shook his head, "Can I at least peek out and see if they're gone?"

"Very carefully," Hannah instructed.

Derrick inched his way past the edge of the building, looked around for a couple of seconds, then gave an OK sign with his left hand.

"Thank god," Hannah said, inching closer to the sidewalk.

"Are we going to have to do this all night?" Mason asked.

"Probably," Alice said.

"Do I even want to ask what happened between you guys?" Derrick asked.

"Probably better not to," Alice said, with a knowing look at Hannah.

"Yeah, let's just drop it," Hannah said. "But keep an eye out for them. Constant vigilance!"

"Oh boy," Derrick said.

The group made their way back onto the sidewalk and headed for Market Street. They turned right to avoid Leah and Rachel who had gone the other way.

It was a little windy, which felt good in the sticky heat, but in the distance, the clouds were thick and dark gray.

"Shit," Mason said, "looks like there's a storm coming."

"Ugh. We just got here," Alice said.

"Maybe it will pass quickly," Derrick said, grabbing Hannah's hand a little tighter as they wound their way through the crowds.

They passed crowded bars and restaurants, not going anywhere in particular and found themselves nearing Carroll Creek.

"Hey guys!" Mason yelled out. "Look, that's gonna be us when we're old!"

Hannah looked in the direction where Mason was pointing toward some outdoor seating on the side of a Mexican restaurant.

A foursome of people in their late twenties to early thirties sat sipping margaritas. Two men and two women. Hannah laughed along with

Mason and the others at the thought of being that old and still hanging out. One of the women was even wearing a yellow shirt just like Hannah.

The group made a left across Market, and Hannah perked up at the sound of a trumpet playing. Hannah was surprised when they arrived near the water's edge on the other side of the street, but didn't see a band playing. The trumpet must have been coming from some other place.

"Hey guys," Mason said, pulling his wallet out of his back pocket. "Look what I got from my cousin."

He opened his wallet, pulled an ID card out, and handed it to Derrick first. Derrick laughed.

"Not bad, but . . ." Derrick handed the card over to Hannah, who looked at it with Alice.

"Do you think we could use it to buy beer or something around here?" Mason asked.

"Dude, on a good day, you look seventeen," Derrick said, laughing. "I think they're going to card you at graduation."

Alice and Hannah laughed, then chimed in with a few more comments.

"All right, fine," Mason said, putting the fake ID back into his wallet. "I'm just getting prepared for college. That's all."

"Frostburg State will love to have you," Derrick said, then grabbed Mason's shoulders and made like he was going to push him into the water.

Mason recovered and the boys pushed and shoved a little while laughing and joking.

The wind had picked up even more, and the gray of the storm clouds crept ever closer to downtown Frederick.

Hannah heard the trumpet again and her curiosity was piqued even more about where it was coming from. Especially with the storm approaching, she thought whoever it was would have packed up.

"Hey, do you guys keep hearing that trumpet?" she asked over the wind, but the other three didn't hear her.

"Let's go back up on the street," Derrick said, waving an arm to corral the group back onto Market. A few raindrops fell as the group left the creek and made a right onto Market.

They walked along quickly, discussing where they should go to ride out the storm. Passing back over Patrick Street, Mason still wanted to go to a bar to try and use his ID, but the group shot that suggestion down again.

The rain drops were bigger, heavier, and they were falling faster. They had to hurry up.

"Don't ever call me again, asshole!" Hannah heard someone yell just a couple of storefronts up. She instinctively looked up to see a man and woman in nice-looking clothes with the unmistakable body language of people having an argument. The man looked entirely dejected and the woman, furious.

Just when she was about to turn to her friends and ask if they saw the people fighting, the sky opened up.

"In here!" Hannah called out to her friends, opening the door to The Curious Iguana. The others followed her into the bookstore.

They hadn't gotten too wet, but the people filing in behind them were soaked. The store started to get steamy.

"What are we going to do in a bookstore?" Hannah heard Mason ask somewhere behind her, but she was already lost in the stacks.

Hannah picked up books, flipped through the pages, felt the weight in her hands and enjoyed the covers. She could see Derrick in a corner of the store looking through a celebrity chef cookbook. He was going to culinary school after they graduated in a few weeks.

Hannah walked up the little staircase to the small landing on the right-hand side of the store, eyeing more books, when she heard the sound again.

A trumpet.

A small chill went up the length of her back. She thought that she shouldn't be able to hear the trumpet in here. Not this clearly. She looked around for Derrick or Alice or Mason but none of them were close enough to her to ask about the trumpet. She put it out of her mind and turned her attention to a travel book.

It was a little too crowded in the shop for her liking. She liked a little space where books were involved, but at least there was no one on the staircase.

She lifted the long strap of her purse over her head and set it down on the floor in front of her.

She closed the book a few minutes later, and the sights and sounds of the bookstore flooded her attention again.

It looked like the rain was slowing.

She reached down to grab her purse and felt only air. Panicked, Hannah looked all around her for her purse but didn't see it.

No one had come up that staircase while she was reading. What could have happened to it?

With a pit in her stomach she descended the staircase in the other direction, trying to reach either one of her friends or a store clerk, but when she hit the bottom she heard a voice calling out.

"Did anyone misplace a purse?" a lady yelled, holding up her bag in a section toward the back of the store.

Hannah called out: "Yes, that's mine!" and felt relief flood her body when her hands grasped the canvas of her bag again.

The lady smiled and walked away.

How did this get over here? Hannah thought and began rifling through her bag, sure that her cash and valuables would be gone.

But everything was there. All of her money, her phone, everything. Someone grabbed her shoulder.

45

"C'mon," Derrick said, "the rain's stopped."

Stunned, Hannah walked toward the front of the store where Alice and Mason were already waiting.

"Let's get out of here," Mason said, with one hand already on the door.

Hannah took a step forward, then immediately backed up when she saw Leah and Rachel walk by the front of the store.

She bumped a large man making for the exit and apologized as he gave her an annoyed look. Then she waved at the rest of her friends to back up out of sight, to the irritation of a few more patrons.

"What are you doing?" asked Mason, looking down the sidewalk. "Oh wait, the girls . . ."

Hannah watched carefully as Leah and Rachel passed by the bookstore, heading in the direction that the group had just come from. She waved everybody on out the door and to the right like an overzealous crossing guard.

When they were all out on the sidewalk, Hannah threw a couple of glances over her shoulder to make sure Leah and Rachel weren't coming up behind them, and when she was satisfied, breathed a sigh of relief.

"Whew. Close one," she said, and Derrick just shook his head at her, a hand on the middle of her back.

They walked a couple of blocks north, the crowds still thick, when Hannah heard the trumpet again.

"Hey," she said loudly, trying to make sure all three of her friends could hear her on the crowded sidewalk, "does anyone hear the trumpet that keeps playing?"

Alice shook her head and Derrick gave her a questioning glance. Mason was looking inside the windows of a restaurant and didn't seem to have heard her.

"You heard a trumpet?" Derrick asked and squinted his eyes in question.

"Yeah, like every few minutes or so. Oh, and my purse—"

But Derrick's attention was elsewhere.

"Hey guys," he said, "let's go in here." He pointed to a specialty oil and vinegar store with a sign out front that read "Lebherz Oil & Vinegar Emporium" with the letters L, O, V, and E highlighted.

"First books, now this," complained Mason, but Alice grabbed his shirt sleeve and gently, but firmly, pulled him inside.

"C'mon, man. There are samples in here," Derrick said, and Mason looked momentarily appeased.

Inside, Derrick immersed himself in sniffing and tasting and looking while the others mostly grabbed some bread cubes and dipped them in butter-flavored olive oil.

"I'm starving," said Mason. "Let's get something to eat after this."

"Sounds good to me," said Hannah, who had tired of oil-soaked bread cubes and had positioned herself by the front window to wait.

Derrick was lost in the rows of canisters just like she had gotten lost in the rows of books, and she knew it would be at least another five minutes.

"Hey, we're gonna wait outside," Alice said, indicating herself and Mason, who was already out the door, and Hannah nodded her head in response.

She turned around to watch her two friends on the sidewalk. Mason was pulling out his wallet again and Alice was rolling her eyes, when she noticed a man staring back at her. But she realized he wasn't outside.

Hannah whipped around looking for the man whose reflection she had seen and didn't see anyone who fit the image. She turned back around and stared at the glass once more but didn't see him. As she wondered about the reflection, a trumpet sounded.

She whipped around once more looking for the reactions of other patrons, but—nothing.

She was the only one hearing this trumpet.

Hannah looked around for Derrick and spotted him testing a dark chocolate balsamic vinegar. Marching up to him, she grabbed his arm.

"Did you just hear that trumpet?"

"No. No trumpets," Derrick said, a slightly worried expression on his face. "But this vinegar is delicious."

Hannah's heart raced as she wondered if the man whom she had seen in the window was the origin of the trumpet sound.

"Are you all right?" Derrick asked and put a hand on her arm.

"I think something's following me," she said and grabbed his hand from her arm.

"Maybe you're just getting paranoid about Leah and Rachel," Derrick said with a warm smile. Hannah heard a chime from her purse. She reached into it and dug out her phone to see a text from Rachel. She held the phone a couple of seconds and let her heart rate go back to normal.

"Maybe," she said but intuitively felt that this man was trying to get her attention.

Derrick finished with the vinegars, and they both walked outside to find Alice and Mason bickering again. It seemed Mason was still trying to figure out in which establishment his fake ID would work the best.

"Man, forget about that thing. It's not going to work, and it's going to be embarrassing," Derrick said, grabbing Hannah's hand and heading toward the direction they had come from.

"Fine," Mason said, "but we've got to eat something now. I'm starved. You want to go to Brewer's?"

"It was packed in there when we walked by. It might be a wait," Derrick said. "What about this place?" He pointed down Second Street to a place just off Market. A couple of parties sat outside in the seating area just off the sidewalk. The name Magoo's was hand-painted on the side of the building.

"Looks good to me," said Mason, and he took off across the crosswalk to the other side of the street.

Derrick looked between Alice and Hannah, and they both nodded their approval.

Inside, the restaurant was dim and cozy, decorated with Ireland-themed posters and pictures. It was mostly full, but the foursome found a table near the back against a long wall, and before long, a server had given them menus.

Mason looked like he might be contemplating using his ID again, but when the server took their drink order, he asked for a Coke.

The chatter between them picked up, but Hannah sat quietly, contemplating her mystery-man with the trumpet. She wanted to bring it up with the group but was afraid to sound crazy. Derrick had treated her well enough, but she didn't want the other two thinking she must be losing her mind.

After ordering dinner, she got up to use the bathroom, as much to get some quiet as to actually use it. Once inside, she closed and locked the door and stared at herself in the mirror a moment, trying to will the man to appear once again. Nothing.

She hadn't heard the trumpet in a while now either. Maybe he had gone or latched onto someone else. But now she couldn't let it go.

She finished up and left the bathroom and saw that back at the table, there was a basket of fried bread. She sat down, grabbed a piece, and dipped it into some marinara sauce before taking a bite.

She couldn't get the mystery man off her mind. Should she tell the rest of them?

The trumpet sounded again.

"OK, guys," Hannah blurted out, generating surprised looks from everyone at the table. "Does anyone else hear a trumpet playing?"

There was a round of no's and wide eyes all around.

"I know this sounds insane, but I keep hearing a trumpet playing everywhere we go."

"What does it sound like?" Mason, of all people, asked her, his eyes sincere and curious.

Hannah was flustered for a moment, having expected a round of strange looks from her friends, and she had to think back.

"Well," she said, "I guess it's kinda like, dun, duh, duhhhhhh . . . It's sort of slow, but the tune sounds familiar."

Mason had his phone out in a second, tapped around a bit and then flashed the screen toward Hannah.

"Does it sound like this?" he asked.

A video played with the tune she had been hearing all evening, and it was labeled "Taps." A man in a military uniform played it.

"Yeah, that's it," she said, perking up a bit now that she was getting some answers.

"Could someone downtown be playing that?" Derrick asked. "There might be live music somewhere."

"No," Mason answered, "it's played mostly in the military, like at funerals and stuff. No one would just be playing it around here. Oh, and also, what you're hearing isn't a trumpet. It's a bugle."

"Huh," Hannah said, mostly to herself. "Oh, also guys, I haven't just heard it outside. I heard it in a couple of places indoors."

"Mason, how do you know all this stuff?" Derrick asked, popping the last piece of fried bread into his mouth.

"I thought about joining the Marines," he said, shrugging. "And both my Dad and my uncle were in the military."

"You are useful for something!" Derrick said, a wide smile on his face. Mason answered him back with a few choice words.

The restaurant bustled with servers and patrons, the din getting a little louder as the dinner hour wore on and the TVs played sporting events.

Hannah described her experiences to the group as they received and ate their dinners, including seeing the reflection of a man in the window.

"What did he look like?" Mason asked in an unusually thoughtful manner.

Hannah took a moment to review her memory. It had happened so quickly, she wasn't sure how much she had retained. She rubbed her forehead.

"Young, like twenties, probably early. Umm . . . he was white."

"What was he wearing?" asked Mason. "Military uniform?"

"No," Hannah said, sure of that answer, but she couldn't quite remember his clothing. "Old-fashioned. I was kinda getting like-a-farmer vibe from him."

"Hmmmm," Mason said and chewed thoughtfully. "What kind of 'old-fashioned'? Like what time period? 1900s? 1800s?"

Hannah thought for a moment, but she wasn't sure that she was pulling the information from the memory of his image. It was more just something she had picked up on.

"1800s."

The four friends sat quietly for a minute, eating, watching, and thinking until their server came by to see if they needed anything. Derrick asked for the check.

"Hey," Mason finally said, as he finished off the last bite of his sandwich. "Want to try to call the ghost to us? I mean, it seems like he's been trying to get your attention all night, Hannah. Maybe he wants to talk?"

Hannah hesitated. Did she want to talk to this ghost? What could she do for him? She wasn't sure she wanted to egg it on. But then again, he had been following her all evening.

"How do we do that?" she finally asked.

Mason shrugged and put his arms out to his sides. "I don't really know. Why don't we head to Baker Park?"

"Why would the ghost come to the park?" Alice asked, mild annoyance lining her face.

"Well, I mean, do you want to stand in the middle of Market Street and try to communicate with a ghost?" Mason asked.

"Fair point," Derrick said.

Hannah took another minute to consider what Mason was offering up, but her curiosity was already winning out over her fear.

"Let's try it," Hannah said, and Mason pumped a fist in the air.

The group paid their bill and headed west up Second Street. The evening air was calm and clear after the storm. They were getting away from the crowds now, and the noise was lessening.

As they neared the park, they could see a few families and some couples milling about or hanging out on the grass, but there weren't too many people around.

"Not too crowded," Mason said and looked pleased.

The group headed onto the grass, and Hannah wondered exactly what Mason had in mind. Apparently, not much.

"Well," he said, turning around to face everybody. "Why don't you talk to it?"

Hannah looked from Alice to Derrick who both wore perplexed expressions on their faces.

"What do I say?" Hannah asked, surveying the area right around them. Her eyes fell on the creek, not too far away. "Hey, how about we go over by the water?"

She led the group over, and as she reached the edge of the creek, she stood there for a moment watching the small current and feeling connected to the natural surroundings.

Mason came and stood beside her with the other two a few feet behind them.

"Ask him something," Mason said, a faint smile on his face.

A warm breeze blew, and Hannah felt just a ping of fear.

"Whatdyo—" she started, stuttering a bit. "Are you trying to get my attention?" She finally got out, figuring that yes/no questions would be best.

Hannah stood there, doing her best to listen. Concentrating so hard on any little sign that might be a communication, she could feel all her muscles tensing. She waited about a minute. Nothing.

"Ask again," Mason prodded, folding his arms over his chest and glancing at her. He was still to her right.

Hannah thought about asking the same question once again but decided on something a little different.

"Is there something you want?" she said, feeling that same warm breeze on her arms. This time she stood attentive but not as tense.

And there it was again. The bugle.

"Oh, I hear it!" she said, and Mason's eyes got wide.

"What is it saying?" Mason asked, grabbing onto Hannah's upper

50

arm.

"No, no. It's the bugle again."

"Still. That's pretty cool," Alice said. "I mean, that's like a direct response, right?"

"Well, you still don't know what it wants," Derrick said, coming around to stand on Hannah's left.

"Keep asking more questions," Mason said, anticipation in his voice.

"You know, I don't have very many choices. I can only ask yes or no questions," Hannah said.

"Well, we're not professional ghost hunters. Just do the best you can," Mason said.

Hannah looked at the creek again and followed it to where it flowed west, to her right. She caught sight of a tree that she had never noticed before and which seemed out of place with the other trees around. But something drew her eyes to it, and she held onto the sight for a few moments. An energy seemed to pass through her as she thought of another question to ask.

She kept wanting to ask, "What do you want?" but knew that the ghost probably would not be able to answer that.

"Do you want to talk to me?" she finally asked. "Specifically?" She felt the question was inadequate, but it was the best she could come up with.

She expected to hear the trumpet again, but after fifteen seconds or so, she hadn't heard anything. She hadn't seen anything she thought might be a sign.

"Did you hear anything?" Mason asked.

"No," Hannah said. She was about to ask another version of the same question when she felt an object hit her square in the back. She turned around and saw a smallish, plastic ball.

She picked it up and immediately heard a man yell, "Sorry!" He held up a hand to indicate that he wanted her to throw it back, and she could see that he had a small boy in tow.

"No problem," she said and threw the ball to the man.

"I guess the answer was yes," Derrick said, and Mason nodded.

"Wait. What?" Hannah said. "The ball just got away from them."

"Hannah," Mason said. "You got hit square in the back with a ball after asking if the ghost wanted to talk directly to you. I think he answered."

Hannah considered. Maybe Mason was right.

"All right. I'm going to need some help with these questions, guys. I'm not sure what to ask."

"Maybe you remind him of someone," Alice said. "Maybe that's why he wants to talk to you."

"Or maybe you're a psychic medium, and you don't know it," Derrick said in a spooky voice. He made mock hand gestures and ghost noises like an adult dressed up for Halloween trying to give trick-ortreaters a good time.

"Maybe it's both," Mason said.

Hannah thought a moment as the unfamiliar tree caught her eye again. There was that experience she had had when she was about six. She had never told anyone about that . . . But in her gut, she did feel that the ghost saw in her someone he once knew.

"Why don't you just ask him?" Alice said. "Ask him if you remind him of somebody."

Hannah took a deep breath and asked the question. They waited.

About twenty seconds later, shrieks of joy erupted through the air, and Hannah turned and looked in that direction.

She saw two people. A man and a woman. Or, more precisely, a bride and groom. They had a photographer in tow, and currently the groom held the bride in his arms, her body entirely suspended off the ground, her arms latched around his neck. They were both laughing.

"Aww, a wedding," Alice said, and Mason grimaced for just a moment.

"Hey," Derrick said, "What if Hannah reminds the ghost of like his wife or girlfriend or something?"

"Or a fiancée," Mason said. "But maybe that's it. Maybe they never got married because he died at war."

The four of them looked around at one another, nodding their heads in agreement. Hannah didn't wait to ask the next question.

"Did you have a wife or fiancée when you died?" she said.

The bugle sounded about five seconds later.

"There it is. I hear it," Hannah said.

"Cool," Mason said. "That was fast."

"Do you have a message for me?" Hannah asked, following her intuition with the next question.

They waited and waited and waited.

"Hmmmm, he seems to have gone quiet," Hannah said, feeling disappointed.

"You guys need to leave the park. Now," said a voice coming somewhere from behind them. Hannah felt a tingle go up her spine before she had really processed what she was hearing.

"Excuse me?" Derrick asked as a man approached their group.

"You guys need to leave the park. This is a dangerous place. Get out of here. Go someplace else," the man said, and Hannah thought he was downright odd.

"Yeah, man, I think we'll be all right," Mason said and waved the guy off.

The man looked at them imploringly for a few moments, then said, "Get out of here while you can." He hurried off to the west following the creek.

"What was that about?" Derrick asked, then immediately burst into laughter, followed by the other three.

They laughed and joked with each other a few moments about the strange man before getting back to the situation at hand.

"Wait a minute, guys. What if that was the mess—" Hannah started to say.

"THERE YOU GUYS ARE!" a female voice shouted from their left. Hannah had forgotten all about them.

Leah and Rachel half-jogged/half-walked over to the group, their arms outstretched and big smiles on their faces. Hannah and Alice exchanged a glance, and Alice cursed under her breath.

"We've been texting you all day! Where have you guys been?"

Derrick and Mason greeted the girls, and Hannah and Alice gave grudgingly pleasant greetings.

"Hey, you guys ever seen a ghost?" Mason said and began to fill in Leah and Rachel on the events of the evening. They oooohed and ahhhhed at the news.

While the group was busy filling in the new arrivals of all things ghostly, Hannah stood with her own thoughts and looked into the gently moving creek.

Had the ghost been trying to warn her about the location of Leah and Rachel? That seemed such a trivial activity for a spirit from the beyond, but she had been obsessed with it when they arrived downtown. Maybe it was just helping her out?

As her thoughts began to consider what exactly the ghost had been trying to communicate, she quickly caught what she thought was a reflection in the water in front of her. A young man with an expression on his face that said, "I tried to tell you." But it was gone almost as quickly as she had noticed it.

"Earth to Hannah." She turned away from the water and saw Derrick looking at her. "What's next?"

"Uhhh, I think I've gotten all the information I wanted this evening. Why don't we move on? Do something else?"

"I'm hungry again," Mason said. "You guys hungry?" he asked the group. Only Leah and Rachel said yes.

The group began to walk to their left, toward Bentz Street, and Hannah was already plotting how to end the evening early and thinking about her new ghost friend. Derrick came up beside her, leaving Mason with Leah, Rachel, and Alice.

"Hey. You OK?" he said with a smile.

"Yeah," Hannah replied. "Just processing everything that happened."

"Crazy, wasn't it?" Derrick said, giving her a squeeze.

"Hey Derrick?" Mason called out from the front of the group.

"What is it, buddy?"

"You think Frostburg has a Paranormal Investigations major?"

Hannah laughed in spite of herself and had the distinct feeling that this wouldn't be the last ghost she spoke to.

The bugle sounded a second later, and she thanked her new friend.

OCCUPATIONAL KARMA

BY A. FRANCIS RAYMOND

"You said your problem was a lack of words?"

I didn't turn around to look at Judy who had just interrupted my not-so-deep thoughts. I kept my arms crossed as I looked down at the people, so many people, of all ages, sizes, and other attributes walking around on both sides of the canal.

"Yeah," I said under my breath.

"And that was your epiphany? Sit back down and tell me some more. We still have twenty minutes left."

I let out the breath I didn't know I was holding. Watching the people on the canal was addictive, figuring out who I was gonna' tap next, whether it was worth it. Whether or not it would help keep the balance in the Universe.

Of course, these are not things I could tell Judy. I liked meeting her once a week because she was so . . . neutral. I touched the patch on my temple. To Judy, it looked like a Band-Aid that I never took off, and in the year that we've been meeting, she's never asked about it. When I touched it, the stats that hovered around everyone's heads disappeared. Then I was just looking at people on the street. I was off duty.

I sat down on the hard chair and intertwined my fingers. Judy waited for me to say something next. That was her way. She didn't need to continually fill the silence by endlessly chattering. Another thing I liked about her.

"I was never a big or long talker with people, you know? I never knew what to say to them."

"So you avoided them?" Judy asked.

"Yeah."

"Do you think this is why you had problems making connections?"

I hesitated before I answered another generic, "Yeah."

"Why are you thinking about this now?"

"Well, 'cause of my retirement, you know? I'm thinking of what's going to happen after."

"I'm glad you're bringing that up. You mentioned it once . . ." She shuffled through her yellow lined note pad that was filled with her notes of all our past conversations, details about who I am (or at least the things I had told Judy) and the things she thought important to remember. I guess retiring was one of those important things. " . . . a few months ago. That's another significant loss in your life, isn't it? The loss of your job? For a lot of people, the end of their career is a major transition."

I hadn't thought about that.

"I guess." Not that Judy understood my job. The final thing I liked about her: I didn't have to tell her everything. I was free to be vague. So Judy, who probably knew more about me than anyone else I'd ever met in my fifty-three years, didn't know about my job. One more year left . . .

I know, you're thinking I'm too young to retire. Does it sound any better to know that I've only been working this job for five years? Sounds like a sweet gig, right? It's not.

See, for the last five years, I've been Karma. (By the way, these are the details I haven't shared with Judy—or anyone else.) As in, you get what's coming to you. As in, Karma's a bitch—except that I'm not a bitch. I'm a fifty-three-year-old man who was pulled into this because I'd led a less than stellar life, and my personal payback was to see to it that other people get theirs. Other than that, it was a job. I got paid a modest sum so I could afford an apartment, eat. All the normal things people do.

But this nebulous thing that people can't put their finger on, this inner working of Karma in the Universe . . . well, it goes back to nearly the dawn of civilization. At least, that's how it was explained to me by the person who I took this job from. Unwillingly, I may add. But like I said, this was me getting mine, and I had no choice. No one does when it comes to comeuppance. The Universe does keep track and dole out rewards for good deeds. It also, harshly, doles out punishments for the bad ones. The Universe keeps *real* good track.

Here's how the rest of it was explained to me. What our ancient ancestors figured out was that while normally, the Universe rewards or punishes people on an individual basis; if several people's karma scores combined overall are ridiculously good or bad, the Universe will dole out something much bigger, with wider-reaching repercussions.

Well, these crazy-smart genius people also figured out that if—by happenstance or any other means—someone's score got righted on its own, the Universe was happy. For example, if some jerk cuts you off, the Universe might get around to giving him his comeuppance, but if he then accidently spills his hot coffee on his lap on his own, the Universe sets him back to zero. Get it?

Which brings me to me and my job. An ultra-secret society was started long ago so people could monitor the karma points of others. If someone did something bad, a society member would give him his comeuppance—no waiting for the Universe. These ancients decided that it was better to ensure that a buildup of negative karma points didn't occur which might cause the Universe to wreak havoc on everything and everybody. Ever heard of Pompeii? Well, next time there's a terrible hurricane or tsunami, you can bet dollars to donuts that there was a buildup of bad karma in the region.

People like me, who racked up lots of negative karma? Well, we are tapped to do this job for a few years to work off those negative points doing things to keep everyone else close to neutral. Yeah, that includes doing some bad things, but when the bad thing happens to be bestowed upon someone else who did something bad first, the Universe doesn't think that's bad. Two wrongs do indeed make a right, at least by the standards our Universe has set.

And just so you know . . . I wasn't *that* bad in my old life. I wasn't a murderer or child molester or even a politician. I was just a normal guy who did lots of little things. I threw plastic bottles out of my window while I was driving. I never once left a good tip, even when the waitress really worked her butt off. I took my co-worker's can of soda out of the fridge once, too, and never paid her back or said anything. To be short, I was just your run-of-the-mill asshole.

Of course, today, we've got some fancy tech to help us. It's pretty common knowledge that secret societies always have more advanced tech than the general public. Even more advanced than the most advanced governments. That's the patch I wear on my temple. When I touch it, my vision is augmented with stats of the people I see.

How does it work? I have no clue. I don't need to know, and I never bothered to ask. It just does. And there's an app on my smartphone that allows me to pull up extra information on people. Think of it as an advanced, and very personal, search engine.

And you now know more than Judy, who I've spent a lot more time with, but I could never bring myself to tell her any of this. I'm pretty sure she wouldn't believe me. I'm not sure you do, either, but that's not my problem.

~~~

After our session concluded, I headed for the ice cream shop on the other side of the little canal right outside Judy's office apartment. I was walking behind a mother with her two young children. The youngest, maybe only a year or so old, was being pushed in a stroller, while the older child, a five-year-old, walked behind. The mom was yelling at him to keep up.

Another young mother was walking fast in the other direction, and the baby she was carrying dropped his binky. Neither mom noticed the dropped pacifier, but the five-year-old had and grabbed it, disobeying his mother's calls, shouting, "Wait, Mom!" His mom turned and saw her five-year-old give the pacifier back to the other mother and her baby.

I had my augmented reality patch turned on and saw the kid's point counter jump up. I made an unseen gesture with my finger towards his mother.

"You know, we're not in a rush," I heard the mother say. "How about we go for some ice cream?"

The kid's face lit up, and his count went back down by one. It's all about balance.

I was in the ice cream shop, sitting with my double scoop of mint chocolate chip at the counter by the window, and gave the kid a wink as he passed by, loaded up with a triple scoop piled high with gummy bears and sprinkles.

I sat there finishing off my own self-indulgent treat. I'd left my patch on and watched the people walk by with the numbers and symbols over their heads. Occasionally, I'd witness a number rise up or down based on something they did, like the kid. I was still on break, so I wasn't about to go correcting anyone's karma.

I did get a chuckle when I saw one man walk by in his suit at a brisk pace, ear bud in one ear and gesturing comically because he was so important. He was at negative 62 when I first spotted him, and back to 0 twenty feet later. That's a pretty big jump in the matter of seconds. That's the kind of thing where this guy's car was just stolen, or his credit card got jacked up. He has no idea that his day just got really bad. Or that there was a reason for it.

I always thought that part was kind of sad. I like the self-correcting nature of the Universe, but if the person never knows why, never has the opportunity to learn from it, then what's the point?

And that's when I smelled him. He sat down next to me.

I wasn't looking at the door and didn't see him come in. I've always called him Johnny, and he's never corrected me. How do I know this greasy, smelly person? He recruited me.

"How ya doin', buddy?" I instinctively moved over a couple inches. Johnny was in the same situation as me. Working off a lifetime of negative karma. He had a few more years in than I did. He looked like he came straight out of some mobster movie. He was too thin for his height, with bad teeth and slicked-back hair. Luckily, I didn't need to see him too often. As my handler, he only came out of the woodwork to talk to me about big or important jobs.

"So, you've got like what . . . one more year of this?"

I nodded as I shoved a spoonful of ice cream into my mouth so I didn't have to speak.

"What if I told you, you could be out tomorrow?"

I blinked and put the spoon down. "What?" Johnny picked up my spoon and took the rest of my bowl of ice cream.

"Yeah, bub, you heard me right. Tomorrow. We've got this one job for you. It's a doozy. But do it, and your slate is wiped clean." He licked the spoon clean as he said it.

I was very skeptical. "Why don't you do it?"

He chuckled. "Because I'd enjoy it too much and that would defeat the purpose." He winked at me.

~~~

I headed back to the canal. As soon as I sat down on a bench, my phone beeped. It was the information I was told to expect about this job.

Right away, I knew this was going to be ugly. I was used to drunk drivers or people who were cheating on their spouses and not taking care of their families. But this guy . . .

Jeff Bowden was his name. Thirty-eight. Never married. Child molester.

The information that came with the data dump showed that he'd successfully lured half a dozen pre-teen girls to one or more parks around town. He was a textbook internet predator, stoking these girls' fears and insecurities, initially pretending to be a boy around their own age and convincing them that he "gets them." Eventually, he reveals that he's a little older, but not before his victim is convinced that he's the only one in the world that understands them, and they seem to willingly go to him. He molests them and turns them away. Why hasn't he been caught and tried and prosecuted according to the law? It's because none of the girls have been able to come forward about it.

My job? End this man's life. That's what my superiors deemed fitting comeuppance for his terrible actions. Something didn't seem right. While I'd never worked a job this big before, I'd heard stories from Johnny and it was very eye-for-an-eye. Killing a molester seemed over the top.

What weren't they telling me? I re-read the dossier a few times to be sure I didn't miss anything. Did they, powers that decide these things, really think that murder for molestation was the way to right the wrong?

I looked up from my phone. My job never required me to kill anyone before. I know others have, but this would be my first. And then I'd be out.

It was the late afternoon. The sky was getting dark early. Storm must be coming. I needed somewhere to go and wait it out. I needed to be in Baker Park after dark. Jeff was expecting to meet his latest victim shortly after the sun went down. Someone else was going to intercept her, and I was going to go in her place.

Probably would be best to do all this on a full stomach, so I made my way over to Brewer's Alley for some beer, some pizza, and to wait out the storm. I sat at the bar and got lost in my beer and the game on TV. I didn't even notice the storm had come and gone. The sun was back out for a short while before dusk.

I decided to take a walk to Baker Park and scope it out. I was vaguely familiar with the layout but hadn't been there in a while. I walked back down Market Street, past all the shops that were getting ready to stay open for a late night. Once I hit the creek, I followed it from Market Street as it wound past some restaurants and led me to North Bentz Street. Once I crossed that road, I'd be in the park proper. I could hear the waterfall where the creek opened up. The path continued to follow it as did I.

As I was walked, there were some teenagers hanging out on the grass.

"You guys better get home," I called out.

"Yeah, old man," I heard one of them shout back.

"It's not safe," I said but my words trailed off. They weren't interested in listening to me.

As I walked, I opened up the map on my phone. The path splits. If I stayed to the left, I'd be crossing College Avenue street-side. If I veered right, I'd be going under the road. That was the meeting place. I went right and under the road. It was just a tunnel. Low ceiling. No lighting except what might leak in from street lamps. The park was technically closed at dusk, so the path wasn't lit. Perfect place to meet with someone if you don't want to be seen.

I decided my best bet was to walk to the end of the park then circle back. My target, my victim . . . well, he should be there by then. I knew exactly how I was going to do it, too. I had acquired some piano wire while walking around earlier. I would approach him from the back, wrap the wire around his neck. It was that simple.

And it was that simple. The guy wasn't even paying attention. Cocky jerk. He was looking down at his cell phone, probably trying to text the girl, wondering why he didn't see her yet. He never heard me, never checked around. I was as quiet as a cat up to the moment I reached around with the wire and pulled tight.

I left him, and the wire, there for someone to find. There was no possible way it could be traced back to me. The only ones who would know were my employers, and for this, I was supposed to be set free. I wondered how it was going to happen, exactly. A letter? Would my AR tech just be turned off?

I checked to see. Nope, I still had access. Maybe I'd be allowed to keep the tech, but I just wouldn't be given any jobs anymore.

I headed back up street-side and used my phone to request a cab. I wasn't sure where I was headed yet. I wasn't terribly hungry. But I could go for some dessert. There was a small restaurant in nearby Brunswick that had really good homemade baklava. Yeah, getting away from here sounded like a good idea.

~~~

Several minutes later, a fairly nice looking blue sedan pulled up. The window slid down. "Where to?" the driver said.

"Brunswick," I responded. "Head to the center of town." I closed the door behind me as I got in the back seat.

"Sure thing," he said and pushed a couple buttons on the phone letting his service know he'd picked up his fare.

As he made his way up to the main highway, I noticed that he kept giving me glances in the mirror, but he wasn't talking. This struck me as a little unusual. Most of these drivers will either try talking to you or pretend you're not there.

I turned on my AR and nearly had a heart attack. This guy's numbers were low. So low that he . . . I did some quick research. Serial killer. I was in the car with a goddamned serial killer who seemed to be sizing me up.

If ever someone had to go, this was it. And I could do it, too. No wait, I couldn't. I'd ditched the wire. I could have wrapped it around his neck while he was driving. Yeah, we'd probably crash, but I'm sure I'd be OK.

But this guy . . . how was he walking around with no karma to get him? Why was I tracking down some guy, who while a pretty bad guy in his own right, wasn't *this* bad. This is the guy that should have earned me my early retirement if he was wandering around my neck of the woods.

~~~

What happened next is something I really don't want to talk about, but I understand you're collecting data for my replacement, so here it is.

The cab driver, Mr. Superbad, I'll call him, because I never did find out his name. I know you guys know, but I don't. Anyway, while I was lost in thought, Mr. Superbad pulled off the main highway and onto some dark back road shortly after we got out of the city. I was already feeling very suspicious, so I called out, "Hey, I wanted to get to Brunswick."

"Shortcut," was all he said. Apparently, he didn't feel the need to be believable, because he wasn't. Was it something about me, or was he this arrogant with all his victims?

At this point, I still didn't believe I was going to be a victim. Except that when he pulled over on a dark road, he pointed a gun in my face.

"Put these on," he said, dangling a pair of handcuffs.

I hesitated for a moment, again lamenting the fact that I didn't have the wire I'd used earlier.

"If I don't?" I asked. This was more about buying some time, but my brain wasn't coming up with anything. The AR was still on, and his number had dropped even more. Just remember: pointing a gun in someone's face other than in self-defense is bad for your karma.

Once I had the cuffs on, he led me out of the car. I heard a second set of footsteps crunching on the ground and turned around.

Johnny. Johnny? There was no augmented reality reading on Johnny—there wasn't ever for anyone in the business.

He looked at the ground and tsk'd at me.

"I really didn't think you were going to do it," he said. I didn't have any words, just a lot of puzzlement on my face. He must have known or sensed all my unasked questions, so he continued.

"It was a freakin' test, ya know? To see if you've changed? You've been doing this how long? You know it's an eye for an eye. Not a leg, or a whole dead body, for an eye."

My whole body went numb as the realization of what I'd done caught up with me. I was supposed to question it, to not go along with what was expected of me. I was supposed to have been better.

"That's why we choose guys like child molester Jeff. 'Cause maybe half the time they do get killed and really, it's not a loss. But I thought you would have been part of the other half. It's a shame really."

He walked away after that and I heard my driver-slash-serial killer giggle from behind.

And well, do I really have to tell you the rest? My body was eventually found, I was "John Doe'd" by the police and that guy is still out there, with an even lower karma score.

I'm at a loss to understand why he's being used in the service of Karma and not being dealt with appropriately. I mean, I accept my fate. I lived a terrible life and I wasn't ever able to fully make up for that.

But I do hope the next guy gets him. If not, Frederick is going to be the center of a pretty significant disaster soon.

SET IN STONE

BY CHARMAINE WESTON

Xaro whirled from the jewelry store window and crashed into something hard and hot. Her forehead bounced off a thick shoulder, causing her to stumble backward on tangled feet. Fortunately, large hands cupped her shoulders and pulled her back before she sprawled on the sidewalk.

Ow.

"Oh man, are you OK?" The man's hands lightly squeezed her shoulders and held her steady. Xaro's hand clasped the man's wrists in response.

"Yeah, I'm . . ."

Nodding to unrattle her rattled brain, her dark eyes roamed up a long torso encased in a blue T-shirt and traveled up the tan throat to his bright eyes. The familiar blue eyes, the glowing aquamarine of the Mediterranean, reminded her of family trips and reunions. But they belonged to the hot mechanic who worked near her bakery. "Jason?"

Did that sound spontaneous enough?

"Yeah, ah, um." His hands dropped away, his wrists slipping from her grasp as he squinted at her.

Xaro straightened, shoulders falling back and breasts thrusting forward, as she waited. Jason's eyes roamed over her face, then down her simple long-sleeved T-shirt and belted skinny jeans. She shifted from one wedge sandal to the other as his gaze slipped back up her body. And he squinted some more.

Crud. Really?! Her heart clogged her throat as seconds passed in silent squinting.

Finally, he snapped his fingers and Xaro's heart bounced. "Sherry?"

She suppressed a sigh. "Xaro."

"Right, sorry. Zee-hea-ro." He offered a half smile at his careful pronunciation of her name. "You work next door. At the bakery, right?"

"Yeah." Xaro shook her head. "I mean . . . I mean, no. It's Zah-row. Well, actually, my name is Itxaro." *Stop babbling.* Her gaze followed his as those big blue eyes flicked to his buzzing cellphone. *Why can't I breathe? Why can't I stop?* "You know, I-T-X-A-R-O. It's a Basque name. I was named after my great grandmother, but too many people mispronounce it, so my friends and family usually call me Xaro."

She shrugged a shoulder and sucked in a shallow breath. Her cheeks burned beneath his gaze.

"Anyway." Xaro couldn't stop even as his eyes moved away again. "Are you here for First Saturday? I had the day off, so I thought I'd take it in."

"Yeah, me too." He glanced at his buzzing phone again. "I planned to meet some of my boys here, but I'm gettin' 'done to death' and 'catch you later' texts. They bailed on me."

"Oh, that's too bad." She squeezed his arm sympathetically. Her palm glided over warm, golden skin. Her hand tingled.

Wow.

Her eyes roamed over him again: neck, jaw, smirking lips, laughing eyes. Jason's eyes twinkled.

Darn it.

She snatched her hand away and turned back toward the jewelry store. Her eyes roamed the other people reflected in the store window but from the corner of her eye, she watched his eyes roam down her length again. Sunlight glinted off his chocolate-colored hair, creating subtle mahogany streaks.

He's so handsome.

Her fingers itched to touch it, touch him. Her hands lifted to her own hair instead and shook the thick mass off her shoulders.

"You wanna hang with me?"

"Ah, sure." *Too fast. Shoot.* Her head dropped a notch. Xaro turned back to him.

Avoiding his gaze, she gulped a quick breath then released it through pursed lips. *One, two.* She shrugged. "I mean, my friends bailed, too. So why not?" *Better.*

"What do you want to do first?"

Xaro wanted to visit the tea shop down the street. She wanted to find a tea set for her mother's collection, but teacups, ladyfingers, and cucumber sandwiches were probably too girly for Jason. Plus she'd eaten a big breakfast already. Still . . .

"What are you in the mood for?"

"Coffee and doughnuts. I can't function without 'em."

"All . . . all right."

Jason spun away at her agreement and strode down the sidewalk and around the corner. Xaro trotted behind him. As they walked, his chatter about all the doughnut flavors he'd tried floated behind him.

Thank the lord, there wouldn't be a quiz later. She wasn't listening. Instead, she admired his denims, revealing white Calvin Kleins below the hem of his shirt. With every step, his muscles bunched and contracted in a way that made her mouth water.

It worked. I can't believe that had worked.

Xaro had watched Jason for months, stammered over his orders at the bakery, and tried to find the perfect way to meet him as she hovered outside the garage.

But bam, a quick bump, and Jason had finally noticed her. She was on a date with the hot mechanic next door. They were spending the day together.

She grinned to herself and did a mental jig.

A few minutes later, Xaro nearly bumped into Jason again as he slowed in front of her. Her mind snapped back into focus, on his hand. His warm rough hand brushed her wrist; his hand slipped around hers. Her hand tingled at the contact; a heat bloomed, creeping over her palm and up her arm.

Don't sweat. Don't sweat. Don't sweat.

He tugged her closer before striding across the street. She trotted to keep up with his long stride.

Maybe wedges and skinny jeans weren't the best options. Normally, comfort trumped stylish, but she'd chosen this outfit, this accidental meeting, to catch Jason's attention.

The doughnut shop's door swung open, releasing the heavy scent of sugar and vanilla that saturated the air. The aroma seeped through her pores and into her lungs, traveling through her body until the thick scent hit her stomach, making it clench around her breakfast of waffles, eggs, and bacon.

As she sucked in tiny doses of air to ease her stomach, Jason ordered a few doughnuts and a pair of coffees to go. He leaned against the counter and stared over her shoulder through the big window while they waited.

Xaro didn't need to look behind her. Despite the glass, chatter and laughter from people strolling along the storefronts filtered through the window. Women paraded past, their reusable shopping bags rustling at their sides.

Jason watched the increasing activity behind her. His lips curled, nipping his lower lip as a pair of women giggled. He tracked their progress past the large window.

Her fingers brushed her necklace's last row. Her fingertips touched a cool stone. She promised herself she wouldn't use it, but . . . "*Arreta niretzat.*" The Basque words throbbed between them.

"What?" His gaze flashed to her.

"What?" Her fingers found the ends of her hair and twirled them.

Jason shook his head. His smile spread wider. "You look different today. Nice." He added the compliment quickly. Standing from his slouch, he grabbed the bag of doughnuts with one hand while he slid the coffees toward the condiments. "Nice necklace."

"Thanks." Her own smile grew. He'd seen the necklace before. She wore it everyday, everywhere, with everything. It was probably too much for today's simple outfit, but that didn't matter since she needed its good luck.

Jason gestured to the sugar and cream. At her nod, he loaded both cups with sugar and cream until the dark liquid was as pale as salted caramel ice cream. Never mind that she didn't like coffee.

It was thoughtful. That's what counts.

He handed her a cup, pulled a cream-filled pastry from the bag and lifted the bag with oil blooming up its paper sides toward her. Vanilla, sugar, and cream hit her nostrils again. She grabbed the first doughnut her fingers touched—chocolate-glazed—and stepped away from the nauseating scent.

"Thanks."

He smiled as he chewed and finished the first doughnut in three big bites. A blush bloomed on her cheeks again.

Yes, him.

"Let's see some art."

Sipping coffee and eating doughnuts, they wandered along Market Street. They paused to admire random trinkets in store windows. They inspected crafts, fabrics, and art.

"It looks like we can reach into it and touch them." Several painted canvases leaning against a store wall caught Jason's attention. He pointed with a chocolate cream-covered finger to the series of still lifes and nudes. "They look so real."

"Lovely work," Xaro contributed. Eyebrows raised, Jason threw a look at her.

A woman in Birkenstocks and a loose summer dress strolled toward Jason. Rocking on her heels, Xaro looked on with pride as Jason spoke with the woman about technique, paint preferences, and brush strokes.

My boyfriend can talk to anyone about anything.

Throughout the weeks, whenever Jason had visited the bakery, he had smiled for everyone. He had ended up in random conversations with other customers, but discussing art added culture and class to him.

Xaro blinked, her attention refocusing in time to hear "think about it" as the woman handed over a business card, which he shoved into his pocket.

"What was that about?"

Jason lifted an eyebrow at her. Xaro had stood right there and missed the entire conversation. "She wants me to model for her next class."

"Ah, good choice." She grinned.

"Obviously." He smothered his smile but winked at Xaro. He steered them toward a crafts store a few doors down.

"Let's go in." Jason crumpled his empty doughnut bag and coffee cup and tossed them in the trash. Xaro inched over to the trashcan, muffling the heavy thump of her full cup and half-finished pastry hitting the bag.

Inside, they prowled the store. Xaro stroked a brightly-colored quilt patched in wild patterns. Jason declared it too girly.

He picked up a pair of beer steins etched with woodland scenes. Xaro shook her head and pointed to a feathery purple dreamcatcher.

He snorted and pointed to a stuffed pink and yellow pony. Xaro snorted back.

It became a game to find all the items the other person would reject.

Gold heart-shaped wind chimes. Nope.

Rainbow paintings of children playing in a field. Nope.

A frog pillow. Hell nope.

Eventually, Xaro selected a leather key fob with a dragon burned into its side. Jason loved it. He chose a thin bracelet woven from silken ribbons for her. They bought each of their items and strolled toward the door. Jason's hand touched her lower back as he guided her from the store. Her knees wobbled at the touch.

Outside, soft guitars, a slow rendition of a Shakira song with a flamenco flare, flowed on the breeze.

Jason swayed and bounced on his heels to the beat. He paused and bumped his hip to hers; then, he slid across the sidewalk, away from her.

Xaro laughed as he snapped his fingers and shimmied. His rhythmic foot taps lost among the bustling pedestrians, Jason slid close again.

This time, he grabbed her hand, lifting it high above her, but she shook her head despite her grin. So he dropped her hand and slid across the sidewalk once more, still bumping his hips to the music.

One arm arced above his head, and the other curled around his waist as if he prepared for an elaborate courtly bow or a bullfight.

Xaro clapped and laughed again as people, ignoring Jason's antics, bustled between them. His arms snaked around her waist and hips, pulling her close to his chest, so her cheek pressed against warm cotton.

Her belly pressed his.

Xaro sucked in a breath. His scent—cedar, chocolate, and coffee— seeped into her. She shivered.

Jason lifted her against him and spun. Around and around they turned; the seductive guitar hummed louder. Her legs floated around him like ribbon on a breeze.

A dozen steps from the musicians and their crowd of listeners, he lowered her to her feet, but kept one arm around her waist. His nose tapped hers.

Yes, him.

This time, when his hand clasped hers, she twirled and dipped with him in a tango that probably looked nothing like the real dance. Still, she swayed and swung her hips; she trusted him as he dipped her at the end of the song. The ends of her hair brushed the concrete.

Yes. Yes. Yes. Him.

He held her there, suspended above the sidewalk, as he leaned over her. Then Jason smiled and winked. Above her head. At someone behind her.

Xaro's head fell back. A redhead in cutoffs and a flimsy silk blouse blushed at Jason. Sighing, Xaro squeezed his shoulder, her short fingers digging into the soft material. "Let me up."

He quickly lifted Xaro back onto her feet.

To his credit, he turned his back on the watching redhead and dropped a five-dollar bill in the open guitar case. But as the sky opened up and released hard icy rain, he glanced over his shoulder.

The redhead was a few stores away.

Her friends tugged her into a bookstore quickly filling with pedestrians escaping rain. A group of teenagers followed them through the swinging door then several more crowded through. Jason gripped Xaro's wrist as if to follow, but she pulled back.

"It's too crowded. Let's go there instead." She pointed to a handmade crafts shop in the opposite direction.

Jason glanced toward the bookstore again.

"*Ahaztu bere.*" Fiddling with her necklace, she brushed her fingers over his damp forearm. He shivered and focused on her. *Good.*

Jason scooped Xaro against him and hurried into the crafts store.

Two magic spells in one day was too much. She couldn't use another spell on him or they'd never be a good match. Xaro had learned her lesson

68

with Alix. Despite her mother's warnings, she'd used spell after spell to keep his attention, until the spells had stopped working on him. All the love and attention her spells created became anger and violence. Xaro didn't want that with Jason.

Soaked pedestrians shuffled out of the path as Jason swung the door open. Xaro and Jason shuffled into the small space, then pressed close to each other when more people squeezed in behind them.

When the door finally closed again, Jason swiped his dripping face and looked down at her.

His breath, still sweet from the doughnuts, blew across her cheeks as he lifted strands of her hair from her face and eyes. Black strands clung to his tan fingers like ivy to a tree, but he didn't bother to detangle himself. Instead, his wide thumbs sloshed the water from her cheeks, her jaw, her bottom lip. Her tongue followed his finger's path across her mouth.

"Here." His chest and arm brushed her side as he dug in his front pocket. He produced a crisp napkin. His shirt was soaked and his jeans darkened with a water line from the rain, but the napkin remained dry.

She giggled, and he patted the rain from her face.

"Thanks."

His lips smothered her whisper as he slanted his mouth across hers. His hands cupped her neck lifting her head higher for his seeking lips. He kissed her again. Xaro leaned into him.

Kiss him back. As his mouth pressed hers again, Xaro pressed into him, her lips moving against the softness of his, collecting his sweet breaths.

After a moment more, Jason eased away. His nose brushed along the length of hers.

Just like The Notebook.

Warmth bloomed through her body. Her heart thumped against his chest.

"Let's look around." He pulled her further into the crowded shop, and she, her arms wrapped around his forearm, floated beside him.

She didn't see anything except the wedding arrangements in her head.

~~~

The rain had stopped minutes after it began.

An hour later, their damp clothes were almost dry, and Xaro had chosen her wedding colors, flowers, and meal. Still, she blew out a relieved breath as they approached a table at Ayşe Meze for dinner. The delicious aroma of oil, peppers, and garlic engulfed her at the door. Since her stomach finally settled from the doughnuts, she was starving.

And her aching feet needed a rest.

Pausing for him to pull out her chair, Xaro sighed again when he slumped into a chair across the table. He pulled a menu toward him and flipped to the drink section.

Jason ordered a Corona and gimlet while Xaro seated herself.

OK, his manners weren't great, but they'd had fun so far.

He really seemed to appreciate art . . . and not just the nudes. He was spontaneous and romantic . . . sometimes. When he'd noticed her shoes bothered her, Jason had stopped her, peeled off her shoes, and carried them while they walked. And he had no problem with their long walk along the main drag, so he was super fit.

Xaro eyed the muscles moving beneath his golden skin.

Definitely, super fit.

After gulping down half a beer, Jason ordered the lamb rib chops. She ordered the vegetable kebob.

"So where'd you get the necklace?" He gestured to her throat with his mug.

Xaro pressed her hand over the necklace covering her chest from throat to cleavage. Glowing against her umber skin, glossy stones of red, black, yellow, pink, and milky white dotted its eight rows of gold chains. "It's a family heirloom from my sister. She—"

"Yeah, yeah. Really pretty." He downed half his gimlet and waved two fingers at their waitress for another round. "My old man gave me his favorite toolbox. He was a mechanic, too. He'd had it over thirty years, so it was rusted and dented in some places. But . . ." He swiped his mouth and clinched the cloth napkin in a fist against his thigh.

He's comparing my necklace to a toolbox?

She touched one of the large white stones; in the sunlight, it took on a faint blue sheen. The necklace meant more than some beat up toolbox.

For eight generations, as was tradition, every woman in her family had worn the necklace, filled her row with the necessary stones, and passed it on to the eldest unmarried female when the wearer married. Her sister had given it to her. Her mother had passed it on to her sister, and her mother's mother had passed it on to her.

And because of their Basque heritage, the women in her family never wore the necklace for long.

Except for her.

Frustratingly, Xaro had had the necklace longer than anyone else to date. Her sister had passed it on after eighteen months. Her great-grandmother had passed it on after only six months.

Xaro had worn the necklace for more than five years. Five. Years. She'd endured five years of bad dates who made inappropriate assumptions, cheaters who didn't want a real relationship, and lovers who made better friends. The necklace's magic should help her find a husband, but to Xaro, it emphasized her bad taste in men. Most rows held a few stones, never more than a dozen, but the necklace's final row representing Xaro held nearly two dozen stones. *Five years of wrong men.*

70

As she watched Jason eat and talk, bits of food spraying the tablecloth or tumbling to his T-shirt, she worried she'd have the necklace another five years.

She frowned. *He needs a haircut.*

His brown hair swept past his collar and his bangs fell over his forehead and into his eyes. He'd swiped the hair from his gaze at least a dozen times so far.

And his nose had been broken before. How had she missed the bump on its bridge that angled left?

"Anyway . . ." Jason lifted a shoulder.

Xaro realized she'd missed his talk about his father's toolbox. Jason swiped his mouth again, but still missed the sauce dotting the corner of his narrow lips.

Hmm, they'd felt full.

"It's nice to have something from family."

Jason's comment drew Xaro's wandering attention. He paused as she nodded agreement. She leaned her chin on her upraised palm.

"It's like a reminder. They experienced this life, too. They found their way, and we can, too. Those reminders give us a bit of hope, you know?"

Xaro nodded again. *That was so true.* Eight generations gave her hope; the women in her family always made good matches.

With a smile, she extended her napkin across the table. "You have a bit of sauce." She dabbed at the splash by his lips.

"Aw, man. More chewing, less talking, huh?"

Jason ordered another gimlet and a Corona as he finished his second round. Despite his comment, he kept up a steady stream of conversation. He made her laugh with stories from the auto shop and memories of working for his father during high school.

His deep voice hummed along her skin and settled in her chest. She leaned her chin into her palm as she listened and picked at her vegetables.

"You've got this, right, Xaro?" He sucked down the last of his beer. "Since I bought the doughnuts and coffee this morning?"

Xaro blinked at him. She waited for his laugh and "gotcha," but Jason just lifted his brows expectantly. "Ummm, OK?" After checking the bill, she rifled through her wallet then opted for her credit card.

He'd buy their dinner another night.

"All right, then." When the waitress returned her card, Jason tossed his napkin on the table and heaved himself from the chair. "There's more to see."

They wandered along the road, pausing to listen to street musicians. When he spotted a fudge and ice cream shop, he grabbed her shoulders and steered her into the small store and ordered a cone for each of them.

As they left the shop, discussing their favorite flavors, Jason stopped, rocked on his heels, and pulled her close. Leaning, he brushed his lips over hers. A delighted shiver moved down her body.

Jason tilted his head and brushed his lips over hers again. His tongue darted out, lapped lightly at her lower lip, and tasted her mouth.

Xaro released her breath and leaned into him. His lips pressed harder against her parted ones as her hands, and ice cream cone, slid up his chest, across his shoulders and snaked around his neck.

"Cold." Shivering, Jason laughed and leaned away. The cold chocolate dripped onto his neck.

Rising on her tiptoes, her eyes steady on his, her heart pounding in her ears, Xaro licked the drops of icy dessert away, and Jason released a heavy breath.

He pressed another quick kiss to her lips. "Come on, temptress."

Xaro wrapped her free hand around his bicep. Swaying slightly, Jason steered them away from the main road and turned onto a residential street. Here, fewer people roamed.

Jason told Xaro a ridiculous tale about a transmission repair. He stretched and swung his arms expansively as he embellished. His arm arced around and hit a man passing them.

Wow, he was tall. The lanky man with a buzz cut was at least a foot taller than her and probably several inches taller than Jason.

"Hey! Hey! Watch it, man!" Jason barked. His arms tensed beneath her hand.

"Me?! You hit me!" The tawny-skinned man rounded on Jason as he thrust his chin out and glared down at him.

Jason lurched closer to him and jabbed his dripping cone toward the other man's chest. "Because you were in my way." For a moment, his cone circled the space between them. "Apologize."

The man opened his mouth to argue, but one of his friends gripped his arm and tugged him away. "Zab, let it go."

"Let's go, Zab. He's drunk." His other friend agreed.

Xaro patted Jason's bicep with a restraining hand. "Sorry, guys." She tossed an apologetic smile toward them. The tall man's gaze snapped to Xaro when she spoke, but she concentrated on her angry date. "Jason, just apologize."

"I'm not apologizing to him. He was in my way."

"Yeah, but you hit him."

"I'm. Not. Apologizing."

"Fine, whatever." *No matter, he's gone anyway.*

The stones of her necklace tumbled over her fingers as she debated. *A spell could calm him down, but another spell so soon . . .* Xaro had used three spells in one day only once. *And that had had horrible consequences,* she thought as she twirled the black stone on her row of the necklace.

"And don't tell me what to do!" The guys were about a block away, but glanced back at Jason's bellow.

"You're not my wife." He flung his melted ice cream cone at her feet. The cold splash over her toes told Xaro this was over. Magic wouldn't fix Jason, and she couldn't accept him as is.

Xaro's eyes narrowed as she watched him list back and forth. He inched closer; his knees bent, and his head ducked down as he approached. A wicked smirk bloomed on his lips.

"You want that though, don't you? To be my wife?"

She turned away, but his hand encircled her wrist. She tensed and yanked at his grip, but he pulled her closer.

"You want me." He breathed against her ear.

"You. Are. Not. Worthy." Xaro's voice quavered over the words.

"Worthy?" Jason chuckled. "Worthy of what? You?" His chuckle morphed into a full blown snorting laugh. He dropped her wrist. She backed away. He stalked her, matching her step for step. "I could've had you months ago. The way you follow me around the shop, all wide-eyed and needy. You're like a little lapdog begging for a rub."

Xaro turned her face away and sucked in ragged breaths.

He grabbed her and yanked her into the muscular arms she admired only hours ago. Now she twisted against his hold, struggling against him as he refused to release her.

"Of course I'm worthy."

"No. You're. Not." Her voice was low and hard. She calmed. Standing on her toes, Xaro pushed her face close to his. Her nose was millimeters away. Her black eyes narrowed as they delved into his, looking deep for his soul. Her lips pulled taut over her teeth.

"*Maltzur hau arima indetsua. Tranpa bere izpiritua.*" The Basque words echoed with power.

Confusion flitted over his features. Then Jason tensed, his nostrils flaring. His neck stiffened as the tendons bulged beneath his smooth skin, which flushed a dark red.

Xaro jerked out of his grip. His hands remained balled in fists; his arms froze in front of his chest.

"Wha ... wha ... what ..." His words slipped and slid in an indistinguishable slur behind his clenched teeth. A low hiss interrupted them and became a heavy, agonized groan.

He shuddered.

Then nothing.

Jason was gone.

Xaro looked down and touched her necklace. Her fingertips roamed the last row of stones and found it, the new stone among the twenty other multicolored stones on her row of the necklace. A jagged red stone with black streaks, as large as her thumb, centered her gold chain. Her fingertips brushed over cool stones on either side of the new memento.

But the new stone burned against her fingertips.

Staring into the stone for a moment, its dark surface cleared. Xaro watched Jason, inside the stone, scream and beat against its walls. His stone would remain hot until his anger and fear cooled.

Trapped. And angry.

Another unworthy man.

Her fingers moved up the necklace and encountered a large bluish-white stone, one for each row except hers. She straightened her back. Her female relatives had found mates, so she could too, Xaro reminded herself as she stepped back onto the sidewalk.

"Hey, hey!"

Xaro glanced up to see a man loping across the street toward her. With a tall, whipcord lean physique and a buzz cut short enough to offer glimpses of his dark scalp beneath darker hair, she easily recognized the man Jason had yelled at earlier.

She froze mid step. She squared her jaw and lifted her chin, but she still stepped back when he towered over her from a few feet away.

He raised his hands. "Sorry, sorry. I didn't mean to startle you, but I had to come back. My friends told me not to." He jerked his thumb over his shoulder. His two friends hovered across the street. One watched them talk while the other scanned the street, probably looking for Jason. "But I couldn't leave you with him." His eyes roamed her face as if looking for injuries.

"Oh." She blinked; her shoulders relaxed. Her gaze traveled over his face—his strong jaw, Roman nose, and black, bottomless eyes that glowed with unnatural light.

Her head tilted. "You were worried?"

"Yeah, that guy was a di— um, a jerk. A drunk jerk. He wasn't worthy of you." The man finally dragged his gaze from her and scanned around her.

"He's gone." She fiddled with her necklace, twisting the new stone.

"He is?" His thick brows rose over his eyes that dropped to the hand at her throat. His eyes widened, then narrowed at her necklace, where she twisted and thumbed the new stone. Red and black. Passion and violence. His expression darkened with anger.

And recognition? A frown twisted his lips, and Xaro's brows bunched even more.

"I knew he was wrong for you. May I?" He gestured a hand to the necklace, more precisely, the new stone.

Xaro sucked in a breath. She held the necklace protectively to her chest, covering it with her restless hand, but slowly, she nodded and lifted the necklace as if presenting it to him for inspection.

Would he see?

He stepped closer, and the faint scent of sandalwood and peppermint tickled her nose. The backs of his cool fingers brushed her skin; he lifted the necklace higher. Xaro's head tilted as she watched him stare into the stone.

The man carefully shifted the necklace. He looked deep into the center of Jason's stone and smirked at what he saw. When his gaze shifted, she looked, too. His gaze rose to the milky stone on the row above her own. Her sister's row.

Together, they stared into the stone as it cleared. Unlike the other stones that trapped their ex's, the pale stones revealed happy glimpses of her family's marriages.

In the stone, they saw her sister's husband bend to kiss her sister's temple. His fingers brushed along her dark hair before he sat beside her to read a newspaper.

Xaro smiled and preened at the shared moment from her sister's marriage. She didn't peek into the family's relationships, but she wore the happy moments proudly.

My family makes good matches.

The man carefully lowered and released the necklace to her thumping chest.

She didn't notice.

Instead, Xaro's eyes followed the hand that fell away from her necklace. His other hand moved to fiddle with a bracelet, a cuff band encircling his thick wrist. Nearly as wide as her palm, the cuff was a series of small colorful pebbles with thin ropes of gold connecting them into nearly two dozen rows.

Two dozen rows! No more than five stones each. His family was old, and they married well.

Xaro stared at the last row that rested closest to his heart. It held three stones with a golden yellow stone in the center. In her family, the color meant deep love that had gone wrong. For her mother, the single golden yellow stone was for her fiancé who'd cheated with her best friend. The pink one beside it was for the former best friend.

As she stared, she could see the faint figure of a girl clutching pale hair and rocking to and fro.

Xaro's heart throbbed harder.

"What's your name?"

"I'm Itxaro, Xaro."

"Xaro." He paused as if testing the name on his tongue. The glow in his eyes grew.

Warmth spread through her and settled low in her belly like warm honey in hot tea.

"I'm Xabier."

"Xabier. Zab." She breathed the nickname his friends had used. His eyes, deep black pools that exposed his soul, never left hers.

He nodded.

"Do you want to come to Baker Park with us? There's a concert soon." Xabier offered his hand.

"Yes." With glittering eyes and a small smile curving her lips, she nodded and took his hand. Electric heat, his heat, zapped her and swept along her skin. "I do."

THE OCEAN

BY EDWIN STANFIELD

What does she think about? Mike wondered as he leaned back against the brick building and watched Lieutenant Ashley Taylor. She wore spandex leggings and a bright yellow workout shirt from their morning hike that hugged her every curve. She was fit—she spent over an hour in the base gym every day after class—with long slender legs that she crossed awkwardly as she stood. She was a very attractive girl, even more so now in civilian clothes, with her hair down and not curled up in a bun that was required while wearing the Air Force ABU uniform. Despite her tight body and form-fitting clothes, his eyes were fixed on her face as she looked up Market Street.

She is solid, Mike thought. He trusted her. He'd recognized her intelligence long before the class stratification was posted, ranking her first among a room full of capable people. As an enlisted analyst, she'd spent five years tracking terror networks before becoming an officer. She processed information quickly and made good decisions. But he never really had any idea what she thought about.

We've been friends four months already, so I guess I'll never know if I don't know by now.

He'd been back together with Tara over a year—granted they spent a lot of time apart—and he still never knew what she was thinking. Ever. Tara and Lieutenant Taylor were very different people, but they were both quiet and introverted with similar quirky mannerisms. *Is that why I am so interested in trying to decipher her thoughts . . . or feelings? Is it just because we are friends? Or is it because she is an attractive girl, my kind of girl, and I'm lonely?*

Impossible to know, he decided. Tara hadn't talked to him in over a week, and he wasn't sure what was wrong or if anything was wrong at all. He didn't understand. The silence was tearing him apart, but he loved her anyway. *What else can I do?*

The diamond in Ashley's wedding ring caught the sun as she spun it around her finger, and his thoughts drifted. *Will I ever be married? Over thirty, the old man in the class, and still I don't know. Did Tara even want to be married? To me, or anyone at all? No way to know. Apparently, she doesn't even want to talk to me. Don't let them know; don't bring anyone down. Everyone deserves a good weekend. Don't bring anyone down.*

~~~

Ashley stared up Market Street, past the dressed-up couples who'd driven into Frederick from DC for the weekend and the locals who wore jeans and T-shirts and walked with a purpose as if they had somewhere to be. *Half a block up to the next side street,* she thought. *Then I can sprint past that old theater toward the park if I need an open area. Or, if there is a bombing or a tornado, I can see if that church on the corner is unlocked. It might be, and they most likely have a basement I can shelter in. If anyone attacks me, Mike will protect me. He isn't that big of a guy*—something about the way he carried himself filled her with confidence, but she couldn't quite identify why—*but he's been through some stuff. He can definitely handle himself. McKenna will probably try to defend me also. He's a lot bigger and lifts weights all the time. He's such a pretty boy, though. He's probably never been in any real danger in his life. Mike always seems so observant; I just feel safer with him around. It's similar to the way I feel around my husband*—she fidgeted with her wedding ring—*but not quite the same.*

Mike is probably even more observant than my husband, she thought. *Maybe I am even safer with him . . . though my husband is a hell of a lot bigger, and he loves me, so he should do anything to protect me. Right? Something is different though . . .*

he just doesn't have the same edge that Mike does. Thinking about Mike, she turned and glanced at him to find him looking at her.

Her face instantly flushed, she smiled at him and felt awkward. *I'm being weird again,* she thought. *Why can't I just act normal?*

~~~

"Whatcha thinking about, Taylor?" he asked. Mike wasn't a big guy, but he wasn't weak either; he possessed an intense mechanic's grip-strength and what he lacked in power he made up for with endurance. He wore a blue Under Armour shirt and tan hiking pants with cargo pockets that had seen a lot of miles.

"Nothing," she said awkwardly. Just like Tara had done a thousand times.

"You're full of shit," he replied, looking into her intelligent, bright blue eyes. She shrugged, just like Tara would have. *Guys were supposed to be the ones who didn't communicate effectively. What a load of crap,* he thought.

"Hey," she stepped toward him. "We are real people this weekend, *Mike,*" she said very deliberately.

He rolled his eyes. "Yes, Ashley," he said, remembering the pact they'd made to try and use each other's first names for the weekend to feel a little more normal, and a little less "Air Force" until they were back in class. "I'm so glad this week is over. The Integrated Air Defense test, a Syria brief, and a Korea brief. That shit kicked my ass."

"You didn't do so bad," she said. He tilted his head as they looked at each other, trying to decide if she meant it or if she was just being nice. *Impossible to tell,* he concluded. He guessed if it got too bad, the instructors would have some sort of counseling session with him to let him know. They had already lost two of the eighteen they'd started with four months earlier, and as far as he could figure, he was close to the new bottom of the class. Embarrassing really, he'd been in the military since he was eighteen, and more than half the class was fresh off the street. This was different though. Up to now, he'd done nothing but turn wrenches on airplanes in foreign countries and combat zones all over the world. Now work was sitting in the dark windowless classroom cranking out research from a secret computer network.

The door opened beside him to the North Market Pop Shop, and he could hear McKenna's booming voice followed by laughter. Jess giggled behind him.

"It's not my fault, you're just not fast enough," he said in his loud nasally Jersey voice. She kicked him playfully in his calf.

"I'm paying for dinner! Not negotiable!" Jess was short, maybe five foot one, attractive with light skin, curly black hair, and a compact muscular build like a gymnast. Her husband was deployed to Iraq in a Psy-Ops unit outside Mosul, doing stuff that Mike wasn't real clear on.

"Well you better get a whole lot faster!" McKenna took a drink of his strawberry kiwi soda. Mike looked at the brand-new hiking shoes that McKenna bought specifically for his first walk in the woods and shook his head. Mike liked him. McKenna was a loud, obnoxious ex-Jersey schoolteacher who spent most of his free time studying or at the gym. He was six foot two with broad shoulders and a solid frame. His wife had elected to teach abroad while he did his Air Force training. McKenna hadn't seen her since Christmas.

Over the months, the class had split themselves up naturally. All the single people hung out together, as did the married people who'd managed to bring their husbands or wives with them. The four of them were the remainder. In committed relationships but at school alone: Ashley's husband unable to leave his engineering job; McKenna's wife teaching abroad; Jess's husband in Iraq; and Mike's girlfriend didn't count for anything as far as the military was concerned. She had another month of teaching in Chicago before her summer break began anyway.

It'd been a four-hour drive from the middle of nowhere to bring them into town for the weekend. They'd spent the morning hiking in Gambrill State Park and now walked up Market Street in the afternoon sun.

"Of course you got a strawberry soda," Mike said shaking his head. "Dirty Jersey metrosexual . . ."

"You're the one missing out. It's not my fault you live a miserable little life with no massages or facials or fruity drinks," McKenna responded.

Mike shook his head again.

They strolled south down Market Street. The girls in front looked in shop windows, and the guys would stop and wait, just as if they were with their own girlfriends in some other life, some easier life, where you could just be happy and reach out and put your arm around the girl you love.

Mike thought about Tara. He wanted to check his phone, but he didn't. It would just make him feel bad when she hadn't called.

The girls disappeared into a trendy looking clothing store. "I'm going to sit this one out," Mike said, and he leaned against the exterior of the building.

McKenna shrugged and pulled his phone out of his pocket. "It's around nine at night in Kuwait now?" Mike asked, knowing why McKenna was checking his phone. Mike had spent so much time in the Middle East, the time change was burned into his mind.

"Yeah . . . but she flew to Greece for the weekend with some of the other teachers. They got a long weekend."

"That's cool, man. I hope she's having fun."

McKenna shrugged and exhaled slowly. "Yeah," he said flatly. Mike studied his face as McKenna stared down at his phone and thought it best to let it drop. His own thoughts consumed him. He hoped Tara was doing something fun. She was a teacher, too. She worked hard and took a lot of things to heart that it'd be healthier not to, even lost a student to gang violence the year before.

Mike shook his head. *Life,* he thought. *Shit's rough. Like trying to cross an ocean.* He remembered looking down at the vast, harsh expanse of the Atlantic in the night, as he'd done many times through the para-troop door window of a C-130. *But you wouldn't know it standing here, on Market Street in Frederick, Maryland. A nice, happy-looking little American city.*

The girls reappeared, and they continued down the street. McKenna tossed his empty soda bottle into the trashcan. Jess—still holding her empty bottle—kicked him again. "Recycle! How many times do I have to tell you?!"

"Do you have any idea what the carbon footprint of the average American is? One soda bottle is negligible!" McKenna retorted.

Jess had her hands on her hips and flexed her short muscular frame with a playful attitude. "It matters!" she yelled leaning forward. "Mike! Tell him!"

"Sorry, lady. I recycle my cans and bottles, but I gave up on everyone else a long time ago."

Jess, annoyed, looked toward Ashley for support but could instantly tell her mind was somewhere far away.

~~~

Ashley's mind was racing. *He could absolutely be a serial killer,* she thought. *Why else would a middle-aged man be in a trendy downtown girls' clothing store? The way he looked at me!* She shuddered as shivers went down her spine. Ashley looked sideways back at the storefront windows to see if she was being watched. She didn't see him. *Could he have slipped out a back door?* She glanced around to see all three of her friends looking at her. She felt her face turn red. *I'm doing it again,* she thought. *Act normal!*

~~~

"Stop blushing!" McKenna said. "We love you, you beautiful, awkward girl." He threw an arm around her steering her south down the sidewalk, and they were all walking again. "Wow, that's pretty cool," McKenna said two blocks later, pointing at a mural of an old man with angel wings painted on the brick wall of a building.

"Hey, can you get my picture?" Mike asked. "I'll send it to Tara."

"No way! You're nothing like an angel!" Jess replied. "Hmmm . . . you are old, though . . ."

"Come on! Thirty-four's not old!"

"Yeah it is. You were in the Air Force when I was nine!" Jess was the youngest of the four of them, but by no means the youngest in their class. They had several ROTC lieutenants who had only left college a few months before. "You were a sergeant in two wars before I graduated from high school. You probably even got the letters we wrote in elementary school!"

Mike laughed. He did remember boxes of letters from school children showing up at his tent in the desert back in the day. It seemed like a long time ago. He never would have guessed that some of those kids would grow up and join the military themselves, and the war would still be going.

"Are you out of school now, Stretch?" He gave her a pondering look. "I feel like you should be taller."

"Shut up!" Jess said, laughing as she hit him in the ribs.

"Doesn't matter anyway. We're all lieutenants now," Mike said, down-playing his previous experience.

Ashley took his phone, smiling, and snapped a picture of Mike leaning up against the wall looking up at the old man angel looking down at him.

He smiled when she handed the phone back, but when he went to send the picture, he saw the last week's worth of messages that had gone unanswered.

```
I love you girl
I miss you babe
I hope you're having a great day
Thinking about you
I'm always here if you need me
```

~~~

Ashley saw Mike's smile falter. It was quick and subtle, but she was sure she'd seen it. *Sadness, deep sadness. Just for a moment. It can't fade that fast. He is hiding it. But why? Was it because he saw a picture of himself? That doesn't make sense. Something is happening that he isn't saying.* Mike looked up from his phone and their eyes met. She felt connected to him for a moment. As if something was shared between them, or he had told her some secret no one else knew.

Mike gave her a weak smile. *Seems forced . . .* Ashley squinted, studying his steel gray eyes. Then it was over. McKenna was talking again. "Come on, there's a margarita place down the street."

They made their way down the busy sidewalks, a few more blocks around window-shopping tourists, until they reached La Paz, a Mexican bar and grill with outside seating.

~~~

They sat at a wrought iron table in the pleasant afternoon sun and passed around their second pitcher of margaritas. All partook except Mike, who abstained for some reason that was unclear to the other three.

"No! I hate him!" Jess was giggling. "Everything we do, doesn't matter what it is, he's amazing at it." She paused. "It drives me crazy! He'd never been snowboarding before, so I thought it'd be fun to take him when I brought him to meet my dad in Colorado. I thought finally we'll do something, and I'll be better at it."

"Let me guess?" McKenna said in an even louder than normal voice that came out with alcohol.

"He was amazing!" Jess exclaimed, throwing her arms up. "It was like he'd been boarding his whole life! I hate him! I didn't even want to date him, or anyone at that time, and now look." She held up her hand and pointed at her wedding ring. "He wins at everything . . ." She shook her head. "I guess that's why they need him on that team in Iraq. He couldn't just work a normal job . . . he's got to be the best at everything." She drank her margarita and the conversation dropped for a moment.

McKenna slapped Mike on the shoulder. "What the hell's your problem? Have a drink! You're missing all the fun!"

"Nah man, I'm good. I feel perfect right now after that hike. I don't want to change a thing," Mike lied. He'd been around long enough to know alcohol was a mood amplifier, not a mood changer. Besides, he didn't need any truths slipping out to ruin everybody's good time. "I'll have some beers with you guys tonight after dinner."

McKenna looked around the table. Jess was looking into her drink and Ashley had stopped laughing and seemed to be contemplating something distant. He turned back to Mike. "Tell us about your girl. You're the only one not talking."

Ashley snapped back into the present and looked as if she was going to say something, but then she squinted and pursed her lips instead. Mike felt her look at him but didn't return her gaze. Whenever he looked at Tara like that, it was like she could see every feeling he'd ever had.

"Well," Mike began. "She's amazing. She's smart, she notices things others don't, and she really cares about people. She loves being outside; she's not afraid to get dirty and go backpacking for a week." He paused. "It's not that, though. There's something else. I don't quite know how to describe it. When I'm with her it's just like . . . It's like nothing else matters. It's like I really believe everything is going to be great. I love her. I don't know what else to say."

Ashley was still looking at him, he could feel it. He let his eyes move up to hers. Her light blue eyes looked happy, and she was smiling. "Aww . . ." she let out and touched his arm.

"More margaritas!" Jess said, having either hidden or worked through her earlier emotions. She topped off everyone's glasses with what remained in the pitcher.

They toasted to love and passing tests. McKenna flagged down the waitress and ordered another pitcher.

~~~

Ashley felt more like she was floating down the red brick path by Carroll Creek than walking; the margaritas had taken the edge off. Maybe it wasn't just her. She watched Jess playfully attack McKenna's side as they walked in front of her. Jess ran giggling down the path as he chased her. Then, he acted as if he'd shove her in the creek. Ashley drifted down the path. Mike walked beside her, but she barely noticed. *I could hide out under there, if something happens,* she thought, looking at a small pedestrian bridge crossing the creek. The margaritas were fighting back, and she smiled. Her thoughts seemed ridiculous, but even still, she wondered how deep the creek was below the bridge.

~~~

Mike walked beside Ashley, wishing Tara was with them. *It is a perfect day, and it'd be really nice to hold her hand right now.* Even as he thought it, he was wondering how she'd get along with the other girls . . . *Should be good. They are all super nice, but she might not want to hang out at all, sometimes she just wants to be alone.*

When they reached Baker Park, they all stood for a moment at the edge of the flood control spillway. Twenty feet down, the water churned before it traveled through a massive culvert and disappeared under the street.

A large snapping turtle sunned on a rock just before the water dropped off and mixed below. Mike looked down at it, its distinct alligator tail protruding from its shell. *Big enough to take my hand clean off,* he thought. It amazed him that nature, especially the parts people were afraid of, still found ways to survive right in the middle of town.

He looked at the other three, wondering if they'd noticed the turtle. McKenna was already staring at his phone, Jess was affectionately watching the dogs chase each other around in the dog park across the street, and Ashley was clearly concentrating on something as she stared down into the water below.

~~~

Ashley stood watching the water fall, mix, and turn before flowing under the street. *This is where they'll dump my body,* she thought. *They'll drag me here in the dark and throw me over the edge . . . I'll just bob there in the water beneath the street. No one will know what happened to me.*

Thinking about her body floating under the street made her remember the cold, piercing eyes of the man who'd looked at her in the clothing store. She spun around quickly to try to catch him watching her from a distance. The other three looked at her. She felt her face turning red. *Stop being ridiculous. Why can't I just act normal,* she thought.

"You doing all right, Lieutenant Taylor?" Mike asked.

She glanced at him sideways, and smiled. "It's Ashley this weekend, Mike." He smiled back and patted her on the shoulder.

~~~

Jess's easy enough to read, but I'll never understand what Ashley's thinking. With Tara, I'll really never know. Mike's mind was crowded with acceptance and rejection, sex and love. It all rolled into some indescribable feeling that didn't allow him to think clearly. He was quite sure that Tara never wondered what he was thinking. Nor did Ashley, Jess, or McKenna for that matter. *I am adrift,* he thought.

They stretched out in the grass beneath a tall willow tree near the bell tower. Mike looked up at its branches gently swaying in the breeze, making a soft rustling sound. It felt nice. The branches made just enough noise that he couldn't hear the terrible ringing in his ears that seemed to occur in the quiet before he went to sleep at night.

Too many airplanes, he thought. *Too many missions, too far from nature for too long. People have become too removed from where they are meant to be, how they are meant to live. Now, our ears ring. We stay too far apart from the girls we love; our bodies break down or get eaten up by cancer. It's not natural.* He shook his head as he thought about it. *Staring at a screen in a windowless vault, cranking out research might be better. It'd certainly be quieter and safer, but it comes with its own set of problems. It was no more natural than being on a noisy ramp full of aircraft.*

This is how people were meant to live, Mike thought as he glanced over at his friends. McKenna, stretched out in the shade of the willow tree, was already fast asleep, no doubt aided by the earlier drinks. Jess had stripped down to her sports bra in the afternoon sun. She didn't seem to be the same person he saw in class, in uniform behind a computer screen. She laid out with a book made up entirely of letters from an infantry sergeant in Iraq to his young sons that promised to have a terribly sad ending. Mike couldn't easily connect it with anything on the visible exterior of her happy and fun-loving personality.

~~~

Ashley was stretched out in the sun next to Jess, ear buds in and her eyes closed. She listened intently to her podcast. The afternoon sun felt warm and nice on her skin. She felt good lying next to Jess with the guys close by. Just enough of the margarita buzz persisted that she didn't feel so uptight. She listened to the host describe the crime scene details, evidence, eyewitness accounts, and psychological patterns of a serial killer who stalked his all-female victims in national parks. It completely fascinated and terrified her. Ashley often preferred to be alone, even from her husband, but sometimes it made her too nervous to listen to her podcasts by herself, or even in a public place with people she didn't know. Now she hung on every word as the broadcaster described the particular traits the killer liked in his victims. She opened her eyes and glanced over her body. Then she sub-consciously looked over at Jess, ran her eyes from Jess's bare feet where she'd kicked off her shoes in the grass, up her short muscular legs, curvy bottom, the light skin on the small of her back and then skipped to her face when Jess looked up from her book. Curly black hair fell to one side of Jess's face as she locked eyes with Ashley. She scrunched her eyebrows and smiled at her.

Ashley's face tinted red. *She saw me looking at her! This is super weird.* She tried to smile but it felt awkward. She didn't think it looked like a smile on her face. Jess was eyeing her with a confused look of amusement. Then, she started laughing and shaking her head. Ashley felt a wave of relief. *Maybe that's what boys feel like when they get caught staring at us.* She gave Jess another side glance, and they both laughed again.

~~~

Mike, propped up on his elbows, looked away from the swaying branches and at the girls. *How do they always know what each other are thinking?* They were opposites. Jess—social, fun, and loud; and Ashley— quiet, introverted, and always far away in her thoughts. *One more thing I'll never understand,* but he was glad they were having fun. He smiled and shook his head then the smile faded a bit as his mind crossed to Tara. *I hope she is somewhere having fun, too.* He slipped off his elbows and went back to watching the willow branches gracefully move in the breeze.

~~~

Ashley woke up in a wave of fear as low, drawn out thunder rolled through the park. She looked beside her. Jess was gone. She sat up quickly as an overwhelming sense of panic swept through her. She took a deep breath. The sky had gone dark with heavy black clouds. A fat raindrop landed on her shoulder. There was a bright flash and every muscle in her body tensed. A sharp crack of thunder followed. Ashley involuntarily let out a yelp-like whimper.

"You all right, kid?" The voice came from behind her. With heightened alertness, she twisted and jerked her head to look. She felt a wave of relief to see Mike reaching down to help her up.

"Where is everybody?" she said in a voice that she wasn't sure had hidden her anxiety.

"McKenna really wanted to play Frisbee. He and Jess went to look for a place to buy one, but that was a while ago."

He pulled her to her feet. There was another bright flash. She looked tense and inched closer to him. It was uncharacteristic for her to stand so close; she had always valued her personal space. When the thunder crashed, she shuddered and fought an instinct to move even closer.

"Are you scared of lighting?" he asked.

"Mike, I'm scared of everything!" she said with a quivering voice. He gave her a confused look, as if he wasn't understanding what she was saying. "I'm scared of everything!" she repeated, surprising herself with her own vulnerability. "I'm scared of lightning and fires and terrorists and cars and even people I pass on the street! I'm afraid all the time!"

"All right," he said calmly, though he still looked to be processing what she had said. More heavy raindrops fell. "Well, let's move. It's about to start dumping rain."

Her muscles were tense. For a moment, she thought she would break into an open sprint, then she didn't feel as if she could move at all. She wrapped her arms up tightly against her chest. Mike gestured towards the bell tower and began to move in that direction. Ashley felt herself start to follow him but then stopped.

"Mike, no! We have to stay away from tall things!"

"Whatever you'd like," he replied, but when she looked around, there didn't seem to be anywhere else to go, and the rain was falling steadily now. She gave him a look then ran for the tower.

They stood together under the medieval looking doorway as the wind blasted the stone wall behind them. Then the sky opened up and heavy sheets of rain joined the bright flashes of lighting. Thunder boomed.

~~~

It made Mike smile; he'd always enjoyed a good thunderstorm, especially if he had something to stand under. He watched the branches of the trees in the park whip around in the wind and liked the sound of the rain pounding against the ground and bell tower. When he looked at Ashley, though, with her arms still wrapped tight around herself, his fun faded away. *She really is scared.* He wanted to hold her hand, or put his arm around her to make her feel better, but he didn't. *Life is hard enough,* he thought, *the last thing she probably needs is my dumb ass putting my arm around her.*

~~~

"Hey," he said, and she locked onto his steel gray eyes. "Anything I can do?" There was a flash behind them followed by an instantaneous boom. They were in the heart of the storm now. Ashley shuddered.

"Why aren't you scared?!" Ashley yelled. Mike looked at her confused. "You've been in aircraft mishaps and car wrecks and shot at and all kinds of craziness! Shouldn't you be scared!?"

He seemed lost for a moment as he gazed back at her. "I . . . I don't know . . . I try to avoid bad situations, but whatever comes up, I just deal with it the best I can."

"But why aren't you scared?!" she demanded. "Nothing bad has ever happened to me, nothing. Never attacked, never robbed, never had an accident, never broken a bone. I've been in the Air Force five years working a desk job and never deployed." She was backed as far up against the door as she could get, and her heart was beating fast.

She still felt panic. *Why did you say all that?* she thought. There was another explosion of thunder and she screamed inside her mind.

"I think I understand," Mike said. "I always thought I'd just live my life, do the best I can, and if I get clipped, I get clipped. I guess I never really cared all that much. But the past year, it's been a little different. Being with Tara, I began to dream something good might happen later. Maybe lots of good things, things I don't wanna miss out on. It made me start to care. Somebody's loved you for a long time, and you probably have lots of plans for things in life you don't wanna miss. So that's why you're scared." He paused. "Hey, look, it's going to be OK, though. It's just a storm."

Something Mike said had connected with her and a sense of calm began to take hold. Ashley felt the panic start to leave her body. She was still locked on his eyes, almost afraid her fear might return if she looked away. She couldn't decide why, or what made her tell him everything to begin with. The lightning and thunder were spacing out now. Her thoughts circled away.

"I'm glad you feel like something good is going to happen." But when she said it, she saw it again on his face. There was a flash of sadness before he could control it. *Something is wrong, something he's not saying.* Thunder cracked in the distance, but she didn't shake this time.

~~~

Mike's feelings had betrayed him. As he looked at her, it seemed her eyes could see straight through him. He felt exposed, as if she could see every emotion he'd ever had. Tara could do the same thing to him. There was no way to hide.

"She hasn't talked to me in over a week," he confessed. His voice quivered as if saying it out loud made it real for the first time. "I don't . . ." he trailed off as a wave of feelings came from somewhere deep. Ashley reached out and touched his arm.

"I'm sure she's just . . ." Ashley began, but Mike was shaking his head.

"She did this before, just quit. It wasn't her fault . . . I wasn't there when she needed me. She didn't talk to me for two years. I couldn't take it. I was losing it. I stopped doing everything except for going to work and flying on missions. It was the deepest, darkest pit I've ever been in.

It never got any better. The happiest moment of my life was when she came back. Ashley, I don't think I can make it through that again." He swallowed hard and felt a wave of guilt. He didn't want to burden her with his problems. He didn't ever want to bring anyone down.

Her intelligent blue eyes were locked on his. It felt like she could see everything he was feeling, though he couldn't pinpoint those feelings himself. Guilt and vulnerability but something else, too—a connection, an understanding, a momentary lack of solitude. She squeezed his arm. "You're going to be OK," she said. Her voice was confident and steady. He felt himself frown, knowing deep down that all might already be lost.

"I don't know what I can do to . . ." he began, but she cut him off.

"Whatever happens," Ashley said, "you will be OK." He swallowed hard. Thunder rolled somewhere in the distance. When he finally looked away, and the rain had stopped, all his fears were still real, but something else had changed.

~~~

They could hear McKenna's loud, distinctive laugh before they reached their table in Brewer's Alley. By the number of empty glasses and the stupid smiles on their friends' faces, it was obvious that they were not on their first round of drinks.

"I couldn't find a Frisbee," McKenna said before he and Jess broke out into laughter. "You guys all right? Did you get stuck in the storm?"

"We did all right," Mike said, and Ashley gave an awkward half-smile.

"Come on, guys! Sit down! I've got oysters and crab dip coming!" McKenna said. Mike pulled up a chair next to him, and Ashley sat down by Jess, who in an unexpected show of drunken affection leaned over and hugged her.

Ashley went rigid, smiled awkwardly and started to turn red. McKenna and Mike both began to laugh.

"You're all right, Ashley," McKenna said. "It's not you being weird this time!"

"Shut up!" Jess yelled and kicked him under the table without letting go of Ashley.

"So much violence! You should have joined the Army."

Jess peeled off Ashley's shoulder long enough to stick her tongue out at McKenna. "Oooh . . .that kinda turns me on!" McKenna said, smiling.

"Shut up!" Jess yelled and kicked McKenna again.

When the appetizers showed up, they all laughed at McKenna's detailed and vulgar description of the proper way to slurp down a raw oyster.

They worked their way through the starters and ordered dinner and more drinks.

When the waitress came back with everyone's food, she put a porterhouse steak and baked potato down in front of McKenna. Before he could take his first bite, his smart phone buzzed on the table and lit up with a picture of his wife.

"I've gotta take this, guys," he said, jumping up and leaving with his phone.

"If you're not back before the steak gets cold, I'm eating it," Mike called after him. *It's awfully late in Greece right now . . . Maybe everything's all right, though,* Mike hoped as he bit into his pulled pork sandwich.

Less than a minute later, he knew things were not all right. Over Jess's shoulder and out the bay window, he could see McKenna pacing back and forth on the sidewalk. He was moving quickly, and his face seemed tense. Then, he looked to be yelling, but Mike couldn't make out the words. He went back to his sandwich.

Jess, despite being so small, was devouring her food. Ashley ate politely next to her with a far-off look in her eyes. *Impossible to know,* Mike thought as she fidgeted with her wedding ring.

Mike's thoughts snapped back to McKenna, who had unknowingly paced right up to the outside of the window, and Mike could hear him yelling.

"How could you even think that?! Everything I do is for us! Do you have any idea what I'm going through right now?! You're far away, and I'm trying to learn all this complicated shit and pass this class, and trying to find us a good place to live at our next base, and trying to sell our house, and coordinate all our stuff getting moved from Jersey into storage. Everything I'm doing is for us!" Then he'd passed, and Mike couldn't hear him anymore.

Mike looked at the girls. Jess was focused exclusively on her food, and Ashley was still far away and fidgeting with her wedding ring. He wondered what Tara was doing. *It's Saturday night.* He hoped it was something fun. He hoped she would talk to him soon.

They were all finished eating by the time McKenna returned. The waitress looked confused when she brought the checks and saw his full plate still sitting in front of him.

"Oh . . .you put me on the bill with this girl?" McKenna said, snatching the check.

Are we all covering something up? Mike wondered, impressed by McKenna's ability to hide his emotions and put on a good face.

"We're not together," McKenna said, pointing at Jess across the table, "we're together," he joked, throwing his arm around a confused and then embarrassed Mike.

"Get off me!" Mike said, pushing McKenna.

"You see what I have to put up with?" McKenna said, looking at the waitress. "He almost never takes me out and then acts embarrassed when he does."

Jess yelled and leaned over the table, trying to grab the bill, but McKenna held it out of her reach. She stood up and went into a frenzy, trying to attack McKenna across the table. A smile crept across the waitress's face.

"You're fine," McKenna said. "That is my lovely wife right there, clawing at me." He slid his credit card into the bill folder and handed it back to the waitress while holding Jess at bay across the table with his other arm.

"Whose turn is it, honey?" Ashley said as she looked at Mike.

"I think I'm up, darling," Mike replied, and she smiled though still blushing a little as he handed the check back.

"I'll bring you a box," the waitress said to McKenna, motioning toward his full plate.

"No, no," McKenna replied. "I'm not even hungry, and I don't do leftovers."

"Are you sure?" she asked, and McKenna nodded.

"Bring a box," Mike said.

McKenna shrugged. "You're going to carry that around the rest of the night just for some leftovers?"

"I'd carry a box around all night for half a cheeseburger. You spent more on that steak than I spent on food in half my twenties." McKenna shrugged again.

~~~

They ventured down the street and found themselves in a bar called Firestone's half a block later.

"This bar looks like it was designed for frat boys who were just smart enough to get jobs," Mike said as they walked in.

"I think it's nice!" Jess said, grabbing Ashley's hand and pulling her between patrons toward the bar.

"This looks like my kind of place," McKenna said, stepping through the door.

Mike smiled and shook his head, then went serious. "You doing all right, man?"

McKenna looked surprised for a second. Mike cocked his head and looked at him, as if to say, "Really man?"

"Yeah, I'm good," McKenna replied. "Just dealing with some bullshit. Are you OK?"

Mike choked up for a second; it caught him off guard. He swallowed hard. "Yeah, man. I'm good."

~~~

Jess and Ashley were carrying beers back through the crowd. The four of them pressed in around a high-top bar table. A band started playing, and the bar was loud. They had to half-shout to hear each other.

Ashley stood next to the table. Her legs were crossed in a way that seemed comfortable to her, though it looked unstable and awkward to anyone else who looked at her. She forced herself to stop analyzing possible escape routes in case of a fire or bombing or an attacker in the crowd.

As she drank her beer, she looked around at all the different people in the bar. She tried to guess who the locals were, and which guys and girls were couples. *Am I being weird again?* she asked herself, quickly glancing around the table at her friends. It didn't seem like any of them were talking. *Too loud,* she guessed. Her eyes met Jess's, who smiled and moved her head from side to side with the music, making her curly black hair bounce back and forth. *She always knows what to do, and she's so fun no matter what the situation is. Why can't I be more like that?*

Jess took it up a notch and did a little improvised dance. Ashley smiled and reached out. The two girls were dancing in place together. It was too crowded for them to really move around.

Ashley smiled wide. For a few minutes, she was really enjoying herself. She couldn't stay out of her own mind for long, though. She scanned the room. McKenna had made friends and was talking loudly with someone. Mike was staring at his phone and looked unhappy. She looked back at Jess and saw that she had stopped dancing. Jess was looking at someone a few feet away. She was shaking her head and holding her hand up, pointing at her wedding ring. Ashley turned back toward Mike and saw him casting a malicious stare in the same direction. *How does he always know what's happening?*

"Watch my drink. I'm going to the bathroom," Jess said in her ear so she could hear. She pushed her way through the crowd. Mike motioned her over.

"What just happened?" she asked.

He waved his hand dismissively. "Don't worry about him." He handed her his phone, pointing at it. There was a BBC news article displayed, just released. Four US Army Special Operations soldiers had been killed outside Mosul, Iraq.

"Aww . . ." she said feeling a frown cross her face. A moment passed before she could force it away. "Mike, you really need to stop thinking about this stuff for a minute, though, and try to relax. At least until we go back to class."

"That's where Jess's husband is," he said, and she felt her face flush. Their eyes locked for a long moment. Her stomach dropped and her legs suddenly felt weak; her mind began to race.

"Don't tell her. The names won't be out until the families are notified. If no one calls her, it's all good. She deserves to have a fun night without worrying about all of this. We have a bunch of guys there. Not as many as before, though . . . there's a good chance it's his unit."

Ashley felt herself nod. *Mike is right. No good can come from upsetting Jess now.* She felt a wave of fear and wondered if the bar had a back door in case the front entrance became blocked.

Then another wave of panic. She was collapsing and couldn't identify why. She felt a rush of relief as she heard Jess laughing and felt her catch her from behind. Jess had pushed the back of her knees to make her fall.

"Come on!" Jess yelled. "McKenna bought me dinner again! I'm buying drinks for all of us!"

The two girls shoved their way to the bar to order. The music stopped. The band had finished their set and was taking a break.

Ashley felt it before she saw it or heard her. Jess went cold and rigid in front of her, standing at the bar. Then, she was scrambling in her small purse for her smart phone. Ashley looked up at the TV above the bar. A news ticker streamed across the bottom of the screen. It was too late. Jess had her phone unlocked and the news alerts open. She turned, and they looked at each other as Jess's eyes welled with tears. Then it was all too much and became audible. Jess was crying aloud. She couldn't help it.

What do I do? Ashley thought in panic, looking at her crying friend. The people closest to them backed away, a cushion of space formed around them in the crowd. She sensed the whole bar looking at them and felt panic. It was only a second before a dark-haired man in his late twenties with a solid build stepped up, boxing Ashley out, and was trying to talk to Jess. Jess wasn't having any of it.

Ashley felt as if she were losing control. Then McKenna was there, towering above Jess with his tall, muscular frame. He wrapped his arms around her and pulled her away.

There was yelling behind them. She felt her adrenaline spike.

"You don't dance with her, you don't talk to her, you don't pay any attention to her, and she buys you drinks! If I had a beautiful wife like that, I wouldn't treat her like you do!" the dark haired man yelled. The crowd got quiet, and McKenna yelled something back.

I don't know what to say; I don't know what to do! I don't know what to say; I don't know what to do! All her instincts screamed for her to run, but she didn't want to abandon her friends. Mike stepped in front of her, and she felt a rush of relief.

"Hey, why don't you take her outside. I'll meet you guys in a few," Mike said, and McKenna nodded. Jess buried herself in McKenna's shoulder before trying to go back to her phone to read more of the article.

Ashley watched McKenna pull Jess away. She began to follow them when more yelling behind her sent shivers down her spine. *It's OK,* she told herself. *We are leaving . . . wait, something is wrong.* The wave of panic came over her again when she realized Mike wasn't moving with them.

She turned towards Mike. "Grab the leftovers," he said pointing at their table. "I'll meet you guys outside." His voice was calm and steady.

"What are . . ." she began, but he just winked at her and turned towards the yelling man and his friends. *What do I do? What do I do? What do I do!?* Her mind raced as she watched Mike move toward them.

"Oh, what? You're going to stick up for that sorry S-O-B? You're just as hopeless as he is. You wouldn't dance with your girl, either! I'm surprised she's not crying, too!"

People shuffled out of the way as Mike closed the short distance between them. Ashley watched them, terrified. She turned and looked at the door. McKenna and Jess were gone. *What do I do!? What do I do!?*

Mike stopped a foot short, squared off with the yelling man, and crossed his arms.

"What? Can't talk?!" the man shouted, and he leaned in toward Mike. He pointed a finger at Mike, who simply stood there with his arms crossed. "You just gonna stare at me?" the man continued.

Ashley was standing two arm lengths behind Mike and couldn't see how he was reacting. She was fighting her instincts to move for the door. Her phone buzzed in her hand. McKenna had texted her.

Taking a cab

Her emotions heightened. *We are on our own. If something happens to Mike, I'll be completely alone.* The crowd was still silent. There was more yelling; none of it was Mike. The other man was standing there with a group of guys while Mike was all alone. She scanned the others for hidden weapons, but she couldn't tell.

From behind, she saw Mike tilt his head to one side. She imagined that he was making that annoyed face he always had in class when someone suggested a scenario he knew from experience to be impossible.

More yelling. She nearly jumped, but Mike didn't flinch or speak. He just stood there—cool, collected, squared-off with his arms crossed.

The man leaned his face just inches from Mike's and his hands had now formed fists. Ashley zipped her phone inside the pocket of her workout shirt and felt her grip tighten on the bar stool tucked under the table; then, still staring at the shouting man, she thought better of it and wrapped each hand around an empty pint glass sitting on the table. Her pulse accelerated. She took a deep breath. *It's about to happen, I can do this.*

Just then, the dark haired man seemed to surge forward toward Mike. Ashley let out an audible sob and her eyes forced themselves shut as her forearms shot up defensively in front of her face. The next second seemed to last forever but the inevitable sounds of a scuffle never came. She exhaled slowly as she peered over her forearms still holding the beer glasses. The man made another fast aggressive head and body thrust but stopped short just before contact as Mike stood there motionless, calm and steady with his arms crossed and his head tilted. The larger aggressor screamed in frustration as Mike slowly shifted his head, slanting it all the way to the other side without breaking eye contact.

"F— YOU!" The man looked away and the two bumped shoulders as he headed for the door. His friends gulped down what remained of their beers and slammed their pint glasses on the table before filing out behind him.

Mike didn't move, his eyes stayed locked on the dark haired man and then his friends until they were gone.

It was all over. Ashley felt herself exhale slowly as her body trembled. Mike had turned around and nodded at her. "Are you trying to steal the bar glasses?" he asked and gave her what seemed to be the first real smile she'd seen from him in over a week.

Looking down at her hands in confusion she quickly placed the glasses back on the table.

She opened her mouth but couldn't manage to speak. "Ready to go?" he asked, but she still didn't respond. "Grab the to-go box," he said, pointing at the table, then put his hand on her shoulder, and guided her toward the exit.

Mike spoke to the bouncer at the door to make sure no one was waiting for him on the street before they stepped outside. "Let's walk," he said. "It's nice and cool out now." Mike suddenly seemed incredibly complex. There was some dynamic in his personality that she was noticing for the first time. She couldn't quite identify what it was.

"Are you all right?" he asked.

"I feel a little shaky."

He looked at her, concerned. "Cold?" She had her arms crossed holding herself tight and her shoulders scrunched up. "You didn't drink that much . . ."

"How are your feelings so intense about your relationship, but then you don't care at all when you're in actual danger?"

He looked at her as they walked. "Danger?"

"Mike, there were three of them! You were all by yourself!"

"That was just a couple of guys blowing off some steam. Normally when you let people yell long enough, they'll start to feel stupid."

They walked in silence for a moment. They passed a drunken girl talking loudly on her cell phone and another one barefoot and crying with smeared makeup, carrying her heels.

Ashley was trying to wrap her mind around it. He just didn't make sense to her.

"I can't believe McKenna was going to leave this whole steak," Mike said shaking the box, and she laughed. She didn't know if he was just trying to divert her attention and lighten things up or not, and she didn't care. It felt good to laugh.

~~~

94

Their friends were both asleep when Mike and Ashley reached the hotel room.

Mike laid down in the dark next to McKenna. He stared into the gray void of the ceiling and wondered what Tara was feeling or thinking or doing as his eyes slowly adjusted to the dark. It seemed a long time passed. His thoughts circled around the last time he'd seen her. Their last conversation replayed in his mind. *She hadn't seemed upset.* He was trapped in his own mind. The only thing he wanted was his phone to ring and hear her voice on the other end.

His ears rung in the silence, years of irreversible damage from flying around the world on machines designed to haul cargo, crew comfort being a distant afterthought. The life of a heavy aircraft maintainer. He could feel McKenna's slow rhythmic breathing beside him and hear Jess breathing deeply in her sleep on the other bed. Mike tried to divert his thoughts to something happy, all the fun times he'd had . . .but everything seemed to connect back to Tara. A long moment passed. The room was still except for the sound of his friends breathing in their sleep. Something was missing; he didn't hear Ashley. He turned towards the other bed and found her looking at him in the dim light. Their eyes met. The silhouette of her face changed in the dark as she smiled at him. Mike wondered what she was thinking. *Impossible to tell*, he concluded.

We are all adrift, he thought. *At least we are not alone.*

TED AND THE TIME PLUMBERS

BY J. J. MAXWELL

Ted closed the apartment door and turned on the lights. He expected nothing to have changed but let himself—for the moment—imagine a future. To dream what it could be like.

She'd be sitting on the couch, PBS on the big flat screen, two wine glasses on the coffee table, hers already started, his awaiting his arrival. Perhaps she'd be making jewelry or working on stained glass—some kind of cool, skillful hobby.

She'd turn to him, give him a big smile, ask him about his commute home on I-270, and tell him they could decide either to go out for dinner with some other couple, or better yet, run to Wegman's, get the ingredients for pan-seared scallops with snow peas, and make a nice dinner for just the two of them. She'd get that grin, and he'd recognize she'd already decided.

That'd be awesome.

But the light that shone down from the recessed fixtures reflected not the home of a happy couple, but unfinished Xbox games piled on the floor and a kitchen trash can brimming with empty takeout containers and Lean Cuisine boxes. He draped his jacket over the sole stool next to the kitchen island, tossed the laptop bag on the couch, and dropped the mail, his keys, and wallet onto the counter next to the sink. He retrieved his phone from his jacket. No invitations. No hellos. No just-checking-ins. Ted walked to the bedroom to escape business casual. No woman's clothes were invading the closets or conquering the drawer space. He stopped in the bathroom to reload his inhaler. In the cup on the bathroom sink only a single, solitary toothbrush stood guard.

Back in the living room/kitchen, he reminded himself (again) to brighten up the place: remove the stale-smelling layers of dull dust, replace the dead, flaking ferns drooping from the window sills, and hang something cool on the unadorned walls. A colorful blanket (perhaps a small quilt?) would make the gray leather couch, and the room, a lot less monotonous. You wanted the place to look right if someone special came over. You know, just in case. But pondering there was no one special—and no opportunities to think of—weighed down his spirit.

Ted decided that was dumb. *Nope, not going to do it. There's no point in getting all mopey about it.*

He focused on the positive aspects. On-demand Manchester United instead of awkward, forced introductions in some crowded, hot, noisy club. Scarfing down leftover lasagna from Il Porto in sweats and a Pixies T-shirt rather than cajoling friends to meet for dinner (most of whom had either already married, moved away, or were fading into his life's background noise with the rest of his twenties). Chugging Coke from the two-liter bottle appealed as a rebellious act against the absurdity of struggling to garner a busy bartender's attention to refill an overpriced whiskey and water.

So, full of righteous bachelorhood, he delved into the fridge for the baked pasta but came up empty. It wasn't in the freezer either. "Well, that sucks," he said, swinging both doors shut.

For a moment he considered heading downtown for an early dinner, but the idea of streets swelling with the merry makers on First Saturday dissuaded him otherwise. The forecast for scattered storms further verified the decision.

Alone in a sea of loud, inebriated, rain-soaked people? Thanks, but no thanks.

With baked pasta a no-go, Ted's mind searched for recipes as his hands groped through the near-empty pantry. He pulled two items that brought him to a culinary cross-roads: could one mix Ramen noodles with pizza sauce? Would it taste anything like lasagna? He decided to let the 1100-watt microwave answer that riddle when his phone, propelled by an unexpected text, slithered toward the countertop's granite edge.

```
Ted?
```

An unknown number.

```
Who is this?
Alicia
From the conference
I hope you remember me
```

Alicia? Ted's heart accelerated. He tried to restrain the grin spreading across his face from blossoming into a booming, beaming smile. He almost texted her back a challenge—did *she* recall being a smoking hot red-head? But Ted had learned the hard way—in a series of emotionally muddy relationship missteps—that while the better part of valor is discretion, the better part of early romance is often restraint. *Don't scare her away. Tone it down. Way, way down.*

```
Sure, I remember you
And, yes, you've reached me
How r u? What's up?
I'm in Frederick
Carroll Creek I think
Can you still show me around Frederick?
Dinner?
```

OMG it's really freakin' her. After not hearing from her for what three . . . no . . . four weeks? Awesome. Totally, totally awesome. No sucking down soda from a two-liter bottle tonight. *Still, don't appear desperate.*

```
I do have plans
```

He looked down at the packet of dried noodles and the jar of probably expired sauce.

```
But they're flexible.
So we can—
```

His fingers wanted to type 'hook up' but he reigned in their fervor.

```
—meet. When?
I have somewhere to be by 6:30
Can you come soon?
```

Ted looked at his watch. Almost 4:30.

```
Be right there. Thirty minutes or less or the
pizza's on us!
```

He waited for the response long enough to realize she hadn't gotten the joke.

```
What?
Never mind. Be right there.
```

So off to the bathroom to fix the hair, to the closet for some hip (but not too hip) threads, and toward the door he went, rationalizing away the gathering storms and the incessant, growing throngs awaiting him downtown. Really, he told himself, these were mere minor inconveniences; a girl—no, a woman, a smart and beautiful woman— waited for him. One future image filled his mind: Alicia, holding two white wine bottles, and the two of them play-fighting about which to pair with the scallops.

~~~

He almost missed it on the way out. Old, yellowing, and weather-beaten, the envelope jutted out from under the grocery ads, pre-approved credit offers, and junk mail. It carried neither postage nor a return address, but that's not what he noticed. The envelope was handwritten and addressed to his full legal name: Leslie Theodore Bullins.

'Leslie' was a name he hid from the world. A name worn by generations of men in the family, Ted didn't care for it. Especially when it raised memories of schoolyard and lunchroom teasings that a boy with a so-called girl's name attracted. He accepted he had to keep it, that he'd never stoop to changing his legal name for fear of insulting those paternal ancestors who'd borne it for an entire lifetime, some with great pride. But he didn't broadcast it, didn't share its existence, and didn't expect to see it scribbled on an aged piece of snail-mail.

So although his meeting with Alicia beckoned him, he delayed long enough to tear open the envelope, and to read the small shred of paper that fell into the sink, its chicken-scratch almost illegible. *"Leslie,"* it read, *"don't trust her."*

What 'her'? What woman possessed anything about him to betray? And as he headed down the stairs, out the door, and onto Motter Avenue, he couldn't think of anything he'd said or did with Alicia that would warrant such caution. The note was a mystery for sure, but one that would have to wait. He had other priorities—like not screwing up again.

Well, that may not have been a fair assessment. He'd only made one real error, but it was a big one. And because of that he hadn't been able to reach out to Alicia after they'd met. He was lucky she'd found him.

They'd met at an analytics conference. He'd arrived early and picked a table farthest from the stage but dead center so he'd still possess a good view. After strewing his belongings across the best seat at the table, he'd retrieved free joe and free fruit from the vendor hall.

She was there when he got back. He struggled not to stare. But she'd chosen the chair next to his, which made stealing glances irresistible.

Wow. He'd read beauty isn't defined by exceptional features, but by a collection of the most average attributes. That made little sense to a data guy. Exceptions are notable, modes and means not so much. But seeing her caused him to doubt the axiom.

Her nose fit the balanced oval of her face, the thin lips and demure mouth proportional to the small Roman nose. The distance between the gray-green eyes, perfect. Red hair, not parted, hung to the shoulders. It was as if she'd ordered the most perfect face, plus every other accessory to match. The complete package.

Except for her clothes. She didn't dress hipster-corporate flunky, underdressed overpaid contractor, or even drab bureaucrat. Old, bedazzled designer jeans paired with a faded-pink, button-down oxford that had seen too many casual Fridays. Plain unbranded sneakers. Nothing stylish or contemporary, and all of it generic and ten years out of date. It was as if she'd accepted a challenge to create a business casual ensemble at Goodwill with ten bucks.

Her bracelet thingy for sure wasn't available at Goodwill. A cross between a wrist sweatband and a fitness tracker, it looked modern, almost futuristic. He wanted to ask her about it. The array of tiny buttons and what looked like a flexible display intrigued him.

"Excuse me," she said, surprising him.

Ted dropped his eyes hoping she hadn't caught him staring.

"Is that . . . that?" She pointed to his Styrofoam cup. Her face contorted trying to find the words.

"Coffee?" Ted prompted.

"Yes! That's it. Is the coffee real?"

"If you consider coffee from a conference urn real, then yes, it's way too real." He threw her a sarcastic grin she didn't catch.

"It smells delicious. And the fruit, is it fresh?"

"I think so," Ted said, confused by her fascination with conference food.

She smiled and craned her neck to look back at the entrance. "So I can just take it? Nothing else?"

"As much as you want." He decided it would be weird to offer getting food for her. The words spilled out anyway. "If you're tied up with your work, I can get something for you."

Her smile melted his backbone. "How sweet of you, but no. I am not sure what I'll get." She stood, and Ted tried not to stare at everything below her neck. "Are these seats assigned?" she asked, shocking his gaze up.

"No, general seating." She gave him a puzzled look. "You can sit where you want," he added.

"Oh, that is good," she said. "So, you will save this seat for me?"

Ted's face flushed. "Of course. I'll be sure no one grabs it." *And if someone grabs it, it will be over my freaking dead body.*

She returned with crammed plates: fruit salad, one chocolate and one blueberry muffin, a croissant, a box of Apple Jacks, various jellies, a packet of cream cheese, at least two plastic cups of fruit juices, and, of course, coffee.

"The food here is excellent I think." She laid out her vendor-sponsored multi-course breakfast and sat down.

Ted choked down a laugh. *WTF with the food?* "Yes. Yes, it is," he said, not believing a word of it.

"I haven't had food like this for some time."

"Working abroad or something?"

"Yes." Her eyes drifted to the stage and back to Ted. She bit into a strawberry, swallowed, and paused before offering what seemed a less than confident answer. "I have been working in Canada."

Ted laughed. "I wasn't aware that Canada didn't have continental breakfast."

Her back tensed, and she sat back into her chair, somewhat reticent. "If I say, 'not the part of Canada I am from,' would that make sense?"

Ted raised his hand with his apology. "Sorry, I didn't mean to offend. Not trying to ridicule you or anything."

She cast her eyes down and lowered her chin. "It is OK, I am not offended." She pulled an errant hair from her face then spoke with a soft, winsome smile. "Please excuse me. I am not so used to it here. My part of Canada is different."

"OK. Sure. No worries." *We'll go with that. What's the expression? Don't look a gift horse in the mouth?* "Don't let me keep you from your food. By the way, I'm Ted."

"Hi, Ted. I'm Alicia." She devoured everything.

Ted watched her eat, hoping she'd wouldn't so satiate herself that she'd refuse an invitation for an early dinner before he had to catch the last commuter train back to Frederick. He had several venues in mind. The deck of the Hotel Washington looked down on the Treasury Building and the White House. The revolving bar across the river atop the Crystal City Reston possessed views of many monuments along the Potomac.

But he waited. Waited for a break in the presentations, a time when he could suggest an opportunity for them after the conference. He didn't wish to appear slimy, like he'd attended the conference with the intent of picking up a date rather than learning better algorithms for parsing data. He waited too long.

"You are quite the expert. I could learn a lot from you," she said setting her hand on his after he'd clarified one of the latest big data terms.

Ted beamed. "Thanks," he said. "It's nice being appreciated."

She patted his hand. "Some men, some men like you, are more valuable than others."

Ted felt his heart skip.

Her pupils suddenly narrowed, her brow furrowed, and her smile flattened. Ted feared he'd done something wrong.

Her gazed shifted over his shoulder. Ted turned and noticed a small group entering the darkened room, splitting up, heading in multiple directions, searching for someone or something in the crowd. "I have to go now. But I need to go to Frederick one day I think."

"I'd like that. Here." He scribbled down his contact information. "Call or text me if you want. I'll happily show you around. Frederick's great."

"Very acceptable," she said, rising. "That would be nice. Goodbye, Ted. Until I see you later." With that, she raced away toward the hallway that ran next to the conference room.

Ted watched her leave.

You jackass!

She hadn't provided him any way to reach her: no text, no email. Nada. He jumped from his seat and pursued her. She had only been a dozen yards ahead of him when she passed through the door. He followed after her into the hall but found it empty.

Ted's head hung low. He placed his head against the wall and slowly, repeatedly kicked it with his toe. "Stupid, stupid, stupid. Rookie mistake, asshole. Rookie mistake. Never forget to ask for her number. Never."

Now, as he made his way from his apartment towards the creek for this serendipitous rendezvous, Ted harbored some doubts. Sure, the note might be warning him not to trust Alicia. Perhaps she'd break his heart, have a boyfriend, or was going to use him in some weird, diabolical way. But that seemed unlikely and eons away.

He hit the inhaler to keep the asthma at bay, checked his appearance reflecting in the passing storefronts, and decided instead of caching uncertainty, he'd fill his steps down Patrick Street with enthusiasm, curiosity, a bit of cockiness, and buckets of hope. It did motivate him past the obstacles impeding his progress. Baby-strollers powered by young parents sprang into sidewalk traffic like road-raging drivers merging onto I-270. He was sure the old man and young female driver in the station wagon had almost aimed for him when he crossed Market. In front of the Curious Iguana bookstore, he dodged four oblivious teens in his path, then had to juke out of the way to avoid an entanglement with a too-long leash connecting a very friendly dog to a very inattentive owner. The early First Saturday revelers were out in earnest now, ambling and searching for good eats, better drinks, and the elusive bargain.

~~~

When Ted reached the intersection where Carroll Creek crossed Market, his enthusiasm again wavered. He realized he'd made another rookie mistake.

Alicia had never told him where on Carroll Creek to meet.

And he hadn't been smart enough to ask.

He tried to text her, but no response. *Am I too late? Shit. Shit. Shit.* He noticed the suspension bridge that crossed the creek and made a beeline to it. As the highest point over the creek, it was his best bet of spotting her—if she was still around.

He looked in all directions, but she was nowhere. When the bad weather rolled in, he'd never find her. The sunlight, like the barometer, was dropping. He checked his phone again. Did her phone die? *Maybe she'd run off for something?* His heart sank.

He leaned back against the railing, hoping that if he couldn't locate her, she might find him. He turned again, looking east, and this time a figure appeared where one hadn't been before. At the top of the large steps bisecting the amphitheater's tiered seating, she stood, looking at him. It was the same outfit she'd worn to the conference. He headed off the bridge, his pace quickening with his pulse. Soon he could make out her face, the hair. Everything was the same. Exactly the same.

His gait extended, having found her, and he sprung to the top tier of the amphitheater. "Hi Alicia, it's great to see you! I hope you haven't been waiting too long. I got here soon as I could."

Ted smiled. He didn't know whether a handshake or hug would be in order. He extended a hand but got the best hug ever. A hug where their bodies almost melded together. It was a hug like finishing a 10,000-piece puzzle. The joy of realizing that nothing is missing.

"It's great to see you." Her eyes looked at him. Through him. "You came alone, yes?"

The statement shocked him. "Uh, yeah." Why would she think otherwise?

She scanned up and down Carroll Creek. "That is very good," she remarked. "I am looking forward to our time together. But I require certain items immediately. Can you tell where to get them?"

"Of course. What do you need? Shopping's good around here. You can tell me on the way." He turned, headed down the steps.

But instead of following him, she stopped in her tracks. "It is better you stay here."

His shoulders dropped with the disappointment. "Uh . . . OK . . . but it'll be easier if I show you—"

She raised a hand like a stop sign. "It is a private matter. You will wait here, yes?"

He tried not to stumble over his next words. "I'll be happy to."

She gave him another big hug.

"I will get these items myself, then we shall, how do you say, make it a date?"

Ted tried to keep himself from flying out of his shoes. So she thought it a date, too? That meant no boyfriend, no husband. And she was alone, no third-wheeling friends. "Sure. I can wait."

Ted sat down in the grass next to a tall willow. "What do you need?" he asked.

"A knife, small and sharp. Flares. Some bright clothing. Something you might wear so cars can see you. A flashlight and some rope. And a medical kit. A large medical kit. I require these."

"Sheesh. What kind of meeting is it?"

She grimaced, her face sagging into uncertainty and self-consciousness. "Perhaps when it is over I will tell you more."

"Sure. Whatever. I'll be right here."

"And then fresh food for dinner, yes? I crave fresh food."

"Like sushi?" Ted said. "You can't get much fresher than sushi. Lazy Fish is good."

"Sushi?" she asked.

"Raw fish and rice wrapped in seaweed," he replied, almost incredulous. *How can she be uninformed about sushi?*

"It sounds delicious. Now you tell me where to go and when I get back, we will get sushi."

Ted gave her directions to Trails End and Edgeworks and watched her scurry away. She didn't so much walk as dart from place to place, peering up and down the creek, around the corners, and down every passage. She paused at Market and stood for a moment, looking back before she wheeled, crossed the street, and disappeared from his view.

~~~

After about fifteen minutes, anxiety crept up his toes, arriving as a slight tightness in his chest. He hit the inhaler. *She wouldn't ditch me, would she? Why call me out to do that?*

He put his hands to his forehead, leaned forward, and rubbed his eyes. *This will work out, right?*

"Dude, you need to lighten up," a woman's voice said. "You look, like, totally bummed. It's First Saturday, happy people are milling about, eating fine food, imbibing fine libations."

Ted's head snapped up. He hadn't heard steps.

It wasn't Alicia. Someone younger. Earthy, crunchy. Her overalls reminded him of a potter or high school art teacher. The type who overdoes the mellow thing and zones out while Phish plays in the headphones. Her eyes, though, were a serious, inquisitive contrast. Her mouth was also small, and the words that poured from it crafted, tainted, Ted suspected, with practiced charm.

"I'll make you a deal," she said. "You tell me what's up. If I can't solve it in five minutes," she reached into a pocket and pulled out a pile of cash, "I'll give you ten bucks."

Ted stared at her. *WTF?*

"Ten bucks," she repeated. "Here, I will even let you hold it. Call me Cheryl."

He shook his head. "Look . . . Cheryl . . . I'm actually waiting, I mean with someone. Thanks, but no thanks."

She thrust the money into his hand. The bracelet on her wrist was identical to Alicia's. "Come on, what do you have to lose?"

Ted looked down at her outstretched arm. "My friend has a bracelet like that. What is it?"

"She does? Well, that's strange. These are very, very rare." She paused for a moment and sat down beside him. "I know what you need. You need a drink." She pivoted to face three others standing at the base of the amphitheater.

They were an odd lot. One resembled the caveman from the insurance commercials, but he wore an AC/DC concert T-shirt, torn designer jeans, and sandals. Next to him stood a tall Asian woman, mid-thirties, sporting a skirt and blazer combo. The last was a teenage boy who could have been from the South Pacific or even Latin America. He stood straight and rigid, in almost a military bearing, if the military were to wear Run-DMC sweatshirts and ancient corduroys that screamed for a disco beat.

"Hey, Pythagoras!" she yelled.

Caveman turned.

"Go get my friend . . . hey, what is your name?"

"Ted."

"Hi, Ted. Py, go get Ted a beer."

"You're the boss," he replied.

"Um . . . I don't really feel like drinking."

"Trust me," she said. "It will ease our conversation."

The words leapt into his mind. *Don't trust her.*

She sat next to him as if they'd been friends forever. This wasn't right. Ted wasn't ugly, but he wasn't heartthrob material either. What was the interest in him? Was she hitting on him? Why? She couldn't be lonely—her friends were right there, albeit looking concerned.

She gave Ted an enormous, becalming smile and placed her hand on his shoulder.

"So, spill, Ted. What's up?"

Ted's skin crawled. He did not trust this situation. At all. Even if her looks were, well, so disarming, she seemed so deliberate in her actions, and that raised his suspicions. Too practiced. Too polished. Yet she also carried this super organic, timeless, mother-earth quality to her. She seemed so genuine in her appearance, if rather plain, though, in her features.

Freckled skin, flat, long, light brown hair, no makeup, hazel eyes— the girl next door you consider just OK, but one day puts on a prom dress and make-up and you're like 'Whoa, she's totally hot!' Then you feel foolish and stupid for not asking her out earlier, because now she's not only out of your league, but you're not even playing the same sport.

"Look, I'm waiting for my friend to get back."

"Ah, is it a girl? I bet it is. Girl troubles, huh? Well you can share with me."

"No, I don't think so." Ted said. *Time to go.* He'd watch for Alicia's return from somewhere else. "I have to go," he said, and stepped down towards the creek when Cheryl grabbed his hand with a strength much stronger than her skinny arm should possess.

"We need to talk, Ted."

He tugged hard to get free, but she held him fast as if he wasn't pulling at all.

"LET ME GO!" shouted Ted, this time pulling with both arms against her grip.

"Not yet," she said. "We need to talk. It's OK, you can trust me."

Ted felt the wave of fear that comes when you become removed from being in charge of your own physical welfare.

"CHERYL!"

Ted looked down at Cheryl's crew. The one named Pythagoras was pointing frantically at his bracelet. It, too, was like Alicia's. It was blinking red in an ever-quickening pace.

"Crap!" Cheryl shouted.

Ted felt heavy drops, and thought he heard thunder.

"Sorry," said Cheryl. The lightning struck.

~~~

"DON'T LET GO!" Ted heard her scream, but with her iron grip closing fast on his hand their bond seemed inseparable.

Her hand strength became the least of his concerns. For a few seconds Ted was very comfortable, floating awash in a bright, warm viscous clear pool. As the light faded with the warmth, so did the calm. Ted was suddenly drowning, then melting in a gelatinous goo that blistered and melted his skin as he was haphazardly dragged over and into obstacles that punched at him with sharp, penetrating jabs or whacked at him with body-blows that stretched his now elasticized form flat and in multiple directions. He tried to keep his breath, but each impact forced the air from his lungs. When he inhaled, the air was yellow and tasted of ammonia and chocolate. When he exhaled, his breath appeared blue, smelling of spoiled milk. He tried to keep his eyes open, but his lids fluttered open and closed as did his consciousness. Then a blackness came, crawling up from somewhere below, reaching and clawing its way to his face. He craned his neck to turn from it, looking up and away, seeing nothing but his extended arm, and realizing the only sensation recognizable was Cheryl's solid, protective, parent-like grip.

All motion stopped, draining away a pale gray slush from his existence. He sloshed his way back to a consciousness not yet capable of keeping up with his clearing senses.

"Welcome to the Pipes," Pythagoras said, his teeth in a wide, smug grin. "Enjoy the trip?"

Cheryl stood above him. Her grip slackened, and his hand fell away.

Pythagoras and the other two stood a few yards away, and like Cheryl, they appeared unaffected by whatever had just occurred.

Ted couldn't talk. He wanted to. But his mouth, like his body, was weak and clumsy, and even if his mind found the words, which it was struggling to do, he wasn't sure his mouth could form them.

Pythagoras leaned close to Ted's face. "Death or Mind Wipe?" he asked.

"Cut the shit," Cheryl said.

"Fine. Just trying to save the kid some time."

Cheryl raised an admonishing finger to him. "If you want to help him, clean him up and escort him to chambers."

Pythagoras raised both arms in a huff of protest, but Cheryl pointed the commanding forefinger in Ted's direction.

"Now, Py."

Pythagoras shrugged but pulled Ted to his feet before half-steering, half-carrying him through a tight tunnel that glowed with blinding green and red light.

Ted looked down at his inept strides, saw brown, and sensed a balmy, wet squishiness in his pants and shoes, realizing a final ignominy. He had evacuated his bladder and bowels.

"Yeah, that happens," said Pythagoras, glancing down at Ted's soiled shoes.

"What just happened to me? What did you do?"

"Well," replied Pythagoras, "wouldn't you agree that time travel's a joy?"

Ted heard 'time travel', but only nodded, his cluttered, waking mind unable to register the words.

His eyes still squinted, but he forced them to open. The red-green brightness speared through his skull, and his eyelids protectively shut. His mind replayed the words.

Time travel? Did that guy say, 'time travel'? "Did you say time travel?"

"Why, yes . . . yes, I did," Pythagoras said. "Now, kindly, zip it." He led Ted to a small room. "You can clean up and get dressed in here."

The door shut and Ted stripped. A powerful shower cleaned him as his vision cleared. He saw a box on the wall. "Cripes, really?" Ted said when he opened the box.

Ted, clad in a Morrisey shirt, cargo shorts, and Dr. Scholl's clogs, emerged a few minutes later. Pythagoras' face blossomed into a shit-eating grin.

"This wasn't my idea," Ted blurted. "There weren't many choices in the box."

Pythagoras gave up and burst out laughing.

Ted clenched his teeth, and for a moment his anger almost propelled his fist toward Pythagoras's wide, amused eyes. He took a deep breath instead.

"Yes, hilarious. But you know what isn't funny? All of this. Who the fuck are you? What is all of this?"

He attempted to stand tall, taking a few steps before he stooped over, his stomach cramping. He fell to his knees, cradling his stomach. "And why do I hurt? What did you do to me?"

"Uh. Duh. Time travel, dude," Pythagoras said. He reached into his pocket, withdrawing a Clark bar. He took a big bite and spoke, mouth full, the crumbs falling freely. "You've traveled through time, disobeying a bunch of temporal and physical laws in the process. The body doesn't care much for it. Everyone knows that." He took another bite. "At least they should."

"Did you . . . ?"

"What . . . crap myself? Hell, no. That's what this is for." He gestured at the device on his wrist. "Well that and they enable the whole time travel gig."

Ted stood and tried moving again. The pain was tapering off. He felt oddly limber and very relaxed. He was also breathing better. Deeply and easily.

OK, they must have drugged me. I need to come to, to figure out where I am. To get away. To get back to . . .

Alicia.

She's going to think I ditched her.

"Whatever that was wasn't time travel," Ted said. "Not like it is on TV. And time travel's been debunked, asshole."

This time Ted stood taller but shrunk when he saw Pythagoras had more than a few inches on him. Nonetheless, he tried to appear and sound commanding. "Tell me what's going on," he barked. "Tell me right now."

Pythagoras wheeled. "Wow. You are going with that? I mean you've experienced the miracle of traveling through time, and you doubt it because TV taught you it should be different? What did you expect? Some colorful spinning tube? Man, that's pathetic."

Pythagoras peered down a tunnel. "Look, I'm not answering any more questions. You'll get your answers later. Now, as I believe I have already said, zip it. Follow me."

~~~

The Pipes, as Pythagoras had called them, were immense and confounding. Ted struggled to keep pace with Pythagoras as they clambered through the odd-shaped tubes. He doubted two adults could pass one another without substantial contortions.

As Ted followed Pythagoras, he'd hoped to spot an avenue for escape, but the Pipes crushed that hope. They ran hither and thither, sometimes so steeply up Ted's breathing grew labored or down so abruptly Ted feared falling. When traveling on the rare, long, relatively straight ascents or descents, Ted anticipated arriving into some open area or substantial destination, but he reached more disappointment: only more intertwining intersections. Often, the tubes crossed one another and more than once hair-pinned into sharp turns that double-backed, thereby erasing any progress just made. Ted sometimes lost sight of his guide and ambled along alone until eventually finding Pythagoras wearing a face of frustrated impatience. Chucky Cheese's playpens sprung to Ted's mind, but only if they were the product of a madman, ran without end, filled a large mall, and had been designed solely to torture the claustrophobic.

He tried a different tactic. Pulsing veins of fluorescent red and green ran along the walls and ceilings. Ted searched for a pattern. Could red, like emergency lighting, lead to an exit? But the viney lights shone from the pipes asymmetrically, diving and rising, crisscrossing one another forming organic meshes and webs. Some passageways shimmered brightly in mostly green. Others shone mostly red. From many others, only a feint yuletide tinge held at bay an otherwise encroaching blackness.

Ted sighed. Even if he slipped away from his escort, he doubted he'd find his own way out. Reluctantly, he followed. He felt like a fragile, nervous child afraid to leave his parent's side in the confusing aisles of the super-duper mega-mart.

They finished a long, steady climb entering a large cavern forming a massive atrium that reminded Ted of a giant, multi-level mall. Far across the atrium, a multitude of veins converged into a crimson and jade river that waterfalled into a large pool that formed the lowest level. At the center of the pool, a vortex swirled and noisily sucked the fluids down like a bathtub draining.

Ted walked to the precipice and looked down. A sudden tug pulled him back from the edge.

"Don't get too close."

Ted turned. Cheryl's eyes sparkled with the hues of the pool. Pretty.

"Follow me."

Ted followed her to one of many doors facing the falls. Before entering, Pythagoras pulled at Ted's elbow, slowing him. He spoke to Ted in a hushed voice.

"Hey kid, just so you realize it, everyone who falls out has to choose. No exceptions. Get used to it. Death or Mind Wipe. Make a decision soon. It's easier."

Ted stopped short of the door. "Fuck you," he said.

"Suit yourself," replied Pythagoras.

Ted's eyes scoured the atrium. Maybe one of the doors led out?

Pythagoras stepped into his line of sight. "Don't get any ideas, kid. Don't make this worse."

Ted made a break for it, trying to wriggle past Pythagoras toward the doors. He found himself flipped onto the floor looking up into the caveman's face.

"You're making it worse."

Ted tried to resist but stronger muscles held him down. His heart pumped faster and harder and a sudden sweat rose on his brow. His breathing became more rapid and labored. Death or Mind Wipe. What if this was some murderous cult? In some "they find-his-body-years-later" way? He tried to get back up, but Pythagoras had him in some immobilizing lock. He reached, grasping for a grip or any leverage to pull himself free. His hand closed on a red vein running near the floor. His mind opened to a blurry scene of a harbor, old sailing ships, and the smell of chimney smoke mixed with sea breezes.

"Let it go," he heard Cheryl say before she yanked his hand clean from the vein. The images disappeared. "You might get sucked there with no way back."

"Let me go. I don't want any part of this."

"Sorry, kid, no can do."

"WHAT THE FUCK! I DIDN'T ASK FOR THIS!" he screamed. The panic and frustration loaded his eyes with tears. "And I had a date. A date for Saturday night. That's all I wanted."

"Don't we all," Ted heard.

Then many hands were on him, dragging him through the door.

~~~

When Ted awoke, he was sitting catty-corner to Cheryl at a large gray, rectangular formica table. In front of him, his clothes were clean and folded. He searched them for his wallet, phone, and inhaler. All were missing.

"Where's my stuff?" he asked.

"Later. If we can get it back to you, we will," Cheryl said.

He wanted to force the issue, but a wave of pain surged through his head.

"Take it easy," she said. "You're not all here. Not yet, anyway."

The table dominated a large common area. Alcoves and nooks bordered the space, each designed for an aspect of cooperative living.

In a kitchenette dominating one wall, the tall kid from the creek was constructing a massive chili dog. The area resembled the food bay of a 7-Eleven, replete with a hot dog machine slowly rolling greasy dogs and sausages, and a nacho station stocked with chili and three different sauce pumps. After piling on the toppings, the kid pulled a bag of Funyuns from the prepackaged chips, pies, candy, jerky, and cookies laying disordered on four shelves. A large display case revealed a wide variety of sodas, energy drinks, fruit juices, iced teas, and cold coffee concoctions. Next to it, a dirty, empty coffee pot stood on its warmer, surrounded by creamer packets and Styrofoam cups. Two microwaves and a small stove were on a counter next to a fridge, a sink, a stove, and another display case packed with frozen burritos, pizzas, and other snacks. A mishmash of paper plates, straws, plastic utensils, cups, and napkins populated a large milk crate itself atop the stove.

Across the room from the food, the Asian woman sat on a well-worn, peeling leatherette couch in a TV room listening to an iPod, her head and feet bouncing in rhythm with the music. Around her were an antique boom box and a hodgepodge of electronics Ted at first couldn't identify. When he did, Ted had to scoff at why anyone would choose to use a VCR, play on a PS2, or use an iPod. Had they never heard of streaming or Best Buy?

To the left of that, a small library lay carved out of a wall, with a plush, but old recliner, a variety of well-read magazines stuffed into a wooden newsstand, and a large, disorganized bookshelf. The numbering on the book spines disclosed their true owners. In some library or libraries, gaps existed where these volumes truly belonged.

A door opened along the furthest wall and Pythagoras appeared, adorned in a cowboy hat, rodeo shirt, overalls, and boots. Adjacent doors were ajar, providing glimpses of unmade beds, heaps of unruly clothes, and floors overloaded with shoes. It was reminiscent of his quad at University of Maryland, had College Park chosen to compress then cram fast-food stores into the dormitory suites.

"It's Ted, right?"

Ted turned and nodded.

"Hi, Ted. Welcome back. The first trip is the hardest. Your brain chemistry gets funky. Makes you panicky. Exert yourself too soon and, bam, you're out."

He looked at her, his head still clearing. She smiled. Ted considered it unconvincing.

Pythagoras sat next to Cheryl, and the others joined them at the table.

"Let me start with 'We Don't Know'," Cheryl said.

"Huh?"

Ted inhaled deeply again, surprising himself. No asthma today. The air was cool, clean. Clinical but good.

"'We don't know' will be the answer to many of your questions because, at the risk of sounding over-simplistic, we really don't know. And don't know equals don't know. So, understand that when the answer is 'We Don't Know,' what we truly mean is that 'We Don't Know.' We're not keeping anything from you."

Ted tried to hide his eyes rolling. That's what someone trying to hide something would say. *Don't trust her*, he remembered.

"Now," she continued, "for the basics. You are dead. Sorry for that. And time travel exists. You just did it."

She paused.

"Those of us in the room, and anyone you may have passed on the way, are what we call a Temporal Maintenance Unit, but 'time team' for short. We protect an era of time. Your era, in fact."

"Bullshit," said Ted.

She stared back at him. "That's Wing." The Asian girl waved at him blank-faced, uncommitted to the greeting. "Over there is Todd."

Todd chin-nodded. "Whassup?" he stated, rubbing his eyes and yawning. He pulled a knife from his pocket and flicked it open and closed, open and closed.

Cheryl glared. Todd put it away.

Pythagoras placed his hands behind his head, leaned back, slipping the hat's brow into napping position over his eyes.

"You are in a complex—basically an enormous machine—we call the Pipes. The red veins channel the past, the green the future. When you want to travel, find the right vein, push the time band to it, and off you go. They also bring you back. We don't know how it works. It just does."

Ted looked at her and at the faces around the table. None of them cracked. Ted believed even the most professional actors couldn't have taken Cheryl's explanation, obviously some kind of joke, seriously.

"I have a question," said Ted.

"Shoot," Cheryl said.

"I don't give a shit about your story."

"That's not a question," said Todd.

Ted scowled at him.

"Fine. Why am I here and when and how do I get out?"

"Tough luck," Pythagoras. "You fell out of time just like the rest of us. Welcome to the party."

"You were touching me when the lightning struck." She stood up. "I'm craving an egg roll. Anyone else? Wing, you field this."

Wing walked to the beverage display case. "You want a Coke?" she asked Ted. "Right now we have original and New Coke. Coke from the '70s is pretty awesome."

"What's New Coke?" asked Ted.

"They changed Coke from sugar to corn syrup in the '80s. But they did it by offering a decoy called New Coke. When people demanded the old Coke, because no one liked the New Coke, they offered something like the old Coke. They called it Coke Classic. But it wasn't real Coke. It had the corn syrup. Pretty clever."

"Uh, yeah, sure," said Ted. "I always drink a 40-year-old soda when talking about traveling through time and being dead. By the way, exactly when do I get to meet myself and then get to be my best friend? When do I break down the door and come to my own rescue?"

Wing just shook her head. "Pathetic. Jerks get New Coke. They always get New Coke."

The soda hissed as he opened it. He took a swig. It sucked.

Wing continued. "The bands we wear enable time travel. But they also have safety measures built in. Normally they recharge from the surrounding environment. However, when the bands sense they are powering up too quickly or powering down too fast—from like an explosion or massive decompression—"

"Or a lightning strike," interrupted Pythagoras.

"—they perform an emergency transport back here, bringing whoever is wearing them, and anyone else who may be in indirect contact with the band. Cheryl saved you. She had a choice to make. Let you die or take you with us."

If they were joking, they weren't laughing.

He could feel himself sweating. Cheryl tossed him a small towel.

"Here. It's a lot to process."

"But there is something else, Ted," Cheryl said. "There is something wrong in your era. Very wrong. And, well, it started when you met a girl. At a conference. Do you remember?"

Ted shook his head. He continued wiping his neck, face, and hands. Cheryl took the towel back, crossed to the sink where she wrung it out, re-wetted it, brought it back.

Pythagoras crossed the room and grabbed a Mountain Dew. "What we don't get," he said, "is that she doesn't fit the pattern for a runner and that's confusing. What can you tell us about her?"

Ted cocked his head to one side and raised his palms up. "About who? And what the hell is a runner?"

He paused.

"And one more thing. If you can travel in time, then you have all the time you want to catch whoever you're after. Didn't think of that in your story, did you?" His face couldn't contain his gloating.

Todd grimaced and glared at Ted. "If the person you're chasing also travels in time, it negates that advantage. But you didn't think of that now, did you, Ted?" He raised a foot to his chair and tightened his Chuck Taylors. Ted's face fell slack.

"A runner is a person who escapes into an era other than their own. A runner is someone who escapes into the past or the future because they've given up on their present, whenever that may be," Cheryl said.

"Right. Of course. I still don't have a clue who or what you're talking about."

"Of course you don't," Pythagoras replied. "But let's imagine her name is Alicia, and you were planning to meet her for dinner or something. And let's speculate this Alicia you haven't heard of might be very dangerous. Most runners try to slip away unnoticed. Not her. She left blood in her wake when she ran."

"So, what you're saying is you're keeping me here, alive, because I might have information on her? In that case, prepare to have me around a while, because I ain't telling you shit."

"Well, that seals it. I'm wiping him," said Pythagoras, getting up and pouring the rest of the Mountain Dew into the sink. "Who wants to hold him down?"

"Check that, Py," said Cheryl. "We need him." She sat in the chair next to Ted and turned to him.

"What we are saying, Ted, is that we need you to help us catch her. Honestly, that's the truth. And right now, the only thing that really matters."

Don't trust her, Ted thought.

"It will be a lot easier if you accept what we are saying." Cheryl fidgeted with her band, spinning it around her wrist. "We do this for anyone who's fallen out. Fallen out of time. Sort of a courtesy."

"YOU CALL THIS A COURTESY?"

"Lower your voice," said Pythagoras. "We aren't heartless. Most like knowing this stuff while—"

"While what?"

"While they realize the life they had is over," replied Cheryl.

"You aren't serious," Ted said. "I mean you aren't really serious, are you?"

"'Fraid so," said Pythagoras.

They sat in silence. Ted wasn't sure they were waiting for him to speak or not. He was the first to break the silence.

"What did this person do that was so bad?"

"It may be easier to show you."

Ted shrugged. "Fine, I guess. Prove something to me."

Cheryl rose. "The rest of you head back and try to make contact. We'll meet up with you soon." She walked to the door. "Ted, you're with me."

He followed her to the door. Next to it were two large boxes filled with wallets, purses, and mobile phones.

"Where's my stuff, Cheryl?" he demanded. "Where's my wallet, phone, inhaler?"

"No idea."

"Well, you clearly have those. Where are mine?"

"Those we did steal. We take the cash and use the phones. We return them when we go back."

"Sure you do."

She sighed. "Just come with me." She grabbed his arm.

"OW! What's up with your strength?"

"Traveling makes you strong."

"Oh." He tried to pull her hand off, but it wouldn't budge.

She released her grip.

"What if I don't want to go with you?"

Cheryl stopped, turned, and took Ted by the shoulders. "Please understand this is bigger than you and me and all of us."

"I don't care."

Pythagoras, Wing, and Todd walked past them into the atrium.

"See you soon," said Cheryl.

She turned to face Ted. "Come on."

He followed her out and into the Pipes.

~~~

They stopped at a small room where she provided him a pair of simple gray coveralls. When he came out of the room, he stopped and looked at the walls.

"I get the forwards-backwards thing, but what's with the shading? Why isn't everything illuminated evenly?"

"When folks travel in time, they take a certain amount of time energy with them. And the veins show that. When there is too much of a time influence—like one time corrupting another—time flows too fast and they glow brightly. They fade when time doesn't flow enough. Our team tries to maintain the proper flow."

"Remove the clogs and stop the leaks, eh? Oh, so you're like time plumbers," he said, grinning.

"Yeah, sort of like time plumbers, I guess," she said straight-faced. Ted had hoped she'd laugh.

After a few minutes, Cheryl stopped at an entrance into a dark, ivy green conduit not over five feet high.

"Watch your head."

She stooped to enter. As he trailed her, he tripped, falling forward into her. She leaned away from him, then pivoted behind him catching him in a full nelson.

"Easy," said Ted. "I tripped."

She eased him back onto his feet. In the cramped space they were face to face and alone. He could see the simple beauty of her face, the sparkling in her eyes. Perhaps on a different day, under different circumstances.

"Watch it," she said.

"I'm a gentleman. A nice guy. Not that that ever got me anywhere."

She looked at him, expressionless, before turning to one wall and tracing a vein.

"It is not standard operating procedure to do this," she said, throwing one of the time bands around his wrist, "but I need you to believe. Touch here." She pointed to where a green vein flowed over a red. Ted hesitated.

"We don't have time for this." She forced his band onto a vein. Ted watched the conduit vanish.

This time Ted handled the travel better. In fact, he had time to pay attention, to see if he could catch a glance of somebody hitting him with a syringe, or to search for a 3-D projector casting the images he was seeing. Anything. Anything to give proof to his doubt. Nothing he saw suggested a manufactured experience.

They emerged behind a crowd gathering in front of a small modular, futuristic house. The surrounding homes were exact clones. The sky above was gray, the ground the color and texture of stone dust. Everything was neat, but bland and nondescript. Even the clothing worn around him. It appeared some kind of a dirty, gray burlap.

"How come they don't see us? Didn't we materialize out of thin air?"

"The bands operate in either observe or interact mode. Observer mode provides invisibility. We can then maneuver until it's safe to interact. Sort of like when someone pops up out of nowhere."

"Is that what you did back at the creek?" She nodded. "That's cool. How does that work?"

She glared at him.

"Right. You don't know."

She led them into a secluded alley. "Ready?" she asked. Ted nodded.

She grabbed both bands and twisted. Ted felt the tepid temperature and smelled the stale air.

"Where are we?"

"Alicia's origination point."

"Her what?"

"Where she started her run. This is about the time they discovered the Pipes. This era, as you can see, is supremely blah. Overconsumption robbed the planet of diversity. The need for survival now regulates everything. The weather, food, clothing. It's not much of an existence but it assures basic survival. The monotony, though, can drive people crazy."

"Like Alicia?"

"Maybe. Probably. Don't know for sure."

"Anyway, when scientists discovered the Pipes, they heralded time travel as a solution. A miracle. Allow folks to travel back to a more plentiful past. And the scientists developed a philosophy, almost a marketing slogan: Careful changes to the past to manifest a prosperous future. Crap like that. But travel made things worse. In fact, a lot worse.

"Folks disregarded the whole careful part. Bringing back too much accelerated extinctions in the past which increased scarcities in the future.

"Worse, most everything they brought back died. There just wasn't enough environmental fertility for things to take. It was a real lose-lose.

"Now one of the traveling rules is you can't carry anything with you except the clothes on your back and, of course, a time band. No tech, no money, nothing. The time teams do get to carry some stuff back. We have privileges, given our mission is hard. Mostly junk or bulk food that won't go missing. Everything else, we consume or use on the mission. The nice part is time travel optimizes health and fitness. We can eat whatever and however much we want. You don't gain weight when you travel. Other benefits, too."

"Like being super-strong?"

She nodded.

"That's cool." He cleared his throat. "So you go back in time without anything—no money, no weapons, no tech, etc.? How do you affect anything? How do you even pay for your Doritos?"

"Ever heard of identity theft? Or pick-pocketing? Petty crime? Or just plain old deception and charm? Take your pick. Time travelers are thieves and scoundrels by necessity. Even us. But our mission justifies our behavior.

"The time teams retrieve rogue travelers. Folks still trying to affect changes in the past and improve the future. And believe me when I say there are a lot of them. Rogue travelers flood your era; in fact, we estimate that one percent of your world may be travelers. You live in a rich, rich time, Ted. It attracts a lot of people. Many civilizations could flourish just off the waste you produce."

She paused, walked to the end of the alley, and waved him forward.

"Who knows how many of those are intentionally stealing from the past and, therefore, screwing the future. We travel to the very bright or dark veins, flash in, and catch who we can, and fix what we can."

Ted tried to draw in a deep breath, but he coughed instead. "Sorry," he said. "Asthma. I need my inhaler back."

"That's not asthma. The oxygen is thin. Regulated like everything else. Not as much oxygen as you're used to. You need a few more trips before that won't affect you."

"They only found so many of these." She pointed to her band. "So the scientists' other stupid idea was to time share the bands. To allow folks to, for lack of a better word, vacation through time. To enjoy real food, see real weather, and get to ride in automated vehicles powered by your time's abundance of energy. It's sad. Most don't travel back in time to witness some historical event, they go back for a dessert, a sunny day at the beach. Live music. A bus ride. To see a blue sky and to lay on green grass. But," she added, "that puts them into competition with those native to the time. You can't get tickets to *Hamilton*, because

117

Hamilton isn't just the hottest show of the year. At the moment, it's the hottest show of all years."

"Why don't they ban time travel altogether?"

"They did. The riots were catastrophic. And for many, it's the one thing that keeps them sane. Its controlled use placates the masses."

"Why doesn't anyone travel into the future?" asked Ted, "Maybe the solution is there."

"We just did." Cheryl said. "See any solutions?"

"Oh," said Ted. "Right."

"But worse, many who traveled forward disappeared. Never seen again. We don't know what happened and can't afford to go looking. The bands are impossible to replace, and we can't afford to lose any more. Future travel is forbidden."

"But we did."

"Not everyone is me. I'm special." She slumped against a wall and gestured for Ted to sit next to her.

"Anyway, at first it was just the rich who got to travel. Then, when money became worthless, everyone did. Yet people who went back broke more and more rules. They couldn't help themselves. Governments had to form the time teams. Guess who they chose for the teams?"

"Who?"

"People fallen from those eras. Those who were inadvertently displaced from their own time. It makes sense: who better to defend an era than those from it? Who understands that era better than them? That's why our team only protects roughly 1970 to 2020."

"So you are from my time?"

"No. Like I said, I'm special. So is Py. Wing and Todd are, though. Todd's from '73. Wing's a Gen-X.

"Anyway, they implemented even stricter rules. Travel no more than twenty-four hours. You can only travel alone. Your loved ones remain in your native time, so something anchors you home. And if you violate the rules, one of the time teams retrieves you, and you are never permitted to travel again. The best idea now is that if we minimize the damage already done, even repair it, good effects might spill into the future. Not sure it will work, but it can't get much worse."

They stopped at the back of the crowd.

"If you wonder why rush hour sucks: time travelers. Why all the good stuff is on back order: time travelers. Why concerts sell out in minutes: time travelers. Why do the wrong teams win? The elections go askew? Time travelers. In fact, one wonders where humanity would be if time travel had never been unearthed. Probably better off. Maybe a lot better off."

"What does any of this have to do with Alicia?"

"You know her now, huh?" Ted stayed silent. Cheryl began walking through the crowd. "C'mon. This way."

118

At the front of the crowd, in the house's front yard, lay a family of corpses. A father and three children. Their throats deeply and neatly cut from ear to ear. Blood trails showed the victims had been dragged from the house and then piled in front with no deference for the dead.

Cheryl pushed Ted to the piles. She wrestled his hand onto a little girl's bloody dead throat and with her other hand turned the face towards them. "Is this real enough for you? Can you believe this?"

Don't trust her.

Ted tried to doubt what he saw and felt. To look past the sallow skin, the blue lips, and the cold, cold, clammy skin. The empty eyes. He'd never touched death. He tried to suppress a gag. And to pull his hand back. Everything about it seemed real. He could not disprove it.

"We are telling you the truth, Ted. Not everyone can handle the truth, but everyone is entitled to it. And this is it. This is Alicia's family." Her grip relaxed.

"HEY! YOU TWO, STOP!" A uniform was parting the crowd.

"Do you understand now?" she asked. "This as a message. She killed her ties here, which means she has no desire to come back." She peered at the oncoming uniform. "Time to go." They darted into another alley. She twisted both bands and they were back in the Pipes.

"Why not just let her go? How bad can it be?"

"Look, Ted, it's like this." Cheryl pulled her hair back into a pony tail, then grabbed Ted and started to run. Ted kept up. It felt great.

"Time moves like a river, but it can flow in almost any direction. Backwards, forwards, up, down, whatever. Time isn't linear because time is special. It's composed of the effects of all the interactions in the universe. People are part of that. It includes all the decisions people are making, have made, and will make. Time, like water, can overcome or wear down almost any obstacle. That keeps what you call the timeline mostly stable. The occasional ripple dissolves into the larger current. But we don't think Alicia wants to make little ripples. Something bigger, but we don't know what. She has a time band. She has future knowledge. And she's mentally unstable. Who kills their own family? We think she wants to change the whole course of the time river. The whole thing. We can't risk that. You can't risk that."

Ted let go a long sigh. "Fair enough," replied Ted. "If you are telling me the truth, and I'm not saying I believe all of this yet, I get it. Enough of it anyway."

They arrived at an intersection. Ted had to shield his eyes from the blinding bright green and red light.

"Is this my time?"

"Sure is," she said. "It shouldn't be this intense."

"Yeah, I get that. Here?" he asked, holding his time band next to the brightest vein he could find.

She nodded.

119

He pushed the band against the vein and, with a flash, they were gone.

~~~

Ted and Cheryl flashed into an elevator in the municipal parking structure that adjoined the Delaplaine Arts Center.

"An elevator?" Ted asked.

"No one suspects much about someone walking out of an elevator," Cheryl said. "It's an ideal place to flash in."

The doors opened. The three other plumbers were waiting. They climbed in.

"Contact?" said Cheryl.

"For a moment, but she lost us. She's preparing for something," said Pythagoras.

"Yeah, she is," added Wing.

"Thoughts?" Cheryl asked.

"Just take her out," said Todd. "A random shooting."

She shook her head. "Too messy. Plus, it won't tell us what she's done or planning to do."

Cheryl turned to Ted. "What were you two going to do?"

"Go for food. Sushi."

"Look," said Pythagoras to Cheryl, but pointing at Ted. "Before this goes any further with him, we need some assurance. Is he with us?"

Ted wasn't sure. But he perceived what being out would mean. Death or Mind Wipe.

Besides, if they did trust him enough to release him, there was a chance he could get away. Then again, he wasn't so sure he would want to be hunted down by them, either. So he nodded and raised an affirming thumb. "I'm in." He'd figure out his true loyalties later.

"Good." Cheryl pulled him aside. "Remember, we'll be close. Think you can get her talking? Once we hear enough, we'll grab her. If you can, distract her when we jump her. Keep her from manipulating her band or we'll lose her. Again. Got it?" Ted gave another thumbs up. "OK, folks, let's go play with lightning."

Ted looked down. "Shit. What about my clothes? I can't meet her dressed like this."

"On it," replied Wing. "I'll meet you there." And—FLASH—she vanished.

"OK, let's move out."

They walked down All Saints Street and then turned right to approach the amphitheater from the rear.

Wing stepped from the shadows and handed Ted his clothes.

"Where did you get these?"

"From last week. I raided your closet. Also, I ate your lasagna. Thanks. And sorry. But mostly thanks. It was yummy."

"That's what happened? I thought I was going crazy. I really, really wanted that."

He caught Cheryl looking at him, a small smirk on her face. When their eyes met, it vanished.

"Game on," said Pythagoras, pointing to the amphitheater. Ted sat alone, head in hands. Cheryl appeared next to him.

"OK, Ted, you're up. After the lightning strike, jump in. Todd, Wing, stay here and provide protection in case things get hairy. Py and I will find some place to listen in."

She turned to him and gave him a grimace crossed with a smile. "Good luck, nice guy."

"Still Death or Mind Wipe when it's over?"

She pulled back. "Inescapable." She turned back to face the plumbers. "Milkshakes for whoever gets her band. Good luck, Ted. I'm taking your time band. OK, everyone out of observation mode in 3, 2, 1 . . ."

The lightning strike was terrifying. And Cheryl had saved his life. Of that, there was no question. Next to where Ted stood, the large willow tree burned, but a gentle rain was extinguishing it fast. Ted took his position.

It seemed like forever while Ted tried to stay dry while waiting for Alicia. Out of habit he reached into his jacket to find his phone. It wasn't there.

"I'm so sorry, Ted. You are so wet. Shall we get dinner now?"

Ted started forward. She had snuck up behind him. "Geez, you startled me. Where did you come from?"

"Yes," she said, "we will eat now I think."

Gone were her older clothes. Instead she wore a yellow hiking rain suit with luminescent orange stripes. She carried a backpack, the price tag dangling from a strap.

"Did you get everything you need?"

"Yes, thank you."

"Good. C'mon, the restaurant is this way. I'm soaked and freezing if that matters at all."

As they crossed the small stone bridge over the creek, Ted heard something familiar. His phone. Buzzing. Loudly. In the one place it shouldn't be. Alicia's pocket.

"Alicia, do you have my phone?"

She pulled it out. "I'm sorry. You dropped it, and I picked up. I should have given it back to you. Here, you should respond," she added, handing him the phone.

It was the last in a series of several texts from the bank. That wasn't so unusual. The bank texted him for every transaction on his debit card. What was unusual were the texts for everything he hadn't bought: A hiking suit ($350), paracord ($35), headlamp ($80), folding knife ($125), backpack ($179), Wilderness First Aid Kit ($379), and flares ($15). All of them without his approval. And all of them Alicia either now wore, or he suspected she carried on her person. He remembered the note. *Don't trust her.*

"Uh, Alicia, what are all these?" He held up the phone for her to see. "Did those fall out of my pocket, too? Did they fall out with my wallet, too?"

He searched his pants and jacket. "By the way, just where is my wallet?"

Ted felt betrayed. Worse—he felt conflicted. Before he had traveled, if she had just asked, he would have bought her the stuff. No big deal. But the shocking realization that what he had heard about her could be true had him questioning his own judgement. Had he not seen it? Any of it? Was he that subject to flattery? Anger welled in his gut, and he raised a single accusatory finger to her face when she pushed him against the side of the bridge in another embrace.

"Oh, Ted," she stammered, her body shaking with sudden sobs, her arms clutching him around the neck. "I'm sorry. I'm so very, very sorry. I should have told you." Her eyes were turning red, her cheeks flushing. She reached into her jacket and handed Ted his wallet.

Ted couldn't read her. She'd seemed so genuine, so frank and truthful at the conference. Shouldn't that count for something? But, still, he couldn't give her a free pass.

"You have to do better than that. Why didn't you ask? I might have just said yes. Instead you left me. Left me by myself, just sitting there. Like an idiot. In the rain. And then you stole from me. On top of that, in case you care, lightning almost killed me."

She was silent for a moment, but then took his hand, pulling him off the bridge.

"Oh, Ted, you don't understand," she said, her voice soft, pleading. "I had to."

Ted yanked back his hand. "Yeah? So tell me the truth. Tell me everything." He pushed her away and crossed his arms. "You need to give me a really good reason why you ripped me off. Why I shouldn't just go call the cops."

She bit her lip. "Can I trust you, Ted? Can I really, really trust you?"

"I guess it depends on what you tell me."

"We need to go somewhere where we can talk. Somewhere private." She took him north past the amphitheater toward the bus stop and train station.

Reaching an empty bench, her eyes searched up and down the creek. *Is she looking for them? Is she looking for the time team?* She sat down and patted the bench for him to sit.

"You aren't going to believe me," she said. "But I swear what I'm about to tell you is true."

Don't trust her.

"My real name is Dr. Alicia Shew."

"And? So what?"

"I'm from the future, Ted. Honestly and truly. I'm from the future."

Ted just stared at her.

"Fuck this," he said. "Give me any other shit you stole from me and get lost." Ted stormed away, heading back downtown. "And bullshit, Alicia." He glared at her. "Bullshit. Bullshit. And more bullshit. And there's no such thing as time travel. Science has disproven it."

She raced in front of him, blocking his path. She raised her hands to him. "Ted, please wait. Please. Listen. I'm telling you the truth. My life," she said stuttering through the words, "It's . . . it's . . . it's in danger."

Ted stopped. "I think you need help, Alicia. I think your boat has broken free from the pier."

"Please." She took his hand, leading him to the bench. "There's more . . . but I'm running out of time. I need to explain. And I need your help."

She sat on the bench again. He sat beside her. "I am a temporal scientist."

"A what?"

"A temporal scientist. I study time. Temporal science does not exist in your time. But it does in mine." She paused. "In my time, my era, we discovered a complex where time travel is possible. My team and I . . . we figured out how to use it to benefit mankind."

It was consistent at least with what he had heard from Cheryl. "You're talking crazy, but I'll play. Keep going."

"The future is bleak," she said. She turned, staring across the creek, lost in thought. "The future is not good, Ted. People are starving, dying every day. We theorized that a limited amount of time travel would enable us to pull resources from the past to the future. To save the future by picking off the waste from the past. A past where overconsumption made waste. A lot of waste. But that waste, especially from your era, is enough to jump start our barren dirt, to help repopulate some species, to bring diversity and life back to our ecosystem."

Again, consistent.

"And it was working. Improvements happened. But in cultures where scarcity is common, those who have resources rule those who don't. The people whom we trained to run the complex turned against us. They now plunder the past for their own ends, their own desires. And they don't care if the rest of the world survives. They eat, what is it called now, snack food? A luxury. They eat snack food while the world starves."

He'd seen it with his own eyes. "Alicia, I need to tell you something."

"Yes?"

Don't trust her.

"Never mind . . . I still don't believe you . . . but I'm listening. Continue."

123

"I was going to tell the authorities. They . . ." She bit her lower lip again, her eyes swelled, and her face paled. ". . . found out, and they killed my whole family." She swallowed hard. "My husband . . . my three precious babies. Left them piled up like . . . like garbage."

She stood and walked a few feet from him, sobbing.

"Alicia . . ."

"Wait, please . . . I need a minute."

He draped an arm across her shoulders and escorted her back to the bench. He understood he shouldn't be thinking how beautiful she was. Especially like this. But she was. Even in her pit of despair she captivated him. And if her story was true, maybe they could have a future.

She reached for his hand, and he let her take it.

"They came for me. But I escaped. I killed one of them and took this device. This device that allows time travel." She held up her time band. "I escaped to here. I was running. Running at the conference when we met. But they've found me again. When I was buying these materials." She held up the gear. "But I eluded them, and I came to get you. I have a plan. A plan to stop them. But I need your help. I can't do it without you."

"Is that your meeting?" he asked. She nodded.

"Their leader is named Cheryl, and she's an anachronism. Most of these . . . these time plunderers . . . hail from my time. But not her. As a child in her era, she was rescued from a car accident by a traveler who did something he shouldn't have done. He brought her back to the time complex. Normally, to minimize any temporal consequences, we would erase the memory of anyone who accidentally traveled with us . . . but . . . we couldn't . . . not to a child. So the decision was made to collectively raise her there. She spent her formative years going back and forth through time. And we think that's what caused her breakdown."

"Her what?"

"It's speculation, but we surmised that seeing humanity making the same mistakes over and over again can't be good for a developing psyche. If she was from a particular era, she might have had the contextual grounding, an understanding in humanity. Instead she grew up away from it. Alienated from it. So now she's a sociopath leading sociopaths, taking from humanity anything they want, anytime they want, regardless of the consequences."

"Wow," said Ted. "That's . . . that's unbelievable."

"The car accident that killed her parents. It should happen in less than twenty minutes. If we stop it from happening, she'll have a normal life. We stop her. We stop them. They won't chase me. They won't destroy humanity."

She stood and stared back to Frederick for a moment before turning back to him and extending her hand.

124

"And if the accident happens when I say it should, you'll have your proof. Proof I'm telling you the truth. All I am asking you to do is to save a little girl."

The totality of her actions, her words, was convincing. And she hadn't needed to take him anywhere to prove it. He took her hand and stood. Alicia pulled him to her and they walked away from Frederick along the creek. She put her arm around his waist, her head on his shoulder. He could feel all of her, open and sharing, vulnerable. She wasn't holding anything back. Not like Cheryl. Cheryl was hiding something. Cheryl would never sob. Alicia was sobbing now. And when she did, he felt her sadness, her loss. And her fear. Her genuine fear.

"I knew it when we met." She looked up into his eyes. "I sneaked into that event. To eat. I was so hungry. And then we met. And I knew it . . . I knew you, dear Leslie, would be the one to save me and the world."

~~~

Ted's job revolved around data. And in the world of data he'd learned to look for a pattern, a consistency of values revealing an insight or dispelling an assumption.

Sometimes it came without effort. Other times it would be more elusive. He would have to keep changing the variables, filters, or parameters. You couldn't predict when, analyzed in the right context, or thrown against the right algorithm, the records would suddenly make sense. But then he'd have it. A record set determined by logic and reason, not hunches or hopes, supposition or suspicion. An authoritative fact. Something with certainty to support a decision. Something to act on.

Leslie.

His real name.

He'd never mentioned it to Alicia. She couldn't have known it without researching him. That implied forethought and planning. She had used his real name, and now he had the data he needed. This beautiful woman, a woman he had hoped to believe in, a woman to whom he imagined sharing everything, had—no, not had, *was*—deceiving him. He knew which 'her' not to trust. The note had been a warning about Alicia.

Ted tried to spot the plumbers without her noticing, but she did.

"What is it?" She spun, her eyes scanning both sides of the creek. "Have they found us? Come, we must hurry." She hustled down the creek pulling at his hand.

He let go.

"Hey, we should go back," Ted said. She stopped and turned. "We can get EMS and the cops. They will help us."

Her back straightened, and her face transformed from tears and grief to aggression and frustration. She caught herself and it changed back.

"Leslie, we are almost out of time! We have to act NOW. We don't have time to get help!" She waved for him to move up next to her.

Ted stood still.

"I don't remember telling you my real name, Alicia. How do you know me as Leslie? And, full disclosure, I don't believe you. Also, this date officially sucks."

She smiled at him, but Ted didn't smile back, and by the time her smile morphed to a scowl, she had already taken him down and now was on him, holding a small knife to his throat. Her eyes were angry slits, her mouth and face drawn back tight. "Oh, well. Too bad for you. We are going to walk away from here, hand in hand like a loving couple. Don't underestimate me."

"There are others, Alicia, and they'll stop you. I've met one of the time teams. They're on to you."

"Oh, Leslie," she said, "I've already killed two of them . . . the ones standing watch behind you back at the creek. You should have heard them whimpering as they bled out, reaching pathetically for these." She pulled from her pocket two bloody time bands. "It's a shame they couldn't reach them in time. But them traveling back to heal, of course, didn't exactly fit into my plan."

She pulled him to his feet. "Walk," she commanded.

Ted looked around. No Cheryl. No Pythagoras. He was on his own.

"Walk," she repeated.

They walked until the creek met the Monocacy River and then continued until they reached a small bridge near Frederick Airport.

"I think I'd survive a fall from that height," Ted said.

She ignored him.

"So what's the plan? What's your evil plot to take over the world?"

He felt the knife poke him in the back. "Silence."

"Is that what you said to your husband, to your kids, when you cut their throats?"

She threw him to the ground, kicking him in the head. He raised his hand to his temple. The tips of his fingers came back sticky and red.

"Need I remind you that your existence is only a convenience," she hissed. Her face clenched, teeth bared. Her breath came out of her nostrils hot, animalistic. "You are money and bait. Nothing else."

"Hey, whatever. I'm getting kind of used to the idea of a drastically limited existence. That's not really going to scare me the way you want. And obviously I'm your bankroll. But bait? For who? No one's going to save me. I can't think of a single person besides me who cares whether I live or die. Even if the others save me, they're just going to kill me anyway or wipe my brain."

Alicia just laughed. "Yes, they have their silly rules. So high-minded. So noble." She kicked him in the stomach, and he fell forward. "And don't doubt that I love my family above all else. And once I kill the rest of the teams, I will get my babies and we will live whenever, wherever, and however we want. Forever."

"Ah, so that's it. You're not here to change the past. Or the future. You're killing the time teams. Smart. Without them, you control the Pipes. You're almost immortal. And have both the past and the future at your disposal. Clever. You'll be rich beyond calculation. My question is, though, did you explain that to your littlest? I mean, did she agree with your plan? Did she extend her neck to make it easier for you? Wait. I bet she even cut her own throat all the while thanking her mommy."

The fury spread on her face. She closed behind him, placed her foot on the back of his knees, forcing him to the ground. She raised the knife into the air.

Ted had seen the homeless man pushing the cart across the bridge but hadn't paid much attention. He did notice when the homeless man flew from the bridge towards Alicia. He couldn't miss it when the man's hat fell from his head revealing Pythagoras's face.

~~~

Ted couldn't believe the speed with which the two fought. But it was clear that Py was not her match. Alicia's technique was superior. The knife found its mark sliding between Py's ribs, and he crumpled to the ground. Alicia stood over him, dominant, and removed his band. Py's labored breathing sounded frantic and desperate.

"One down and one to go," said Alicia. She stood over Ted and bound his hands and feet. "See?" she said. "Bait."

Cheryl charged from the woods, tackling Alicia.

Cheryl rose, ran to Ted, and with her own blade cut his hands free. "Run, Ted. Get help. Anyone you can. Now!" But before she slashed away the knots at his feet, Alicia was on her.

This time the match was more even, but Alicia had more endurance and wore Cheryl down. Cheryl, frustrated, started lunging recklessly, extending herself, looking for the one critical hit—the one knockout blow. Alicia took advantage of Cheryl overreaching, pivoted behind her, used her leverage against her, and seized her in a strangulation hold.

"Fuck you, Alicia, you crazy bitch. Fuck you."

"Now, now, little girl. I wouldn't want you to misbehave in front of your parents."

"My what?"

"Your parents." She let go a little laugh. "We never told you. Never told you how Cheryl, the great defender of the timeline, came to be." She sighed and shook her head.

"Don't forget. You are so special. We would tell you that. But your parents didn't die on a time mission. Any minute now, you and your parents will come down the road and reach this bridge. And a mean old truck will hit your car. Knock it off the bridge and into the river.

Mommy and Daddy dead. Little Cheryl trapped with rising water. So sad. So very, very sad.

"Of course, you will be rescued, and taken to the Pipes. You, the exception. The girl raised in the Pipes. The girl raised out of time.

"But a princess without parents. Wouldn't it be so much better if they survived? If you grew up with a real family? A mommy and a daddy? A real life."

Cheryl's eyes widened.

"Don't listen to her," Ted pleaded. "Cheryl, you were right, you have to stop her."

Cheryl stood frozen.

Alicia loosened her grip. "The easiest course for you is to not interfere." She took a few steps back from Cheryl.

Cheryl didn't move. She looked at Ted.

"Don't fall for it, Cheryl."

"But they say it's best not to take chances," Alicia said, plunging the knife into Cheryl's back.

Cheryl's breath burst from her lungs and her eyes flared with the pain. She stumbled forward and fell. Alicia, though, wouldn't let up. She continued, stabbing Cheryl meticulously, picking her marks to maximize injury. With every stab, Cheryl's groans grew quieter.

Alicia reached over and slid Cheryl's time band from her limp arm. "And now, my dear, you are out of time." She raised the knife skyward.

Ted did the only thing he could, throwing himself between Cheryl and the plummeting blade. The knife slid into him below his navel, up to the hilt. It hurt more when she drew it out.

"Oh, well," said Alicia. "At least this avoids our short marriage and my terrible suffering when my husband dies so unexpectedly, so suddenly in a tragic honeymoon accident." She cackled.

She traced the knife's point along his belly. Placed both hands on the hilt and, with all her weight, slid it into him.

"AAAGH!" The pain was searing. "Please Alicia," Ted cried. "Enough! You win, you win!"

"Of course, I do." She started laughing. "But do you realize the funniest part, Leslie? I thought you were a girl. Leslie is a girl's name, is it not? I was going to kill you and steal your identity. Easy. Single. High income. Perfect for me to assume. Leslie, huh. I even like the sound. But I never thought to check your gender. Imagine my surprise at that awful conference. It was intolerable, realizing I'd have to change my plan. And then to sit there and hear you drone on and on and on . . ."

Ted pulled on her jacket, trying to raise himself up. "I'll do anything, just let me . . ." He felt the knife again.

"Bleed to death?" she laughed. "Certainly."

But he had gotten what he wanted. Clutched in his hand, he held the two time bands he had pilfered from her pockets.

Alicia looked down at him, watching the blood dripping from his abdomen, onto Cheryl, and down to the muddy, sandy soil of the river's edge. "I got to save a little girl." Alicia rose and walked to her backpack.

Get the time bands on them. They can flash to the Pipes, heal, and then . . .

He tried to roll over to get the band on Cheryl's wrist, but something caught Alicia's attention. She wheeled around.

"There will be none of that," Alicia said. She pulled the bands from his hand, dragging him by his ankles away from Pythagoras and Cheryl. Like them, she was strong.

Pythagoras and Cheryl's breathing slowed alarmingly. Py was choking on blood. A sharp pain burst behind one of his knees, then the other. He instinctively tried to draw himself into the fetal position, but was unable. She'd hamstrung him.

Ted tried to focus on Alicia, to figure out a way to fight, but the agony made that impossible. His feet and hands grew cold. It was getting harder and harder to breathe.

"Well, you were persistent, were you not?" Alicia looked in his eyes.

Ted tried to keep them open, but they were too heavy.

"Enjoy seeing them die. Goodbye, Leslie." He forced his eyes open. She walked away. He closed his eyes, sensed something tugging at him, and a sudden bright light.

I'm going into the light, thought Ted. *I'm going into the light.*

~~~

"It's like I always tell you, or us, or we tell ourselves. Whatever. This is so much harder than I imagined. Anyway," the voice cleared his throat, "if you really want something done right, well you just have to do the job yourself."

The light hurt Ted's eyes. His stomach was tender but not painful. And a slight warmth was returning. He could move his legs. The bleeding had stopped.

"But I don't understand . . ." He felt woozy and weak.

"OK, this sounds trite but time, or more correctly, time travel really does heal all wounds. Unfortunately, we don't have enough time for you to fully heal." Someone behind him—someone very strong—propped him up. "But take a second. Here, have some water." A hand shoved a bottle into his hand. The voice was so familiar, but it escaped recognition. He took a large swig and looked up into a smiling face. He choked on the water.

It was a face he saw every day. A face he saw most often reflecting in the bathroom mirror. The face was his own. "OK, Tedster, stop staring. Focus, please," he said. "We need to get back, need to save the day. As usual. Again. It's kinda what we do now. Think you can walk? C'mon, Py and Cheryl are counting on us."

"What? Who are you? I . . ."

"What? You didn't think I'd let it end like that, did you? Dying back there? Time travel, dude. Why wouldn't we save ourselves? Duh. No way. Glad you got my note by the way. Sorry it had to be cryptic. Had to make you a bit suspicious, but without overly tainting the timeline. Plus, if I didn't tell you not to trust her you'd have bought everything she said. You were always so gullible with the ladies. Also, I thought writing it with our left hand was a deft touch. Legible, but unrecognizable. Plus using Leslie would, of course, attract your attention."

"But, but, but . . . how?"

"Yeah, yeah, yeah. Listen, we really don't have time to get into some big, drawn-out discussion." Ted pulled Ted to his feet.

"Wait, you're a . . . I mean I'm a . . . a . . . a time team . . . a time plumber?"

"No, much cooler. I'm a Time Ranger. Time Ranger Ted."

Ted's vision was clear enough to see himself garbed up in black like Errol Flynn from some 1950's swashbuckler movie. With a cape no less. All he was missing was a freaking musketeer hat with an ostrich feather.

"You look like an asshole. And Time Ranger Ted sounds terrible."

"Hey now, go easy. This was all your idea."

It made Ted's head hurt.

"Here's the plan. Flash back, get those two back to the Pipes before it's too late. I'll keep her busy. Drop them off and then come back. You have more work to do."

He tossed three time bands to Ted.

"How do I?"

"Right. You don't know." He placed a band on Ted's wrist. "You don't need to find the right vein. Just focus very hard on when and where you want to go. Then touch here. The band will get you there. Same thing to get back."

Ted nodded.

"Cool," said Time Ranger Ted. "Let's go kick some evil time-traveling, whacked-out, crazy-ass, megalomaniacal bitch butt."

~~~

Aside from a small soreness in his abdomen, Ted's injuries were nonexistent when he materialized back by the bridge. Time Ranger Ted gave him the thumbs up before running toward where headlights of passing cars barely lit Alicia's hiking suit.

Ted sprinted down the embankment to where Py and Cheryl lay. He grabbed Py by his collar and pulled him next to Cheryl. Both were still warm. He placed the bands on their wrists, manipulated his controls, and the three flashed out.

Back at the Pipes, both Py and Cheryl's bleeding had stopped. Cheryl had not yet regained consciousness, but Py was sitting up. Ted was about to flash back when he heard Py's voice.

"Hey, kid."

"Hey, Py. Feeling better?"

"Yeah, almost alive is a lot better than almost dead. Hey, kid, only my friends call me Py."

"Sorry."

"You can call me Py."

"So noted. Thanks. I gotta go."

"Ted?"

"Yeah?"

"Don't take her on alone."

"Don't worry, I won't."

"One more thing. Thanks. Good timing. And don't shit your pants."

"Thanks, Py."

"You're welcome."

~~~

Alicia stood at the end of the bridge, her back to him. She had lit two flares and was pulling the headlamp out of the backpack. Time Ranger Ted was nowhere. *Had she defeated him?*

Ted crept behind her. He had to try. He reached down, picked up a large rock, crept closer, and raised the rock high above his head. His shoe scuffed the asphalt. Alicia whirled, throwing a back kick into his chest.

Ted was thrust hard onto his back. Alicia was over him again, raising the knife.

"You! How is this?" She placed one hand on his neck, forcing him to the ground. "Who's with you? Who did you bring back with you? If you don't tell me, I'll slit your throat, and this time I'll wait till your body turns cold."

She held the knife like an ice pick, high over Ted's face.

Ted saw it before he heard it, the black figure in the air, flipping over Alicia, smoothly twisting the knife out of her hand, before landing in a somersault and rising to his feet.

"Back in middle school, I never liked it when bullies picked on my friends, and I especially didn't like it when bullies picked on me." He hurled the knife into the river. "So whad'ya say I just work out some issues I've carried since the sixth grade. I assure you it will be very therapeutic for me and a crap ton better than what guidance counselors would tell me is," he made air quotes, "the right thing to do."

Alicia sprung off Ted at Time Ranger Ted. Time Ranger Ted easily dodged the move.

"Took you long enough," said Ted.

"Just waiting on you, pal." His face broke into a Cheshire cat grin. "Now watch and learn, Tedster, watch and learn."

Alicia spun, throwing a low kick at Time Ranger Ted's heels, but Time Ranger Ted jumped, and the kick passed under his feet.

"Lesson one: learn to fight." Alicia hurled herself at Time Ranger Ted, throwing numerous punch combinations which he countered seamlessly. "I recommend visiting Bruce Lee. He's great. But Chuck Norris is good too. Especially for the kicking." Time Ranger Ted's leg seemed to shoot straight up before slamming down on Alicia's head. Her hands shot up defensively in response and were, therefore, pulled out of position to block Time Ranger Ted's following front kick from knocking the wind from her. "The important thing is to use different styles for different distances. Tae Kwon Do for further distances, boxing, Karate for a bit closer in."

He turned his back to Alicia and faced Ted. "And you also must learn grappling . . ." Alicia flung herself on Time Ranger Ted's back, swiftly putting him into a sleeper hold.

". . . so wrestling . . . Jujitsu . . . hang on I'm getting a bit woozy here . . ."

Ted could see Time Ranger Ted weakening. He leapt up to assist, but Time Ranger Ted raised his palm, stopping him.

". . . are super helpful . . ." Time Ranger Ted seemed to weaken further, his arms groping, reaching back toward Alicia. Alicia held on tight, clutching him harder. He fell to his knees.

"LET ME HELP YOU!" screamed Ted.

". . . And lesson two . . . never ever ever . . ." said Time Ranger Ted, ". . . underestimate fitness or . . ." his eyes opened widely, and he winked at Ted, "sleight of hand." In his hands were five time bands.

He counted them as he tossed them to the ground in front of Ted. "Py one . . . Chery two . . . Todd, RIP, three . . . Wing, RIP, four . . . Ted five, this one's yours . . . and . . ." He rolled into a reversal move which had him coming up straddling Alicia, "six. This one is Alicia's."

Alicia looked down at her bare wrist, her eyes ablaze with shock and fury.

"Lesson three: take the time band away so they can't flash away."

Alicia turned on her side, bringing a leg up and across Time Ranger Ted's chest and pushing him down and off her chest. Time Ranger Ted rolled on his side before rolling into a reverse somersault and rising to his feet.

"Where did you learn the moves?" Ted asked.

"The Fierce Five," said Ted Ranger Ted. "Great ladies. Big smiles. But don't piss them off."

In his hand was his cape. "Let's continue. Lesson four: have cool gadgets."

Alicia looked at Time Ranger Ted and feinted his way but charged at Ted instead. Ted cringed. There was no way Time Ranger Ted could get there in time, and he could see the whites of Alicia eyes, her pupils wide. She pulled back a fist, and Ted could see it rushing at him, closing on his face. He raised his hands in defense and turned his face away. But there was no impact. He just heard a gentle muffling noise and sensed darkness. He turned back. Time Ranger Ted's cape. It had enveloped her, morphing itself into a body-length sack. In it Alicia struggled, but futilely.

"OK," said Ted, "now that I've experienced the outfit in action it's growing on me." He looked down. "Really digging the cape."

"Yeah, the infinity cape. Pretty badass. It grows and constricts to whatever size and shape you need, like a body bag, a hammock or, and I'm not admitting to this, carry-on luggage. Is that cool or what?"

"Totally."

"OK, lesson five. Use non-lethal when you can." He snapped his fingers. The cape returned to his back. Alicia flipped herself onto her feet, breathing menacingly, her fists clenching and unclenching.

"I can't believe you were ever into her," he said, laughing.

"Well, you haven't always had the best taste either," countered Ted.

Alicia screamed and shot forward. Time Ranger Ted stood his ground, but at the last moment, he cartwheeled, grabbing the five time bands from the ground. He tossed them at her, at each limb at the ankle or wrist, and one around her neck, which closed on it like a wide necklace. There was a quick buzz, and pop, like a buildup of static electricity, and she stopped moving, immobilized. "But understand certain opponents, no matter what, will never, ever stop."

He approached Alicia. "Right? You are never, ever, ever, going to stop."

There was no surrender in her eyes. Only hate and defiance. Endless, eternal defiance. Ted could feel it. Sense it. "What Alicia, and those like her don't get, is time travel is awesome for improving who and what you are, but not for getting you what you think you want.

"OK, finally, lesson six. Always seek to make new friends. Do something for them, and they do something for you." He waved his arm wearing the time band dismissively at Alicia. The time bands holding her glowed rapidly, surrounding her in a pool of soft white light, then turned red and green and vanished.

"Um, what just happened?"

"She's gone. Strewn throughout time. She's dead. Lost forever in forever. Just another day and another win for Time Ranger Ted." Time Ranger Ted winked.

Ted rolled his eyes.

~~~

Time Ranger Ted moved to a guardrail and gestured for Ted to join him.

"Look, no one can know I've been here, OK? If you squeal you will only be hurting yourself, got it?"

133

Ted nodded. "Got it."

"Good. Now pay attention. The time bands. They're not tech. They're beings. Beings that live in time. They're circles, rings, loops? Doesn't that suggest something to you?"

Ted shook his head, "No, not exactly."

"Eternal. Without end."

"Wait . . . what?"

"Look, they built the Pipes. It's a portal between the temporal universe, a.k.a. time, and the physical universe, a.k.a. space. They can travel through time like we travel through space. But they can't crisscross a room, like we can't crisscross a year. But they are cognizant, intelligent. The time teams will realize this eventually. But you can't lead them to it. They have to learn it on their own.

"But once you learn they're sentient, the fun begins. You learn to pick up their thoughts and to feel their presence. And they begin to recognize you. Communications are easy after that. Shortly after that bonding begins. One band, one person."

He held up his wrist. "This is Timmy. Timmy Time Band. Say hi, Timmy." The band flashed twice. "We share a symbiotic relationship. I need him to explore time, and he needs me to explore space. You'll meet him soon."

Ted sat, a smile growing across his face. "But that could mean immortality, perfect health, infinite time to do almost everything, to learn almost—"

Time Ranger Ted interrupted him. He clasped the back of Ted's neck. "Look, we aren't there. Not as an entire species. Some of us, maybe. But most of us, no. If you and Cheryl and the time teams continue in your work, our history and future will straighten out. Undo the damage done, and we'll get there one day. But not today. Not tomorrow either."

Ted peered down at the river. "Yeah, well that's a bummer. I get it. But still a major bummer."

"And on that note, I gotta jet." Time Ranger Ted stood and held up his arm. The five time bands reemerged, attaching themselves to his arm. "Gotta get my friends home."

Time Ranger Ted started manipulating his band.

"But wait," Ted said. "Aren't we violating the grandfather paradox or something?"

"Absolutely. And in just six seconds hordes of angry theoretical physicists will come charging up the river and tell us we can't exist." He glanced at his watch, his lips moving, counting. "Hey, I guess they're running late. Tell them I couldn't wait, OK?" His hand moved again to his band.

"Wait, one last question," said Ted. "Death or Mind Wipe. I have to choose."

Time Ranger Ted laughed.

134

"Absolute knowledge about the past or the future is a curse. With it one becomes stuck in the glories of the past, or idle, lingering, waiting passively for the fortunes of the future. Either causes one to neglect the present. Both lead, usually, to self-destruction. Erasing your memory is an act of kindness, believe it or not. You will end up living somewhere in time, most often on society's fringes and not in the era you're from, but alive. You can build a new, normal life. That's the Mind Wipe.

"Anyway, choose death and you join the time teams. But the work is dangerous. You don't always make it. Like Todd and Wing. That's the Death.

"The life you led before is over, Tedster. But not because of the time teams. Cheryl granted you a new life. Alicia destroyed your old."

"I wish they'd explained that," Ted said.

"They would have. But I don't believe we were open to new ideas at the time. Anyway, you know which one to choose now, I hope."

Ted shrugged. "Yeah, I guess I do."

"OK, Timmy, where to?" The band glowed and hummed. "What, another thermonuclear threat?" He looked at Ted. "Gotta go. A time ranger's work is never done. See me later. You, however, still have work to do." He pointed over Ted's shoulder.

~~~

Ted saw the dump truck approaching the bridge, the driver on his phone, the truck crossing back and forth over the lanes. When Ted turned back, the guardrail was empty, Time Ranger Ted long gone.

From the other direction, Ted could make out the couple in the mini-SUV with the baby seat in the back. It was almost at the blind corner to the bridge. The dump truck had crossed into its lane.

Alicia's flares. The driver will see the flares and avoid the accident. They'll survive. All of them. But her parents have to die. If they don't, Cheryl won't lead the time teams. The damage to the timeline's permanent. They have to die. Her parents have to die.

He raced to the flares and threw them into the river. He ran to the edge of the bridge and leapt off just in time to hear the horn and screeching tires of the smaller car. The dump truck smashed into the smaller car with a loud, deep thud. Then there was cracking as the side of the bridge broke and toppled into the river. The truck's momentum slowly shifted the car closer and closer to the side of bridge until the vehicle itself plunged over, landing upside down in the water.

Someone grabbed him. Pythagoras had returned.

They ran into the river towards the wreck, through the shallow water to the misshapen vehicle. Her parents were already dead. They could never have survived the impact. In the back seat, a small girl, perhaps three-years-old, lay crumpled. Blood was flowing from her nose, mouth, and ears. Her limbs were askew in grossly awkward angles.

135

Ted and Pythagoras worked furiously, cutting away her seatbelt, pulling away the pieces of the car entrapping her. Her body slid free into Ted's hands. Her body broken and lumpy, bones sticking out.

"I'll get her back to the Pipes." Ted shouted.

"No."

"She's not going to make it, Py. We have to go now."

"No," Pythagoras repeated. "I'll do it. This is mine."

Py opened his arms. Ted read Py's face. It was sad and resigned. He passed the girl to Py.

"I'll see to it she does well."

"That's a known. See you back at the Pipes."

"No, you won't. Goodbye, Ted." He flashed away.

Ted climbed to the road. Cars were approaching the scene. Soon EMS would arrive. He swung back down the river's edge to flee the scene, when he made out a figure just inside the wood line.

Cheryl stood crying, leaning against a tree. Her shoulders shook with each sob.

"Cheryl, I . . . I . . . am so . . . so very sorry. But I . . ."

"I saw what you did. You could have stopped it. My parents could have lived. I could have had it. A real family. A normal life. And you . . . you . . . took that all . . ." She turned away from him.

"Away," said Ted. "I took it all away. But I had . . ."

She spun away from him, "I KNOW WHY YOU HAD TO! I KNOW WHY!"

"Cheryl, listen." He tried to make his voice low, measured, soft.

She wheeled around. "GIVE IT TO ME! GIVE IT TO ME NOW!" She pointed at his time band. He slipped it off and handed it to her. Her voice lowered "I understand what you did."

"Cheryl, please, give me a chance, I didn't want . . ."

"No," she said quietly, wiping away her tears. "Get away from me."

The first EMS vehicles were close now, the red lights bouncing off her face. "You are free to go." She didn't look at him when she flashed away.

Ted opened his apartment door. He had nowhere else to go. He tried to watch TV, eat something, read. Something, anything to shut down his brain.

No more First Saturday dates for me. Way too complicated.

The thought made him laugh.

Over the next few days, Ted tried to live normally. To brush his teeth every morning, to not boil over when the traffic backed up without any apparent cause, to watch TV and the ads encouraging audiences to eat, to buy, to use, to consume, consume, consume.

In the end, it all felt hollow. Tiny, irrelevant steps in the enormous reality of what existed. One day he would become Time Ranger Ted. Everything else was just waiting.

On the last few days of the week, he skipped work, forcing himself to stay awake for days, walking downtown at night, through the trees in Baker Park in the morning (even past an olive tree which seemed lost among the hickories and elms). In one afternoon, he completed all the trails at Catoctin Mountain National Park, his vigorous health still with him—for now.

On the way home he bought a fifth of single-malt scotch. He planned to drink it that night. All of it.

He lay down on the couch and looked at the ceiling, trying to find imperfections in the paint job, not realizing it when he fell deeply, deeply asleep.

~~~

"Hey, wake up."

Ted pulled the blanket down from his face. It was a nice, colorful, warm blanket.

Cheryl sat on the kitchen stool. She held a large paper coffee cup in one hand.

"What are you doing here?"

"Drinking a Dirty Hippie from Dublin . . ."

"Dublin Roasters?"

"Yeah, that's it." She put the container down on the counter. "Thanks by the way."

"For what?"

"You paid, you big spender." She tossed his wallet to him.

Ted sighed. "Do you guys ever pay for anything yourselves?"

"Hey now, don't be like that. Don't you like the blanket? You didn't pay for it. I boosted it just for you."

He looked at it. He liked it.

"Wait, from whom? Never mind. I don't want to know. What time is it?"

"No idea."

Ted sat up. His head hurt. The whiskey bottle was unopened. "What do you want, Cheryl? Why are you here?"

She tossed him a time band. "It's yours. Don't lose it."

"Timmy?" Ted mumbled. The band emitted a small flash.

"What was that?" Cheryl asked.

"What was what?" answered Ted.

Cheryl stared at him. "Whatever." She opened an Orange Crush and drained the bottle. "Nice place. You should clean it."

"I was going to, but things got in the way."

"Yeah. Things. Things always get in the way." She walked to the window and looked out onto Ninth Street. She grabbed two of the ferns, took them to the kitchen, and pitched them into the garbage. "I need to show you something."

137

She stood next to the couch and pulled him to his feet. "I'll drive," she said, taking his hand.

They flashed twice: once to the Pipes to change and then once again, back at Alicia's origin point. The streets were full of people staring up.

"What's going on?" asked Ted.

"They've never seen a cloud before."

Ted looked up, and there it was—a tiny cumulous cloud.

"It's miniscule."

"Yes, but this part of the world hasn't seen a cloud in centuries. Thought maybe you'd want to see it."

They flashed back to the Pipes where Cheryl led him back to the team room. "I'm not clear how you defeated her. But your part of the era's shimmering nicely so I'm not going searching just because I'm curious. We have other problems to solve." She grabbed a box of Cracker Jack from the kitchenette. "And I'm not sure that what happened caused the cloud."

"Coexistence is not causality," said Ted.

"Whatever. I need a new team."

"Where's Py?"

"When Py came back, he insisted on a mind wipe. He's in ancient Greece. He's fixing math where a traveler really screwed things up."

"Wait, no, really . . . he's that guy?"

"Yes, really. It's not a super common name." She threw a small grin. "It's a small world and an even smaller timeline."

She walked to the back of the room where she sat on a couch, propping her feet up on a small oval table. "Death or Mind Wipe?" she asked before explaining the options and conditions.

"What did you choose?"

"I didn't get to."

"Right. Forgot. Well then it's 'til death do us part, I guess."

Silence.

"Too soon," she said.

"Sorry," he replied.

Ted frowned. She opened the prize. "Crap prize," she said, flicking it across the room into a trashcan. "Two points."

She stood. "Follow me. But if you are going to be on my team, I suppose we should get to know each other. Plus, I have a ton to teach you."

"Sure," said Ted. "I'm a quick learner."

"You better be." She reached the door and opened it. She gestured him to it.

"How do you feel about scallops and snow peas," Ted asked.

"Sounds good," she answered. She stopped in the open door. "You should know I haven't forgiven you. That will take forever."

Ted frowned. He walked through the door.

"But I like nice guys." She walked out and shut the door behind them.

"But, nice guy, be advised. Your forever starts today."

PAXTON

BY JAMES ALLNUTT

"What do you think, boy? Isn't this just the saddest thing you ever saw?"

Mr. Glover was speaking to his dog, Paxton. He was referring to a sign posted on a telephone pole. It was a notice for a lost dog that included a name, a phone number to contact, and a large cash reward.

"Why do they need to offer a reward?" He scratched his shoulder. It was a warm day, the beginning of spring, and he was getting hot in his large baggy sweater.

Paxton suddenly darted toward a squirrel running by. Mr. Glover managed to tighten his grip on the leash before it was yanked out of his hand.

"Whoa there! I almost lost ya!" He used his hands, barely holding Paxton back. Paxton stared at the squirrel as it made its escape. "Squirrels are our friends. You like having friends, don't ya, boy?"

It was a beautiful Saturday afternoon. People were out in their shorts and t-shirts, spending their day in the small downtown. Mr. Glover stood out in his sweater, khakis, and loafers. He had always dressed like an elderly man, and now he finally was one.

~~~

"Hey! Old man!"

Two boys walked up to Mr. Glover. He was an approachable man. Always smiling.

"You boys want to pet my dog? His name is Paxton."

"Can you get us some ice cream?" one of the boys asked. "We're really hungry. They sell ice cream there." He pointed to the door of an ice cream place right next to them.

Mr. Glover crouched down so that his eyes were at their level.

"Now, ice cream is a wonderful treat, but we can't have it all the time."

"Please, mister! We're starving. Neither of us have had anything to eat all day."

"Really?"

The boy nodded.

Mr. Glover looked at the second boy who wasn't acting as hungry as the other.

"Uh, yeah," the second boy said.

Mr. Glover smiled. He didn't mind being a sucker. He turned to Paxton. "What do you think, boy?"

The one who did all the talking reached out and petted Paxton, scratching him behind the ears. It wasn't hard to see that Paxton liked them.

~~~

"One scoop vanilla and one scoop chocolate, please," Mr. Glover said to the young woman working behind the counter. "Two different cones!" he added before she stacked the second scoop on top of the first. "Thank you."

The two little boys watched as she got their cones ready. Mr. Glover handed the cones to them after paying the young woman.

"And here you two go."

"Thanks," they blurted out while grabbing their cones and trotting out the store.

"Wow," the woman behind the counter said. "Those little brats didn't even say thank you."

"They said thank you with their smiles," Mr. Glover said, smiling himself.

"Good way to look at it," she mumbled with a shrug.

"I have a question for you. Maybe you can help out. Do you know how to get to the post office?"

"Post office? They still have those?"

"Well, I sure hope so. I just moved to town to be closer to my daughter, and she can't even help me find the post office. She's spending the day with her husband. They're hunting. Can you believe that? She married a hunter."

"You can look it up on your phone."

"My daughter got me one of those smartphones but I can't figure it out. She says I can do all types of stuff on it like find directions. I tell her that you can't teach an old dog new tricks."

"Yeah. It's easy. Give it here. I'll show you."

~~~

Mr. Glover and Paxton were on their way to the post office, taking their time.

They came to an intersection and waited for the light to change.

A woman with her young daughter stopped at the corner as well.

Mr. Glover noticed the girl looking at Paxton.

"Hello there," Mr. Glover said softly. "Would you like to pet him? His name is Paxton, and he loves being pet."

The girl blushed and hugged her mother's leg.

"She's afraid of dogs," the mother said.

"You know what I like to do when I'm afraid? I like to sing a little song my grandmother taught me. Maybe I could teach it to you." Mr. Glover began to sing, *"It can be scary to go someplace new, or do something you don't know how to, but I know it's something that you can get through, because I'll always be there for you."*

The girl grinned and walked over to Paxton. She looked at Paxton, then up to Mr. Glover, then to her mother, and then back to Paxton. She reached out her hand and patted him gently on the head.

"Say thank you, Jessica," the mother whispered.

"Thank you."

The light changed. "All right, let's go," the mother said.

"I wonder where they're off to," Mr. Glover happily mused as the mother and daughter walked ahead.

Suddenly, Paxton darted toward the street. The leash was yanked out of Mr. Glover's hand before he could grasp it tight enough. There was a stray cat that had run by, and now Paxton was chasing it across the street.

Mr. Glover gave chase without looking. Halfway across the street, he heard the screeching of tires and saw the oncoming car. He dove toward the sidewalk, but his legs weren't what they used to be. He hit the asphalt hard. Luckily, the car came to a stop before hitting him.

He struggled up to his feet, shuffled out of the road and entered the alley that he saw Paxton run into. There was no sign of Paxton or the cat.

"Paxton! Here, boy!"

Mr. Glover rushed down to the other end of the alley. It opened to a street full of closed store fronts. He didn't see Paxton anywhere.

"Paxton!"

He walked to the end of the block. Without any idea which way to go, he chose a direction at random and shuffled along as quickly as he could.

"Paxton! Here, boy!"

He kept calling out Paxton's name as he searched street after street. Time went by, and he was starting to lose his voice. He made his way to an intersection on the outside of town and gave one last yell as loud as he could. He stood, silent, hoping to hear a bark or see Paxton run around the corner. Instead, he saw a truck do a U-turn right in the middle of the street. The old beat up truck came right toward him and quickly halted.

"Lose your dog?" the man said through the open window.

Mr. Glover heard panting. The truck was tall, so he had to get up on his toes to see inside.

"Paxton!"

Paxton ran over to the window and tried to jump out, but the driver stopped him. Paxton looked scared. The man calmly opened the door, firmly scooped up Paxton with one arm, and handed him over to Mr. Glover.

"Thank you so much! Thank you, thank you, thank you!" Mr. Glover cried. He took hold of the leash and lowered Paxton to the ground.

"No problem," the man said. "There is one thing though . . ." He hopped down and slammed the door shut.

Mr. Glover extended his hand. "I'm Aaron. Aaron Glover. And I see you've met Paxton. Any friend of Paxton is a friend of mine."

"Name's Trent," the man said. "Come over and take a look at this."

He led Mr. Glover to the front of the truck.

"You see that dent there?"

There were dents and scratches all over the truck but it was clear that Trent was referring to the large one on the front left corner.

"I was just driving along, minding my own business, and your dog, what's his name?"

"Paxton."

"Paxton jumped out in the road, right in front of me. There wasn't even enough time to stop. I had a split second decision. Hit your dog or swerve out of the way into a post. So I chose to swerve into the post and this is what happened to my truck."

"Oh no," said Mr. Glover as he tightened his hand on Paxton's leash. Paxton was pulling hard. He wasn't chasing anything. He just wanted to leave.

"So . . ." Trent said, crossing his arms. "Are you gonna make this right?"

Mr. Glover took a close look at the dent. He ran his finger over it. There was a fine film of dirt all over the truck, including the dent. He looked at the accumulated dirt on his finger tip.

"Where was the pole you hit?" Mr. Glover asked.

"It was a few blocks away. I'm not sure which one exactly. I just got out and picked up your dog and came trying to find whoever he belonged to."

"OK."

"Yeah."

"I'm really sorry," Mr. Glover said. "I actually know a little song that makes me feel better whenever an accident happens. Do you want to hear it?"

"What? A song? No, I don't want to hear a song." Trent pointed his finger in Mr. Glover's face. "You need to pay me for the damages to my truck. This is your dog. You're responsible." Before Mr. Glover could say something, Trent went on, showing that he was growing a little irritated. "What? You wish I had just hit your dog? Spilled his guts all over the road?"

"I'm glad Paxton is OK."

"Yeah, me too. But my truck isn't OK. It's gonna take a few hundred bucks to make my truck OK."

Mr. Glover crouched down and turned to face Paxton, who had given up leaving and was now standing behind his legs.

"Well, what do you think, boy?"

Paxton and Mr. Glover looked at each other for just a moment. It didn't take long.

"I hope you have a good day, Trent. I have to go join my daughter and her husband for dinner."

"No. You pay me, or I keep the dog."

"You keep him?"

"I found him, didn't I? How do I know he's even yours?"

Trent took hold of the leash. It wasn't hard for him to wrestle it out of the older man's hand.

"You can't do this," Mr. Glover said.

"Maybe you can put up a cash reward for a lost dog. Show how much he's worth to ya."

Trent threw Paxton into the truck.

"Don't hurt him!" Mr. Glover called, his voice weak.

Trent got in, slammed the door, and sped off.

Mr. Glover took a few steps after the truck, but there was nothing he could do. He tried his best to breathe and calm his racing heart.

~~~

"You find the post office all right? I was just . . . Oh my god, what happened to your knee?" The girl behind the sixteen flavors of ice cream pointed at the bloody stain on Mr. Glover's khakis.

"What?" He had forgotten all about the blood and pain from his fall in the street. "Oh, that? Don't worry about that."

"You sure? We have a first aid kit in the back."

"Yes. I'm fine. I just need your help."

"Sure. What can I do?"

"Can you help me with my phone again?"

"Of course."

She came across the counter and he handed her the phone.

"What do you want to do?" she said.

"There's an app somewhere on here. My veterinarian helped me set it up with Paxton."

"Paxton's your dog? Where is he?"

~~~

It was much later in the day. A storm had come and gone before the sun had set, but now it was night.

Mr. Glover knew if he were younger, he would have been terrified. But he wasn't. He felt calm and confident.

He came to a house. The paint was worn out, and the whole place looked like it could fall down at any moment. There was trash and even some moldy furniture out front. This was where his cellphone had led him.

He could hear a TV inside the house. Its speakers were blaring and its light was flickering across the glass of the windows.

Mr. Glover crept around to the backyard. In the moonlight, he saw a large building. It was a giant shed, almost the size of a barn. It looked even more rickety than the house he had just passed. He opened the rusty door as quietly as he could.

When he turned on the light, the sound overwhelmed him before his eyes could take in exactly what the building was full of. The sound was the barking of dogs. The building was full of cages, about half of them with dogs inside.

Mr. Glover briskly walked along, glancing in and out of the metal bars. All shapes and sizes of dogs looked back at him. Some barked. Some stared curiously. And then he finally found Paxton. He quickly opened the door and hugged his dog.

"Come on, boy."

Mr. Glover started opening other cages that had dogs inside.

"Hey! What do you think you're doing?!"

145

Mr. Glover turned toward the door. It was Trent.

"You think I wouldn't hear you with all this barking going on?" Trent said, walking toward Mr. Glover with clenched fists.

"You have any kids?" Mr. Glover said. His calmness confused Trent, and made him stop for just a second.

"Shut up," Trent said as he continued. "Time for talkin' is over."

"You can't choose who they end up with," Mr. Glover said as he stood up. "My daughter married a real outdoorsman. He's really into fishing and hunting and all that." Trent was closing in on him, when Mr. Glover lifted the bottom of his baggy sweater just enough to reveal a handgun tucked in his belt. He drew it and pointed it at Trent. "He gave me this." Trent stopped in his tracks, his eyes wide now instead of glaring. "To be honest, I didn't really want it, but I figured maybe it would help us bond. We don't really have much in common."

Mr. Glover slowly took a step forward, keeping the gun pointed at Trent. He opened another cage. The dog slowly walked out and smelled Paxton as Paxton smelled him.

"I was never a big fan of guns," Mr. Glover said as he looked down at the gun without changing the direction it was pointed. "They seemed so . . . violent . . . but my daughter married a man who was a big fan of guns so what can I do?" Mr. Glover opened another cage, letting out another dog. "He told me to think of it more as a tool instead of a weapon. And I think I'm starting to understand what he's saying. It's like this gun is a flashlight. And you, you're a dark corner of the basement. See, that doesn't sound so violent anymore, does it?"

This whole time, Mr. Glover had remained as calm and pleasant as when he talked to children. Trent was terrified.

"Look, don't do anything crazy," Trent said. "We can work this out."

Mr. Glover walked a few steps back and held the door open to the cage that he had found Paxton in. It was small and rusty. There wasn't even a water bowl inside.

"Why don't you go ahead and crawl in this cage?" Mr. Glover said. "It is a cage, isn't it? You wouldn't call it a crate . . . or kennel. I think cages are more unpleasant than kennels."

Trent didn't move. He just looked at the open door of the cage next to the man holding him at gunpoint.

"Don't be afraid," Mr. Glover said. "You know what I like to do when I'm afraid? I like to sing a little song my grandmother taught me. Maybe I could teach it to you." The barking of the dogs was beginning to intensify. Mr. Glover raised his voice for Trent to hear him, but kept his soft, almost whispering, tone of voice as he sang. *"It can be scary to go someplace new, or do something you don't know how to, but I know it's something that you can get through, because I'll always be there for you."*

And while Mr. Glover sang, Trent got on his hands and knees and crawled inside the cage. Mr. Glover closed the cage door behind him and knelt down. He turned to Paxton. "Guess we should call the authorities," he said and then paused, seeming to have second thoughts. "What do you think, boy?"

TROUBLE WITH MOUNTAIN FAERIES

BY ANNA O'KEEFE

Kerra stepped out of Hunting Creek Outfitters when the skies opened up, and the rain hit her. It had been a glorious May day when she entered the shop, but now the clouds had broken. Of course her umbrella was safe and dry at home. She turned right toward Carroll Creek and the Delaplaine Visual Arts Center to get to where the car was parked. It was hard enough to move around Frederick on any Saturday, let alone this thing called First Saturday. Adding this crazy spring rainstorm made any progress even harder.

Hundreds of shoppers, dogs in tow, crammed the sidewalks. Kerra was building a rant about First Saturday. She enjoyed a good rant and this First Saturday thing was a perfect topic. Another reason for even more people to crowd into downtown.

Just perfect. How were locals suppose to get anything done? To try finding a parking spot in town was beyond frustrating. Now rain pelted her head. *Just f'n wonderful!*

As the rain changed direction, it pushed into her face. She crossed the road in hopes to find some relief. The rain seemed to change directions. *Such an odd shower, even for spring. It's dancing all over the place.*

The rain brought another sound that sparked alarms in the back of her mind. But the rain moved so quickly Kerra could not spend time on the nagging thought that something was very wrong. Another cloud broke just as she passed the Curious Iguana bookstore. With it came lightning and thunder. The shoppers and their dogs caught in the downpour sprinted for its doors.

Kerra found herself pulled in with the momentum. The Curious Iguana was a small space, quaint and lovely, a pleasant place to spend a lazy hour or so. But with the flood of soggy shoppers now crammed into the tiny space, it quickly began to smell like a pack of wet dogs. *What do the dogs think it smells like?* The storefront windows were steaming from the additional heat given off by the countless wet bodies up against each other.

Without the need to fight the rain, Kerra could make out a sound that stopped her dead. She closed her eyes and tried to hear it again. It was the sound no Keeper ever wanted to hear: the shrill giggle of Mountain Faeries. She whipped her head around as best she could and narrowed her eyes as she started to scan the room. Before she even spotted the Faerie, her phone was out. She pressed a number and waited impatiently for it to be answered. She saw the Faerie smiling at her. A big toothy smile! The cheeky little bugger was sitting on top of a small bridge display at the store's far wall. Thank god no one in the crowd could hear or see him.

But the fact that she could see him and all magical lifeforms was the reason she had been recruited ten years ago by the UN's Altered World Agency. She and others like her were called Charmed Ones. Kerra thought the name was humorous. She never felt in the least bit Charmed by having this ability.

Having forgotten about the phone still ringing in her hand, Kerra jumped when the call was answered by a soft, lilting Scottish accent. She cut the voice off as the Faerie made its way further up the stair railing.

"Horris," Kerra said in a low urgent tone, "what in hell is a Mountain Faerie doing in the middle of Frederick?"

"A pleasant day to you, too, Miss Kerra."

"Pleasant day!" Kerra choked out, her eyes not leaving the magical creature. "I thought you were in charge up there? I thought you had control. You always told me not to worry. And—" She stopped talking when, glancing up to see curious faces looking her way, she became aware that conversation had stopped around her. Taking a deep breath, she closed her eyes for a moment then let the breath out. *Get a grip! Don't need all this attention.*

"Actually, Miss Kerra, it might be a tad worse than just one. As far as I can see it is the whole McDonald clan. Well, the teenage boys at any rate. You have yourself at least a dozen Faeries off the mountain."

The scope of this disaster made her head dizzy. "A dozen McDonald teenagers? Oh. My. God. Who am I dealing with, Horris?" Kerra had always thought of Horris as a touched, little old man and nothing was changing that viewpoint at the moment. He was way too calm for such a disaster.

"Oh, I suspect Ian is the head of this little road trip, to be sure." Horris said, then chuckled.

CHUCKLED! Kerra took a couple more deep breaths. *This breathing thing was not working.*

"I am looking at Ian right now," she said pointedly, staring at the Faerie. "Just figure something out, Horris. Let me know." She ended the call without a goodbye, giving no merit that Horris would come up with any resolution to this growing disaster. *Right, I am on my own.*

Kerra saw Ian pick up the purse of a woman who sat on the top step, engrossed in a travel book. Without alarming the reader, the Faerie slung the purse over his shoulder. He turned and gave Kerra a raspberry. Climbing down the outside of the banister he then leaped for a rack of cards that wobbled slightly.

The Faerie stood up on a man's shoulders and took a bow. With the purse still over his shoulder, he made his way toward the door. She sent mental messages to him: "Put the purse down!" She knew he could hear her. Ian stopped at the cash register, and a chortling sound reached Kerra's ears. Kerra mouthed, "Put it down, NOW!" The Faerie shrugged and plopped the purse by the cashier who was busy with a customer.

Ian and the rest of the teenagers—only a hundred years old or so, young in Faerie years—were known for aggravating campers and hikers up on Catoctin Mountain, which the Faeries call home. If Ian was in town, so were his two brothers and countless cousins. The thought made her shiver.

As the stormed passed, someone opened the shop door and blessedly cool air rushed in. People and dogs began to file out when Kerra heard the young woman on the steps shriek. She had discovered her purse was gone.

Kerra ignored the girl, keeping a bead on the Faerie climbing over the heads of the people leaving the shop. She could no longer see Ian but she knew he was up ahead just a block. A small whirlwind kicked up in the crosswalk.

Fear and panic shoved Kerra through shoppers emerging from store fronts along Market Street. By the time she reached the corner of Second and Market Streets, the wind had whipped itself into a small vortex. A man with three small leashed dogs had just stepped into the crosswalk and the vortex whipped around him and the dogs at his feet. It grew so intense the man suddenly had dogs and leashes tangled around his feet and was completely turned around. Leaves and debris from the gutters had been sucked up in the churning motion.

Above it all, four Faeries flew in circles, laughing and hurling insults at the man and his dogs. One of the dogs made a strangled whimpering noise as a gust of wind twirled him up in the man's arms. People from both sides of the crosswalk watched in total amazement as the man and dogs took a beating. When the Faeries stopped circling, the wind released the man and trailed off behind the Faeries as they went to look for new victims. Kerra let out a low growl from deep in her chest. People rushed forward to lend assistance to the now stunned man and equally confused dogs.

Hanging on a windowpane half way up the building side was a different winged creature. He was younger than the other Faeries she had just seen, not one she had come across before. He was leaping from window to window smiling at his reflection.

In all the vortex mayhem, Ian had disappeared. *Shit shit shit shit shit!* Losing sight of Ian was not going to make this any easier.

It amazed Kerra how Americans thought Faeries were sweet little imps that fluttered around gardens wearing flower petals. They adorned children's books and greeting cards, coffee mugs and countless other trinkets. In reality they were troublemakers, though not the worst of the AW lot she reminded herself. She could have been in charge of zombies—they reeked of decay and had no personalities whatsoever. If you ended up with that assignment you had to have really pissed someone off.

But she had been assigned to Frederick to be a Keeper of the Mountain Faeries. An easy gig was how it was presented when the offer was made. The Faeries could not leave their mountain hold unless given permission. And that hardly ever happened. And yet here she was chasing Faeries down Market Street.

A couple of Faeries flew up behind her. Climbing on her back, grabbing at her purse and messing with her hair. "Get off!" Slapping the air, she turned in circles, to the amusement of those passing by. With a chorus of cackling laughter, the Faeries stopped their aggravation and swooped past Kerra, smiling big goofy grins as they passed. *How do they have such good teeth?* The odd thought went through her mind before she shook herself back to more important matters than Faerie dental plans.

151

The little guy from the windows flipped past her face once again and Kerra thought how she would pull his little wings off and stomp on him when she had the chance. Hearing her thoughts, the Faerie stopped short. He paled and looked hurt. *Someone help me. A sensitive Faerie. What next?*

She needed backup, fast. She dialed another number and the call was answered in one ring. A recording told her that her call was very important to them and leave a message. Someone would be back in touch with the caller shortly.

"Hey, this is Kerra in Frederick. The Mountain Faeries have escaped. I need backup now!" Less than thirty seconds later the phone rang in her hand. A voice simply said, "Help is on its way. Go to the designated portal."

Making her way to Memorial Park, the biggest known portal for the AW community in all the mid-Atlantic area, Kerra was almost jogging. With growing anxiety in her stomach, she turned her back on the chaos going on throughout the main part of old town Frederick. At least the shoppers she passed thought the storm was just the usual spring rain that came and went. *I have to leave the Faeries to do their worst. I have to go to the portal.* Just the thought of backup made Kerra feel less desperate.

She took the route up Second Street, away from the storm clouds still swirling around Market Street and across the whole of downtown. Kerra loved Memorial Park. It did not draw many people. No ponds, no swing sets, no tennis courts. Always quiet and peaceful. Which was fine by her. And the reason many weekend mornings found her sitting on one of its park benches meditating.

Stepping onto the grass, a perfect spring day materialized right before her. Everything glistened from the storm that recently passed through with raindrops still clinging to everything. Allowing herself one quick look back behind her, she could see the dark clouds had spread. A sure sign the Faerie antics were continuing. *Help is on its way. Help is on its way. Help is on its way,* she repeated.

Plopping down on a wet park bench and closing her eyes, she took a few more yoga breaths to calm and get centered. That morning she had seen the mountain, clear and crisp. She remembered the bright green leaves and buds on the trees and how it had lifted her spirits. She chided herself for not realizing something was wrong. Catoctin Mountain was never clear but always clouded over. Faerie energy will do that. But the first rule she learned when taking this assignment was that clear mountains meant trouble. How had she missed it?

Sighing deeply then releasing her breath slowly once again, Kerra let her mind go blank, focusing on the sounds around her—car traffic, a dog barking, kids laughing, birds chirping, squirrels scurrying up a tree.

She felt someone sit next to her. Who had they sent? She looked over to her backup and felt the energy drain out of her. *Oh come on! Not my day.*

A familiar smile greeted her. "Sam." The word caught in her throat. Squeaking in a high pitch. Going for confident and cool, the sound missed by a mile. *This whole mess just got worse.* And she let out a groan.

"Hello Sunshine. I hear you got a wee bit of problem with Faeries?" The smile nodded towards the dark skies to the south of them. At one time Kerra thought Sam good looking. Rugged, funny, and charming. Her grandmother would have said he was well turned out. But he was also childish and self-centered. No amount of charm or fashion model smile could overcome those qualities.

"Are you it?" she questioned in total disbelief. Sam's smile grew larger. So many white teeth. The Fairies, now Sam. *What's up with all these white teeth? That can't be natural. Same dental plan as the Faeries perhaps?*

"Got to get on that plan," she muttered. She looked over to her backup. *Right, there is work to do. I will not allow this man to get to me.* Sam looked her squarely in the eyes and gave her that raised eyebrow that meant everything and nothing at the same time.

"Look, this is no time for your crap, Sam. We have a real problem on our hands."

"Well, a mess to be sure, but Faeries only make mischief. They do not cause real or permanent damage."

"Tell that to the man with the dogs that just got sucked up in the middle of a vortex."

Sam made a dismissive sound in the back of his throat.

"They're fine and now have a story to tell. He will be repeating it until he dies. Perhaps beyond that, depending on how dull his life is."

"Who else is coming?" Kerra wanted to focus.

"Well, Sunshine, everyone else is kind of busy with other things. Ogre uprising in Spain. We are it for now. If we can't get this situation wrapped up quickly more agents will come. But I am thinking we can handle this on our own."

Without the rush of wind, rain, and Faerie wings occupying her energy, the sensation of losing total control sat in her chest and slid down to her stomach. *Why did I take this post?* Her mind was drawing a blank. Suddenly she noticed Sam's hand on her thigh.

"No matter, we will do what we can." Sam continued grinning, patting her knee. "We only need to catch one, even by the tips of its wings, to get the whole crew back up the mountain. Have you talked to Horris? What does he say?"

"What does he ever say? He thinks nothing is urgent. Since he has lived a zillion years he feels he has seen far worse."

"No doubt he has. And I think it is closer to a thousand years."

"Really?" she questioned. "I honestly had no idea," she sarcastically threw out.

Kerra let out yet another deep breath. All the yoga classes she had taken and none of this breathing crap was helping much. She forcefully removed the hand on her knee, taking sudden satisfaction in Sam's wincing as she twisted each finger, a little more forcefully than necessary. But Sam had an ego that could handle it.

"Now what?" she asked.

"We go back to Market Street and get rained on. Hope the weather does not mess up your hair." Sam looked at Kerra's already tangled wet hair with a deep frown on his face.

Kerra jumped off the bench to break Sam's scrutiny and get the focus back on track.

"Don't worry about my hair. Worry about our next move."

They started back down Second Street into the path of another pop up shower that appeared to be moving all over the general downtown area. Sam talked nonstop in a cheery and annoying tone about how much he liked visiting Frederick and how he was always glad when a little problem like this brought him here. He ticked off the shops he wanted to visit.

"Crisafulli's for cheese, Truffles for chocolates, Cakes to Die For— oh those French macaroons!" he exclaimed, kissing his fingertips.

The list was never ending. Kerra had stopped listening as they made their way to ground zero. Sam pulled small pieces of paper from his pocket. "I have requests." Holding the wad of different sizes and color paper, each with an item or two listed on them.

She shook her head. "Do you think you will have time to help me with this little issue before you go hunting for treasures? Or will doing your job interfere with your stocking up on goodies?" The words bounced off Sam's armor of self confidence. Always over the top and full blown.

"No, Cupcake, I can do both. I am clever that way," he said, winking at her. "I remember now why we broke up," Sam said suddenly.

Kerra stopped and widened her eyes in disbelief. "We never were together. Not ever."

It was all just too much. All of it. This whole day had to be someone's idea of a joke. Kerra stopped walking and slid down on the curb. *Screw this nonsense. Especially for a job I don't even get paid to do.*

Sam had gone another half a block before realizing that his companion was not next to him. He swirled around and literally skipped back to her. *Who does that? What grown man skips? Oh, my dear lord. This is the end of my job with AW. End. I am done.*

Continuing the conversation without missing a step, he said, "You don't know how to loosen up. All this will work out. Frederick goes through something like this all the time. Someone accidentally leaves the portal open and all manner of AW beings find their way out."

"That is not what happened here. Someone, something, gave these winged pests permission to leave the mountain. After we get them back we need to figure out how it happened. This can't happen again." Sam sat down next to her after examining the concrete closely.

"All's good," Sam said, as if those words carried some kind of magical power to infuse confidence into the situation. He suddenly jumped up and offered his hand to The Keeper of Mountain Faeries.

She took it, and without any more conversation, they resumed their trek toward the intersection with Market and the moving gray skies blanketing the area. Kerra did not even want to know what had been going on during her absence.

"First things first, Sunshine. Gotta catch one." Just then, a small winged thing no bigger than a dragonfly zipped past them. It was another pre-teen. "Aha, there's one. We need to grab a young one. They are the easiest."

The wind whipped up around them again, led by a fluttering of wings. Pedestrians near them seemed stunned that Kerra was being swept up in a mini tornado screaming, "Stop it! Put me down, NOW! You stupid little pieces of shit!"

Just like that, the wind stopped. Several tiny Faeries flitted past. With a practiced ease, Sam reached up and clapped his hands together.

"Got one!" He slightly opened his cupped palms to show his prize and then closed his fingers around his capture.

"How the hell did you do that?" Kerra asked. Sam shrugged his shoulders.

Suddenly, the captured Faerie bit the palm of his hand.

"Ow!" he exclaimed, opening his hand and letting the Faerie escape.

At least eight Faeries were coming in to the rescue of their captured comrade. Wrapped up in the rescue, none of them noticed the Faerie's escape.

Ian in the lead focused on Sam's hands but Kerra saw him coming and snatched him as he went by.

It happened so fast it totally surprised her. She had a set of tiny wings caught between her ring finger and middle finger, raising her hands up, as if making an offering to the gods. It was a call to the clan. The games were over. Mountain Faerie fun was over with, at least for this day.

Ian folded his arms across his chest in total irritation.

"Not sure you needed me, Cupcake. Well done." Sam offered.

"Sam, stop with the frick'n Cupcake crap. It's insulting. I hate it. So STOP!"

Sam blinked his eyes a few times as the words hit him square in the forehead. And then smiled broadly. "No problem, Kerra. No more Cupcake. How about Sweet Pea, is that out too?" He asked in such a sincere way that it took a second before it struck her that he was still playing.

"No Sweet Pea either."

"Well good job all the same, Keeerrraaa!" he said, pronouncing her name deliberately slowly.

Almost rising to the bait, she realized the juvenile attempt that it was and shrugged, letting the retort drop to the ground and roll away.

"Hold the praise until we have them back on the mountain," Kerra said, looking around for the others that should have shown up immediately. "Where are they?" she questioned Ian.

He reached in his pants pocket and pulled out what appeared to be a small cell phone. Kerra watched in astonishment as he pressed a button and heard Ian's little voice speak into the device saying that he'd been captured. They needed to come in.

In no more than a second, the clouds disappeared. The fading sun bounced off of windows still shimmering with rain. Slow sad fluttering wings started to appear. Kerra smiled broadly at each of them, showing off her own dental plan, but never forgetting to hold tight to Ian's wings. Ian sat down on the ball of her hand in total resignation.

Holding tight to the Faerie, Kerra pulled out her own phone and called Horris as she watched Sam with his phone, appearing to be searching for a contact. *What now? Ordering pizza from Il Forno's?* Before she could stop herself, she asked.

"What are you doing?"

"Well, ordering up Uber of course. That small car you've got will never hold this lot."

Uber? Really? Now she had seen it all. Uber for a band of Faeries. Sam was focused on his ride request when Kerra heard Horris's voice coming from her phone, but it was voicemail.

Ian's phone rang. Answering it, he exchanged a couple of words with the caller. "It's for you," he said, handing the tiny phone to Kerra.

She took the phone and, holding it a few inches from her mouth, she said, "Hello?"

"Aha, Miss Kerra. I see you have gotten one of our young lads. Well done. I knew this would come to a quick conclusion. Will you be bringing them back soon, I guess?"

"Yes. Soon. Sam is ordering an Uber right now."

"Good service, Uber. Use them often."

"Horris, ah, when did Faeries start having cell phones?"

Horris laughed, "Family plan, Miss Kerra. Cheaper the more phones we have. Made good sense to get them all one."

"Well of course. Makes perfect sense to me." She disconnected the call and handed it back to Ian.

He snatched it out of her hand, wiping it on his shirt, as if human kooties would infect him. Taken up with the disconcerting notion of Faerie phone plans, dental coverage, and healthcare, Kerra caught only the end of what Sam was saying. "What did you say, Sam? Sorry?"

"I always thought you hung on every word I said." He shook his head feigning disappointment, and placed his hand over his heart. "You break my heart, Cupcake. Aha sorry, Kerra. You break my heart. Uber will be here shortly."

"OK, thanks." She turned her attention to the captured Ian. "Well since we have time, how about you tell me who gave you permission to leave the mountain?"

Ian turned his head away from her in a huff and re-crossed his arms. The rest of the fluttering mob did the same. Nothing like being frozen out by a band of teenage Faeries to put life into perspective.

Sam laughed in delight. "You didn't think that would work, did you Cupcake? Woops, Sorry Keeerrrraa." *Nope not going to work this time either. Not biting Sam. Keep trying.*

Kerra shrugged. "Worth a try."

Just then, an Audi four-door SUV turned the corner. It came to a stop as Sam hailed it. Uber had arrived. Sam talked to the driver as he opened the back door and motioned for the Faeries to get in. They looked at Ian who shrugged his shoulders and tilted his head to the open car door. Slowly and with much fluttering, the Faeries entered the car. Kerra got in last trying not to squish Ian in the process. Neither the thought of Faerie guts in the palm of her hand nor having to explain to Horris that one of his clan had died in her keep gave her a warm and fuzzy feeling. Best to keep Ian alive until he was safely delivered back to Horris. She managed to just squeeze into the car when Sam shut the door behind her.

The driver took it all in and even though his face was full of all sorts of comments, he did not ask any questions. Kerra guessed he would later tell his family about this odd couple. Why had the woman been talking to herself, why was her hand at such an odd angle? Why was she sitting up against the door as if the back seat was full of other riders? The driver peered at the back seat action in his review mirror and smiled through his tight lips.

Sam got into the front passenger seat. "We are ready to roll!" The driver chit-chatted with Sam as they made their way onward to the mountain ahead. Gambrill State Park was the place the McDonalds called home.

Catoctin grew larger as they got closer. Kerra noted that the mountain was now its normal veiled clouded-gray color. Again she could not believe she missed it.

They drove past the Ranger Station to a small overlook. The Uber driver slowed and seemed hesitant to bring the car to a stop. "This is where you wanted to go?"

"This is perfect, thank you!" Sam answered, in a manner that only worked because of his charm. He handed the driver a sizable tip and climbed out. The driver accepted the tip and shrugged, putting the money in his pocket. With the back door open, Kerra unfolded herself from the seat, holding her hand up and out. The driver continued his observation in the rear view mirror. He clearly wondered why the man stood by the open door and waited even though the woman had already departed. She was still muttering to herself. It took the driver mere seconds to turn around and head back down the mountain, scattering the dirt from the parking spaces and leaving a tail of dust in his escape.

With all Faeries accounted for and Sam in the lead, the group made their way to a hiking path that was hidden by the brush and rocks. Around a sharp bend, a Faerie appeared upon a boulder. Sam smiled broadly and greeted Horris warmly. "Horris! It has been ages. So good to see you again. You look well and fit."

They hugged and back-slapped each other. "I am, Sam my boy, I am indeed doing very well. Thank you for asking. And you? You're well I hope?" Kerra watched this with growing irritation. Her arm was hurting from keeping Ian away from harm and escape.

"Horris. Hello. Can we get on with this? We still need to figure out how they got permission."

Horris turned from the jovial greeting he and Sam were sharing. "Certainly, Miss Kerra. I think it is safe to release Ian."

Peering at Ian in Kerra's hand, Horris raised his eyebrow in question. Ian nodded in total agreement.

"I am sure that Ian will not attempt to extract permission from the same source, correct Ian?" Ian shook his head no.

Kerra opened her stiff fingers and released the teenager into the air. He stood on the palm of her hand, tested his wings and made a sudden swoop up into the sky, followed by the rest of his band of trouble makers. In a second, there was no trace of them.

Rufus, the tiniest Faerie, smiled and bowed low, placing one arm across his middle.

"Thank you for getting us home safely," his little voice said. The group had circled back waiting for him. Ian called out, "Let's go, Rufus!" In spite of her irritation and the long day, Kerra smiled back and said, "You are most welcome, Rufus." The tiny Faerie blinked his eyes at her and swooped into the sky to his waiting family.

"Now, Miss Kerra. I want to extend my heartfelt thanks to you and Sam for getting this matter under control in such short order, " Horris started.

Before he could continue, Rufus was back and fluttering around her head. He got close to her ear. "It's the little one, camping with her dogs," he whispered. Then he was gone for good.

Kerra turned to Horris. "He says it was a little one camping with her dogs."

"Aha." Horris took in what his great-great-grand-nephew had said. "I guess that means we have to go back to the campground and hope they are still there. A little one camping with her dogs. That should narrow it down," Horris said brightly.

Sam looked around. "Long walk back to the campsite," Sam noted.

Horris snapped his fingers and an old Ford truck appeared.

"Nice!" Sam said. "'49?"

Horris, clearly proud of his manifestation, beamed.

"Why yes it is, Sam, my boy! It was just the best year for a truck that did everything. Not one of those overstated things of today. But a simple truck. First time I drove anything was in one of these. It will do for our needs."

Kerra watched Horris slide into the driver seat. "Um, Horris. You're going to drive? Don't you think it will look strange that this old truck is driving itself?"

"I can allow humans to see me. I would prefer not. I can hide my wings but I cannot make myself taller. So I get a lot of stares. But it is something I am willing to endure since we need to find a little one camping with her dogs." He tilted his head toward Kerra, placing his hand up near his mouth as if sharing a deep secret. "Doesn't stop me from driving, though." He ended the statement with a wink. At that moment, his whole little body shook brighter and the wings on his back disappeared. "Let's go!" said the thousand-year-old Faerie. His creased face could not hide how much he was going to enjoy this.

Kerra slid in next to Horris, and Sam got in after her. It was surprisingly roomy, and in a few minutes Horris had maneuvered around the sharp bends. Kerra tried to look but did not see how he was working the pedals.

They made their way down the mountain to the campgrounds. The truck slowed to the fifteen mile-per-hour posted limit. The three of them scanned the campers without trying to look as if they were trolling. Lots of dogs, lots of kids. The campsite was full of families and Boy Scouts. On the second pass through, Sam made a noise, shifting his eyes to the campsite directly in front of them.

Bikes sat scattered on the ground with a variety of outdoor toys. The area was without any of its human inhabitants. Two dogs sat in the middle of the picnic table looking at the road. Evidence of a recent meal was apparent in the empty paper plates and plastic cups scattered about the table. The happy dogs' tails, wagging gleefully, indicated how the problem of leftovers had been solved.

Horris put the truck in park, opened the door, and jumped down. "I got this," he said over his shoulder as he walked toward the furry greeting committee.

"If they are supposed to be guard dogs, they failed at their task," Kerra stated as she watched Horris walk up to the dogs, speaking in a low voice. Muzzles pushed under his hands as he scratched their scruffs and noses. Big wet tongues licked the old face.

159

The dogs both tilted their heads in unison left and then right at the words being spoken to them. One barked once and turned his head toward the wooded area behind the campsite. The other just shook his head up and down in agreement. Horris scratched the fur around their collars one last time, and both dogs gave a final lick to his hand.

Opening the truck door, Horris simply said, "They know the little girl in this family is a Charmed One. They said there were some Faeries around yesterday who were causing all kinds of trouble that would no doubt be blamed on the wildlife. Knocking over trash cans, stealing food, scaring dogs. Not them, they wanted me to know, but other dogs were plenty scared." That statement got a smile from Horris.

"You speak dog, Horris." Kerra said, not as a question but a fact.

"Oh, aye. Faeries are good at all animal languages. These two were easy to understand and very chatty. Yes indeed, very chatty." Horris rubbed his hands together. "Need to find us a Charmed little girl and have a wee chat with her without alarming the parents. I am sure any Charmed child will need to be registered at your AW headquarters." He glanced over at Sam who nodded his head.

Kerra turned to Sam. "You are being unusually quiet. Why?"

"I am in the presence of a true Master. I don't get a chance to see Horris in action often. Might as well shut up and learn." Sam's signature smile radiated through the whole truck cab.

Horris took a staff from the truck bed and started toward the trail the dogs had indicated. He had gone just a few steps when he turned and said, "You two coming or do you think I am going to do all your work for you?" He turned and walked further away as they got out of the cab of the truck, scurrying to catch up with the old man with short legs who was setting such a fast pace that both Sam and Kerra found it challenging. At points he would halt and bid them to stop by raising his hand. Kerra thought he looked like a hunting dog, and yet at the same time, he looked like the ancient spirit that he was.

She was getting what Sam had been talking about. Before that day, she had only thought of Horris as the old man in charge of a group of wayward Scottish Faeries. Shamefully, she had never given him much respect, but Horris had always given Kerra kindness, showing her respect as a Keeper. How many had he seen in his time on this mountain range? And all of a sudden, she wanted to know all about Horris. Know his life, hear his stories. They had to be incredible. If he was truly one thousand years old, he would have been around for many important historical events. She heard herself catch her breath.

Sam looked around at her with a question on his face. Horris simply smiled back at Kerra knowingly.

The thought that had taken her breath away, that had jumped in clear, was a vision of him and his family of Faeries at Culloden. She realized they must have lost their clan there, too. If the Highlanders were fighting, then so must their Faerie clans. She wanted to know more. Horris chuckled softly to himself as he led them further into the woods. Kerra had forgotten that Faeries could read human thoughts.

So lost in her head, Kerra did not stop when Horris next raised his hand to tell them to halt. She bumped into Sam who got startled and let out an *umph*.

"Sorry, Sam."

Sam smiled back. "No harm," his smile said.

Horris turned and stared at the two of them. "Humans!" he muttered in a low voice. "You two quite done playing around? We can get back to the matter at hand?" The words had no heat in them, and no one took offense.

He did not stop for their reply but continued to walk on. The sounds of water splashing and kids playing came from over the next rise. Horris stopped again and raised his hand to say, "Wait." He disappeared over the rise and was gone for what was only a few minutes.

Returning, he held a small girl by the hand. The two of them were deep in conversation. "This is wee Evelyn. She is only four." He looked down at the little girl for confirmation. She held up her tiny hand showing four fingers. "One, two, three, four!" Evelyn said.

"How did you get her away from the family without alarm?" Kerra asked.

"Well, some Faeries can change themselves into almost anything for short periods of time. I left Rufus in her place for a few minutes. He and Evelyn have become quite good friends. No one will ever suspect. I found my young friend here chatting with a red-headed woodpecker. The rest of the family is occupied with trying to catch tadpoles in the stream."

Sam stepped forward and lowered himself to Evelyn's level. He smiled at the little girl so tenderly it transformed him into someone Kerra had never seen before. She was awestruck.

Horris made the introductions. "This is Sam. He works for a whole bunch of people who can see Faeries and who can talk to animals, Evelyn. Just like you do."

"You can?" Kerra blurted. "Are you Charmed, Sam?" What else could be turned upside down today? Sam did not answer. His whole focus was on his new little friend.

"Can you talk to animals? Do they talk back?" wee Evelyn asked Sam.

"Yes I can. They started to talk to me when I was about your age, Evelyn." You could see her sharp blue eyes taking in all of Sam and what he said. After a minute, "OK," was all she answered.

Sam was Charmed. Wow. First Horris, now Sam. Things were changing around her so fast, her mind could not take it all in.

Sam asked, "Did you play with the Faeries yesterday, Evelyn?"

"Not the big ones. I don't like the big ones." Her little face creased in distaste.

"How about the small ones? You play with the small ones?" Evelyn's eyes began to look scared.

"It's OK. You don't have to worry about telling us. We all see and play with Faeries, don't we?" He looked over his shoulder to Kerra.

"We sure do. We were just having a wonderful conversation with several of them today. We played all afternoon in fact." This earned Kerra a huge smile from both Sam and Horris. Horris covered his amusement with a sudden cough.

"OK," she said again.

Just then Rufus's baby brother, Charlie, flitted over the rise and hovered at eye level with Evelyn. She smiled and began to chatter to him. He swooped and chittered back. Clearly they had their own language for communicating.

Horris spoke to Charlie. "Charlie my lad, we need to know who she was talking to yesterday. We need to know how she gave permission to your lot to leave the mountain." Charlie did some more aerial maneuvers and chittered a long stream to Horris.

"Thank you, Charlie. Much appreciate your help. We do not have much more time."

Charlie flew down so he and Evelyn were face to face. She held out her tiny hand and the youngest of the Faeries alighted on it. He chittered and then listened to her reply. Even if the conversation could not be followed, they all got the name: Ian. Charlie flew up and planted a light kiss on Evelyn's cheek.

"She says . . ." Charlie started but was interrupted by Sam and Kerra in unison saying, "Ian did it."

"Well if you knew that," Charlie said, "why did you need me?"

He turned in a huff and started to fly away but heard Evelyn's tiny voice say, "Bye, Charlie." He turned and waved.

"What I caught was enough of the story. Ian told her he was teaching her a fun poem. But it was the incantation for release of Faeries," Horris said.

Kerra started to protest that something had to be done about Ian when Horris lifted his hand for her to be quiet.

"I know, Miss Kerra. I will handle young Ian and his behavior. We cannot have Faeries pushing their will on any human, let alone a small Charmed One like our dear young friend, Evelyn. You need not worry." He then turned to Sam who was still on his knees in front of Evelyn. "I am guessing you will have your hands full with this little Charmed One here?"

"Oh, for sure." Sam said. "It will take a lot of work, but she will need protection and training." Sam got up off his knees and looked Horris square in the eyes. "Why, Horris, you old softy. You are worried about this human child." Just like that, Sam's notorious smile returned.

Horris brushed off Sam's words and said he needed to get Evelyn back to her family.

"We good here, Miss Kerra? Enough for your report?"

"Yes. Enough, Horris. Thank you."

Horris walked back over the rise with Evelyn.

"See you soon." Kerra said to his fading back, feeling somehow silly saying it, but with such an earnest longing she totally did not understand. It had been a strange day. Her tired body and exhausted mind could not make sense of it all. But her spirit was soaring.

A couple of weeks had passed, and Kerra was sitting at the desk in her kitchen, putting the finishing touches on her reports. There had been several; after all, the AW was a government organization, or in this case represented several governments.

She had waited to see if there had been any fallout from the antics of the Faeries in Frederick but found none. She heard from Sam just briefly that plans were being made for Evelyn's training and protection. Her family was from Ohio, in Frederick on vacation, meaning another AW zone was involved. She would not hear about her again. That saddened her. Things had gone back to being quiet. She was free to focus on her day job—her dull, boring, day job. But, it paid the bills.

One morning, she found a strange little note stuck to her front door with what appeared to be gum. She thought it was an apology letter from Ian. Part of his punishment, perhaps? Its writing was completely unreadable. The human ability to write was not something Faeries, it seemed, had perfected. But the signature "Ian" was plain.

She unfolded it and looked at it again, smiling to herself. How did it even get on her door? Who put it there, since she was certain Ian was not coming off the mountain any time soon, nor were any of the other McDonald Faerie clan?

She would ask Horris when she saw him in a week's time. She had gone up the mountain and found the rock he'd been sitting on when they had taken the Faeries back. She left her own note:

Horris,
Would like to come visit. Please, let me know if that can be arranged.
With fondest regards,
Kerra

And as an afterthought she added:

Keeper, Mountain Faeries

She had not heard back from him directly but an appointment showed up on her phone calendar. "Tea with Horris" appeared with a date and time. It was a week from now, and she was almost giddy with the idea. She caught herself looking around her apartment to make sure no one or no thing had observed her reaction.

This assignment was turning out to be OK, she thought. She smiled to herself and hit send on the email that had her reports attached. As long as those mountains stayed misty and gray, all would work out fine.

MR. MCGRADY'S HAUNTED
DRIVING SCHOOL

BY ANNA O'BRIEN

Lucile Hatwick understood her acceptance into Mr. McGrady's Haunted Driving School to be an auspicious sign. Although she'd applied online, telling no one and only half believing she'd be accepted, a light feeling in her chest granted her enough hope in the two weeks between *submit* and *accept* that she just might make it—*it* signifying both her driving exam and life beyond.

The truth behind Mr. McGrady's Haunted Driving School was tenuous, slipping through anecdotes, hyperbole, and gossip equally harmless and malicious. The local paper was never granted an interview with Mr. McGrady, and rivaling high schools within Frederick city limits had yet to compile a complete review or opinion of the business. What the vice principals mostly knew—and they were both under relentless pressure from principals and administrative staff to find out more—was that a few sophomores each year were accepted into the three lesson course and that these students, regardless of previous academic history, then went on to earn A's in their driver's education classes, receive a driver's license, and, to the schools' limited knowledge which was based again on anecdotes, hyperbole, and gossip, to become generally noteworthy[1] individuals.

Incoming freshmen knew of Mr. McGrady's Haunted Driving School through older siblings. Usually only the most observant or socially lubricated—often those exceptionally gifted at sports or remarkably attractive—were aware of the subtle social distinction between upper classmen: those who had completed the course and those who hadn't. Given the small number of students accepted into the course every semester (the actual acceptance rate was also a mystery, since no one knew the denominator of students who applied), a meager mythology was created among juniors and seniors but, like in most old stories, the rules were ambiguous and morals confusing. The driving school graduates themselves appeared unaware of any change in their status and were sometimes found walking the halls between and after classes with a far away look in their eyes.

Lucile Hatwick's sophomore year was filled with various disasters, some commonplace to a girl that age, others heavier, like dragging chains. Having to move in with her grandmother in the middle of the winter because her mother fell in love with a shaman in Papua New Guinea[2], Lucile found herself being taught the differences between dark opal and holy basil and how to knit afghans. She was also given the responsibility of taking care of a house cat and dusting the house plants. ("Don't get them confused!" Amelia, her grandmother, chuckled. "I've done that a few times.")[3]

The lifestyle of a seventy-three-year-old woman gradually became unacceptable to this fifteen-and-a-half-year-old girl. A loner by trade, Lucile's head slowly filled itself with grandiose ideas of traveling the

---

[1] "Noteworthy" being a relative term, as some people have concluded that swallowing fire nightly at a burlesque show, studying the reproductive habits of cockroaches, and chasing whales in an effort to collect their feces for parasitological studies to border the questionable range on the scale of normalcy but, suffice it to say, that whatever the students turned out to be, they were happy which is, in and of itself, noteworthy.

[2] Wanda Hatwick, an entrepreneur by trade, was a woman so loving she had a cardiac arrhythmia. Medication came with intolerable side effects and, in search of something more natural, she came upon the studies of medicinal herbs in the south Pacific. Open-mindedness being what it is, one woman's gumption met a shaman's tentative attempts at learning the internet and before Lucile (or Wanda, really) knew it, plane tickets were purchased and a palm-thatched hut waited, dressed up with pale hibiscus at the entrance. Lucile rolled her eyes and shrugged it off, smarting at something she would only later identify as resentment.

[3] Lucile attempted to dust the cat once. It was only slightly amusing.

globe without a map, exploring forgotten places, maybe writing, maybe taking pictures, maybe composing poems that no one would ever read. She would wear lots of rings on her fingers and keep her hair long in a high ponytail like a warship's flag. This mental romance flourished with the composting of a kind but impractical mother, then grew like a weed with the help of a grandmother who understood the world to be just like it was half a century ago, nothing more, nothing less. Occasional visits by her great uncle from across town only cultivated these thoughts further; lugging his vast collection of vintage postcards to Amelia's rickety coffee table, his reminiscence of old days and old flames were made that much more alluring in Lucile's mind by the faded colors and cryptic handwritten messages on the backs.

Lucile's plan was simple, completely naive, and entirely misguided: to fulfill her nomadic destiny, she would run away. But because she considered herself to be mostly logical, she would first get her driver's license. She had no car, or money to buy one, but obtaining a solid, legal identification that doubled as proof that she could actually do something remotely useful beyond calculating the area under a curve or providing a self-edited version of Richard III's opening monologue, seemed, beyond having some cold hard cash in hand[4], to be a wise step.

When Lucile received the acceptance for Mr. McGrady's Haunted Driving School in the middle of April, she didn't tell anyone. She had heard two senior girls discussing the School in the bathroom a few months back. Jimmy Colter, the loser geek in Mrs. Wilson's geometry class, took the three-lesson course last year and now he's a total hottie, they said. Lucile didn't hear "hottie." She heard "hot opportunity." There is debate whether she willingly misheard or, because of a poorly timed toilet flush, truly at that moment did not hear correctly. Regardless, she knew somehow, this was it.

~~~

Mr. McGrady is tall, six-foot-three at least, but wiry and of indeterminate late middle age. His car is a long, blocky, tan station wagon with wood-paneled sides. Like his car, his clothes are hues of sand and rust: a tan jacket, brown corduroys, a beige button-up shirt with tiny swallows flying across his narrow chest or some other small, monotonous pattern. He is also balding, and large wire-framed glasses with yellow-tinted lenses sit on his large hooked nose. His entire ensemble, including the car, looks sleepy except for his eyes, which are sharp and bright. He always carries a worn

---

[4] The previous summer, Lucile worked at a local ice cream stand. There were no real pistachios in the pistachio ice cream, rum raisin had no rum and too many raisins, and Chocolate Crazies frequently gave people diarrhea, or so she was told. She felt her experience there was something of a metaphor for life but more importantly, she earned slightly over minimum wage.

clipboard and a #2 pencil. He's never been seen eating but is known to accept with grace chocolates from former students. The car is a manual transmission.

Your first lesson is on lonely country roads.

~~~

Lucile was understandably nervous for her first driving lesson. She had never sat behind the wheel of an actual car before. She forgot which pedal was the gas and which was the brake. She forgot how to check her blind spot when changing lanes. She killed the engine four times before they pulled out of the parking lot.

"I'm sorry," she kept saying. Mr. McGrady remained mostly quiet through the struggle, and gradually the station wagon bucked and coughed and ground its way north out of the city. Periodically, Mr. McGrady would absentmindedly—and at the last minute—tell Lucile to turn, interrupting her nervous chatter. Eventually, they arrived at a single-lane covered bridge. The late afternoon sun illuminated the red-painted wood, making it appear as an open mouth. The inside was black.

Approaching the small hill to the bridge, Lucile stopped to check for oncoming traffic. In the moment between releasing the brake and accelerating again, the wagon rolled backward.

"Forward is the only option," Mr. McGrady said. Lucile nodded, silent now and serious. Knuckles white, she choked the steering wheel with a steel grip and pressed hard on the gas. The wheels spun underneath them. The car rolled further back and Lucile glanced in the rearview mirror. Directly behind them sat an enormous yellow pickup.

"Where did *that* come from?" she asked. Mr. McGrady appeared not to notice. The truck blared its horn and Lucile jumped.

"Pay no attention to unnecessary distractions," said Mr. McGrady. Lucile tried moving forward again but killed the engine. The driver of the yellow truck leaned on the horn. A large hairy arm popped out of the driver's side window, gesturing forward, then up in frustration, then rudely. The truck inched closer to the bumper of the wagon. Lucile's eyes bulged. Restarting the engine, Lucile's foot flew from brake to gas and the wagon lurched forward with a grunt on the pavement. They launched into the dark, gaping maw of the covered bridge, the inside lit only by the scant evening sunbeams sneaking in between the wooden slats.

When they emerged on the other side, Lucile realized she had been holding her breath. She let it out with a whoosh, blowing a few strands of hair from her forehead. Back on the pavement, she accelerated and smoothly shifted into the next gear. As the wagon rounded a corner, a group of goldfinches suddenly took wing in front of them, their yellow bodies all the more vibrant in the setting sun.

"Should we call it a day?" Mr. McGrady asked.

168

Lucile nodded. Turn by turn, he directed her back to the parking lot in town. It wasn't until Lucile lay in bed that night, thinking about her first lesson, that she realized she didn't notice where the yellow truck had gone after she drove over the bridge.

~~~

The station wagon is a 1990 Ford Country Squire. It has a thin metal rack on its roof, which is not sturdy enough to hold anything of value or weight. One of the back bolts has come loose so that at certain speeds on certain roads, an audible vibration is created through the rack's frame that is disturbing to most everyone. It doesn't bother Mr. McGrady. The rear passenger door on the left side has a deep gash, and both silver side mirrors are freckled with rust. All door handles stick, and the rear doors are perpetually locked from the inside; to get out, you must roll down the window and jimmy the handle from outside.

The trunk is littered with old clothes, blankets, and decrepit, sad boxes, creating a tidal pool of flotsam that appears to have some depth. If you need to store anything, however, rest assured there is plenty of space back there. Bicycles, backpacks, garbage bags, luggage, and once a hamster cage[5] have been safely nestled in the debris, hugged by it, and swallowed, only to be regurgitated unharmed when needed by its owner.

Your second lesson is in incremental steps.

~~~

Lucile approached the battered wagon with more confidence than she had the previous week. She could feel it again, whatever *it* was, putting a bounce in her step. Mr. McGrady sat in the passenger seat, waiting. He tapped his chin with a yellow pencil. Without looking up, he said, "The countryside calls us again, Lucile. Can you hear it?"

Buoyant, she bobbed into the driver's side. "Sure, I guess."

"Check mirrors, parking brake off, clutch in. Let's follow our noses."

Lucile did as directed and, to her pleasant surprise, drove out of the parking lot and into early evening traffic without screech or hiccup. Soon they were again navigating the country roads of north Frederick County. This time, however, they remained on the same two-laner—Lucile didn't catch the name—for what felt like an unreasonable length of time.

Lucile cleared her throat and glanced at Mr. McGrady who, as during her previous lesson, peered with laser intensity at the battered clipboard balanced on his lap. "Should I be turning soon?"

Mr. McGrady looked up for a moment, pushing his glasses up on his nose with the eraser of his pencil. Drawing his attention back to his lap, he shook his head. "No, I shouldn't think so."

Lucile slumped slightly in the driver's seat, wondering what she could possibly learn from a straight country road. She glanced at the

---

[5] Brown and white hamster named Sophocles included.

speedometer: 35 mph, steady. A few lights glowed on the dashboard—a blue symbol, a green one. When her eyes returned to the road, the sky was suddenly dark enough to be twilight. Lucile craned forward, peering out the windshield. They entered a tunnel of trees.

"Lights on, please," Mr. McGrady directed.

Reaching for a knob, any knob, Lucile turned on the windshield wipers.

"Crap."

Her second attempt yielded the left turn signal. The third try produced two yellow beams that illuminated the road in front of the car.

In the narrow swath of light, the road appeared constricted, like a slender black snake. Bushes at the edge seemed to hug the car, a few errant branches brushing the wagon as it passed. The small shoulder disappeared, as did the dotted yellow line along the center of the pavement. Grit began to ping the wagon's undercarriage and the tires made crunching sounds on what now was a one-lane gravel track. It wasn't straight anymore, either.

Hands at two and ten, Lucile took a curve without slowing. The force of the turn pulled her sideways, the shoulder strap of the seatbelt locking in place, cradling her. She slammed on the brakes, which fishtailed the car, unsettling it from beneath them. Lucile yelped and brought the wagon to a complete stop perpendicular to the direction of the road.

Mr. McGrady looked up from his clipboard.

"I guess," Lucile panted, wiping her sweaty palms on her shorts, "I should slow down."

Except for the idling engine, the road was devoid of other traffic sounds and other life sounds, too. There were no birds, no insects. It was as if they had entered a vacuum. Lucile immediately felt more isolated than she ever had in her past. It was as if this car were the only thing left on the planet. She looked over at Mr. McGrady and felt very small. Suddenly, she intensely missed her mother.

Mr. McGrady spoke, pulling her out of this sudden despair. "A three-point turn, I think. That should help."

The road narrowed to the extent that the wagon, turned as it was, took up its entire width. Lucile put the car in reverse but looking in the rearview mirror, saw only trees pressed into the back of the car. She accidentally revved the engine then hiccupped the car back less than a foot. Branches scraped the back windows like nails on a chalkboard.

Shifting the car into first gear, Lucile looked forward only to see branches encroaching on the hood. She sighed in frustration. "How am I supposed to do this?"

"Sometimes," Mr. McGrady answered, "it's more of a five-point turn."

After a few more attempts of reversing and inching forward, Lucile felt they were more encased in the trees than ever before. She felt squeezed in a vice.

"Perhaps a ten-point turn."

Branches groaned and snapped as the back of the car pushed into them. Lucile winced. Illuminated by the red taillights, the forest glowed like embers in a bonfire. Pulling forward for the twelfth time, Lucile stopped.

"I can't do this." She got out of the car, hands on her hips. "I can't do this."

Looking out into the trees, she had the unnerving feeling they were pulsing. Thinking she saw movement at the periphery of her sight, her eyes scanned the forest. Goosebumps threaded her arms, and she hugged herself, suddenly very unsure. She took one last look at the trees and got back into the car.

"I thought . . ." she started. She looked through the windshield. The headlights beamed into the woods, but now the trees appeared to have exhaled, creating space between wood and wagon. The road felt expansive now. Illuminated branches swayed in a slight evening breeze, the young green leaves waving as if signaling hello.

Mr. McGrady looked up as if noticing for the first time they had stopped. "Shall we continue?"

Lucile nodded, dumbstruck. On her second attempt, Lucile was able to drive the car out of its wedged position on the desolate road. Heading straight again, she took a few deep, shaky breaths to calm herself.

"Which way now?" she asked.

Mr. McGrady was looking out his window. "You've always been headed in the right direction. Just stay your course."

Lucile made a face. She thought they were going the same direction as before she stopped. How could this road take them back? As she debated, she began to notice the sky grow lighter and the road graduate from gravel to pavement, one lane to two. Soon, the dashed center line reappeared and shortly after, they arrived at their familiar starting point, the parking lot. Lucile looked at the clock—thirty minutes. They'd only been gone a half-hour. Impossible[6].

Embarrassed at her mistakes on the drive and her apparent misinterpretations (Illusions? Visions? Hallucinations? Was there something coming through the air vents?), Lucile exited the car feeling empty and exhausted. A step backward, she was sure, in her grand master plan. How could she explore the world if the local roads did this to her?

"—final exam," Mr. McGrady was saying.

Lucile started, unaware she had zoned out. "What?"

"Next lesson will be your final exam," Mr. McGrady repeated, nodding.

"Final? I just started! You haven't even—" she stopped herself. *Taught me anything*, she almost said. Then she remembered: three lessons.

---

[6] Nothing is impossible in Mr. McGrady's Haunted Driving School.

That's what the senior girls had whispered in the bathroom. That's all you get. She reconsidered: maybe that's all you needed.

Mr. McGrady studied her with his large owl eyes behind his tinted glasses then stepped to the driver's side and slid into the car. Lucile wanted to wait for the engine to turn on and for this man to drive off to his home or wherever he spent his time, but she was tired and hungry. She turned toward her own home, leaving the wagon and its driver in the parking lot.

~~~

Internet searches using basic, obvious key words such as "Mr. McGrady" and "driving school" yield a predominantly blue website which essentially functions as an online application for classes. A minimally-designed site with the horror of a hotmail.com-suffixed contact email address is enough to drive most technologically-adept, potential students to better known, better advertised driving schools. But the site gives amateur researchers a thread to pull. While usually a topic laughed off with a shrug and incredulous lift of eyebrows—who me?—there are those students who are drawn to the site hoping to wring out some drip of information that has previously been overlooked by others in their very shoes, shoes that squeak with the conflicting tension between probing harmless worldly unknowns and the far scarier unknowns of the self.

Some intrepid junior detectives[7], working meticulously, discover the McGradys listed in the online White Pages[8] claim no relation to the driving school. More shot-in-the-dark Google searches are equally unyielding—one of the largest hang-ups initially encountered being that no one has been able to confirm Mr. McGrady's first name, much less his home address. Interviews with his driving school students reveal only vague notions of the instructor. "Calm" and "quiet" are most commonly used to describe him. Frequently, he seems mostly forgotten by former students, like a fading photograph.

Perhaps the most remarkable aspect is the fact that Mr. McGrady's Haunted Driving School remains a viable, accepted option for a niche population. It's as if the school calls those looking for something different, existing in a seemingly precarious

---

[7] Historically, writers for the school newspapers and members of the debate clubs are the usual investigators. Once, quite unexpectedly, the mystery behind Mr. McGrady's Haunted Driving School attracted a star high school quarterback. Although Daniel Pearson never took the driving classes, he became somewhat infatuated with the wagon itself, insofar as to attempt to find out its VIN number. Efforts to locate paperwork assumed to be in the glove compartment were discouraged, as every attempt was followed by a disastrous loss at the next football game. Daniel Pearson proved himself to be both smart and savvy but in the end, irresolute, as he connected the cause and effect but then chose sport loyalty over the mien of mystery. He graduated *cum laude* and eventually became a real estate agent.

[8] There are currently 110 listed.

172

balance of attracting those who need something unidentifiable and repelling those requiring a more conventional approach. Those who are accepted continue on a favorable path and those who don't apply are equally content. It's not known if there has ever been an applicant who has been rejected.

It's been said the final exam shakes.

~~~

Lucile's driving exam was scheduled the first Saturday of May. Late that afternoon, she arrived at the parking lot as usual. The sky was a brilliant blue, and the suggestion of the warmth of impending summer hung in the still air. The paneled station wagon sat crooked under the shade of an adolescent maple tree.

"You know, Saturday is the worst day for a final," she grumbled.

Mr. McGrady pushed his yellow-tinted glasses back on his nose. "Any day is the perfect day for something." Lucile fought the urge to roll her eyes.

When student and instructor were settled in their respective seats, Mr. McGrady nodded for Lucile to start the engine.

"Is this it?" she asked. "Is this the start of the exam?"

"Not yet."

"When will I—"

"You'll probably know," he answered, looking out the window at the sky.

Lucile raised her eyebrows but didn't respond. She put on the turn signal to make their usual turn north toward the countryside but Mr. McGrady corrected her.

"We'll head right into the thick of things today," he said. "Turn here instead."

Lucile directed the wagon to the direction of the small downtown. The narrow city streets progressively swelled with cars. Pedestrians, shoppers, and musicians choked the sidewalks. Someone held a cluster of balloons.

"What's going on?"

"First Saturday." Mr. McGrady peered out the window. "Shops are open late, people flock downtown. It's magical. Now turn here."

A left, then a right. At one point, a flurry of fur darted in front of the car. Lucile slammed on the brakes, narrowly missing a black and white cat, followed by a dog, followed by an old man. For a brief moment, Lucile locked eyes with him through the windshield, her own wide-eyed shocked expression reflected back. Then the moment passed and the man ran on, following the scurry of animals.

Mr. McGrady directed Lucile across the maze of one-way avenues that created the grid of downtown Frederick. The late afternoon sun cast a golden glow on the other cars also sitting in traffic, making their faded silvers and blues vibrant once again, like a rebirth. Large puffy clouds rounded the edges of the horizon.

As she drove, Lucile began to feel positive. She hadn't stalled the engine, her shifts were smooth, she braked efficiently and avoided hitting a pedestrian, and she was navigating traffic responsibly, all the time wondering if this was it, if the exam had begun.

When Lucile stopped at the largest intersection yet, Mr. McGrady directed her left: "Market Street."

Throngs of people packed the crosswalk, forcing Lucile to miss her green light. A car behind her honked. She winced. Waiting for the next light, Lucile's hands became sweaty. This was the busiest traffic in which she'd ever driven. And the people! Where did they all come from? Dogs on leashes, women carrying multiple shopping bags, fathers with children atop their shoulders, teenagers zigzagging through the crowd. One particular group caught Lucile's eye and she recognized four kids— two girls, two boys—from her high school. Embarrassed, she looked away, hoping the afternoon glare on the windshield hid her face. The pack ran across the busy street, their collective attention directed inward to their own private universe.

The car behind them honked again, and Lucile realized the light turned green. She eased the car into the intersection and onto Market, a one-way, two-lane avenue. It felt as if the wagon had been swallowed. Lucile could only crawl forward in the stop-and-go traffic. She snuck a glance at Mr. McGrady, sure that the final had started. He was writing on his clipboard. She wiped her palms on her jeans.

The wagon crept up the street but came to a halt where two large crosswalks tattooed the pavement. At this point, Market Street crossed Carroll Creek, a long linear park that sliced through the city perpendicular to downtown. Waiting for a throng of people to pass, Lucile looked down the creek. An ornate pedestrian bridge was just visible arching over the water farther down, the water still as glass and broken only by the greenery of infant water lilies. As Lucile turned away, a large splash caught the corner of her eye.

Amused to think someone had fallen into the water, Lucile looked again. People strolled unconcerned along the brick walk. There: again. Another large splash. Something leapt out of the water, she was sure. Turning to look, she continued to let the car roll forward. Mr. McGrady cleared his throat, bringing Lucile's attention back to the traffic. She braked, barely in time to keep from tapping the bumper of the car in front of them. Her heart jumped, and she leaned against the seat, exhaling toward the ceiling. While waiting for the cars to move again, she chanced a glance back down the creek. A large triangular fin cut through the water and then sank below the surface.

Lucile stifled a laugh. It was ridiculous. As far as she knew, there were only carp in the creek, maybe the occasional turtle. And although there were plenty of people walking along the water, no one appeared to notice anything strange. Her eyes were playing tricks on her, that was all.

She took a deep breath and inched the car forward. Mr. McGrady remained silent.

Passing the next block, where bars and restaurants swallowed and spit out patrons, Lucile noticed the sky darken with heavy clouds.

"Looks like rain," she said.

"Indeed it does," Mr. McGrady replied, tilting his head to get a glimpse of the sky between brick buildings. "One thing to remember when driving in the rai—"

"I can't hear you!" Lucile shouted. A black car with tinted windows pulled alongside them and idled at the next stoplight. Bass reverberated from its body and engulfed the wagon. The steering wheel vibrated, and the rearview mirror pulsed. Lucile was at once desperate to plug her ears with her fingers but afraid the steering wheel would fall apart if she let go. The windows of the wagon rattled, as did her teeth, and then her ribcage.

Lucile did a double take out her window. With each beat, the concrete slabs of sidewalk puckered and rose, creating a miniature mountain chain. The cracking and upheaval continued down the sidewalk like dominoes toward an oncoming group of people.

Lucile yelled. The light changed, and the black car peeled away with a screech of tires and the smell of burnt rubber. The bass dimmed until it was gone.

"—make sure you do that."

Lucile turned to Mr. McGrady, incredulous that he continued to talk through the cacophony and destruction. Heart pounding, she looked back at the sidewalk. Everything was as it should be, not a piece disturbed.

"I think I'm losing my mind," she said.

"It's just an exam," Mr. McGrady smiled. "You really shouldn't take it so hard."

The car behind them beeped its horn. Lucile pulled forward, crossing the intersection. A large raindrop hit the windshield. She groaned.

"Right on time," Mr. McGrady said. The bell tower in the local park rang five o'clock.

Lucile turned on the wipers. The sky was charcoal, and a flash of lightning lit the city block like a spotlight, followed seconds later by a crash of thunder. Wind whipped down the street, buffeting the car, and Lucile watched as people on the sidewalks scurried under awnings and into stores to avoid what was now a downpour.

Traffic came to a standstill. The rain sounded like small angry fists pounding on the metal roof of the car, the whoosh-whoosh of the wipers a metronome. Through the blurred windshield, the taillights of the car in front of them appeared arterial, the gleam of the wagon's own headlights off the rear bumper like glistening fangs.

The windows of the wagon were rolled up and quickly became foggy. Lucile glanced at the assortment of knobs and dials on the dashboard in search of some fan or vent. She reached for one.

"Oh, that doesn't work, I'm afraid," said Mr. McGrady.

She reached for another.

"Nope, not that one either."

Lucile huffed. "Well, I can't *see* anything now."

"Eyes on the road," he replied. "I'll fiddle with it."

The taillights in front of them shrunk. Lost in a cottony haze, Lucile assumed traffic was moving again. Using her palm, she rubbed a clear spot on the windshield at eye level in front of the steering wheel.

Ahead, the road was empty. No cars, no pedestrians. Lucile blinked and squinted and rubbed a larger circle with her hand on the window. She could barely make out a single person standing in the middle of the road one block up. As the details of Market Street faded away, Lucile found herself staring at a young woman. The road had opened up; gone were the stores and restaurants and in their place was a swath of flat land so expansive, it made the horizon seem inconsequential. In the distance toward the west loomed a portentous mountain range, topped with snow. The young woman wore a thick, well-worn leather jacket and boots. She stood resolute, unbothered by the weather.

Lucile leaned forward, transfixed. The woman turned toward the car, stumbled and caught herself. She had long, dark hair pulled back in a high ponytail. She walked with a limp but when she looked up, Lucile saw a smile so broad and bright it flashed like lightning. The woman carried a canvas duffle bag. She swung it in front of her and pulled something out. Lucile squinted harder. A notebook. Loose pages flew into the wind. One landed on the windshield, plastered to the glass by the rain. As the blue ink ran, forming cerulean rivulets that followed the slope of the windshield, Lucile recognized her own handwriting. Before she could distinguish any words, the wipers tore the paper from view.

The woman was walking toward the car, still smiling. Despite the limp, she looked strong and determined. Bright eyes peered into the wagon's headlights. She put a hand up to her forehead as a shade and in an instant, Lucile saw herself.

The woman placed the canvas bag on the pavement, wiped her brow, then put her hands on her hips. She cocked her head and waved.

Without realizing it, Lucile's grip on the steering wheel loosened. She waved back.

~~~

Lucile returned to school the next week. Because no one knew she had been accepted to Mr. McGrady's Haunted Driving School, no one knew she had passed. Some of her more observant teachers, however, noticed something was different about the girl. Mr. Henderson, the chemistry teacher, noticed a deeper exploration in Lucile's lab reports, a greater questioning of results. Mrs. Jenkins, the English teacher, secretly kept one of Lucile's essays because, for reasons she couldn't explain, it had made her weep.

Our Lucile will not run away from her grandmother, as you might guess. She will graduate with honors, and her mother, with her new shaman husband, will attend. Lucile will go to college, then likely graduate school. She will travel and write and explore and open her heart to the world. She will carry a leather-bound notebook. She will rarely drive, preferring dusty trains and bicycles. She will have a limp[9].

Our Mr. McGrady will continue to give driving lessons to those who apply. There will remain more questions about the Haunted Driving School than there are answers. But perhaps one of the answerable questions will be: need you apply?

---

[9] Torn Achilles or fractured tibia or unresolved tightness in the right hip flexor or poorly healed broken toe or gash through the calf muscle—you aren't allowed specifics, only possibilities.

PORTALS

BY SUZ THACKSTON

Sylvie began to cast a circle with salt and sulphur onto the sidewalk. The streetlights were bright on the corner of Church and Market Streets in Frederick. The spring night was thronged with people, yet no one noticed the young woman making her preparations before the angel mural. More surprising was the fact that none of the pedestrians nor the occupants of the cars driving past showed the slightest interest in the popular landmark of the 'Earthbound' mural, an old man with angel wings leaning out of a window.

Sylvie's short purple hair was gelled into spikes. She was dressed in inky black, right down to her soft ballet slippers. She wore no jewelry save for a simple silver ring on the middle finger of her left hand.

If a passerby happened to glance over toward the mural, their eyes would veer away. The faint shimmer of the invisibility shield might pique their interest for a second, but then they would forget and move on.

A man approached from the west. He stopped in front of the Trinity Chapel, peering ahead to the busy intersection beyond the mural, his brow furrowed. He closed his eyes, stood up very straight, and looked again. A small smile tugged the corners of his mouth. He moved forward with a confident stride, pausing only a moment as he neared Sylvie, then *pushed* and joined her in the contained attention-deflecting field. A girl at the crosswalk on Market who had been eying him suddenly lost interest. She stepped briskly into the street and moved on without glancing back.

Sylvie finished pouring the nine-foot circle, muttering under her breath, before she looked up at him. "Mord. Are you ready?"

"Yes." He watched her as she turned and reached for the backpack leaning against the wall under the angel. "Sylvie?" She looked at him over her shoulder. "Thank you for doing this."

Sylvie straightened, holding a round crystal in her palm. "You're welcome." She lifted the crystal, peering at it. "Look at how it catches the starlight. It shouldn't be able to with all this ambient light around, but it does."

"Your invisibility shield filters out the artificial light. Good job."

She shrugged. "I like privacy. Anyone who tries can see us, but they'd have to know where and how to look. It's not foolproof, but we have to chance it. I hope for their sake that no one stumbles in once we've started the invocation."

"I'll add an extra layer of Nothing To See Here outside of yours, just to make sure."

Mord stepped back outside into the street light, and began to pace around the perimeter of the sphere Sylvie had created, admiring how very much his mind tried to forget she was there, to tug his interest into the busy city street. He raised his right hand, visualizing a beam of white light from his forefinger, and traced a circle from the street, across the sidewalk, up the wall to encompass the mural, and out to the street again. When he was finished there was a faint reflection of light shimmering in the air around the girl, but unless you knew where to look there was nothing to catch the eye. Satisfied, he *pushed* through the faint shimmer to get back inside the protected area.

Sylvie had placed on the ground a sheet of moleskin with a sigil drawn in crimson ink. She set the crystal in the very center of the sigil before pouring another shape of salt and sulphur, this one a triangle, with the moleskin and crystal at its center. Nearby was a small iron cauldron full of water which glinted in the filtered starlight.

"What time is it?" she asked him.

"Three minutes until midnight," he replied. "On the dark of the moon."

179

Their eyes met as they both remembered a night two weeks before, when it all began.

~~~

Sylvie closed her eyes and let the music wash over her. Soon it would be time to get up and dance, let it take her, let her conscious mind fade while her primal self took fierce possession. It was a slow process, meant to happen in turgid drops of time. Gradually the human noise and laughter receded. There was only her, and the music, and the cold wetness of her glass as her finger traced a sigil in the condensation.

When there was enough dark space between the mundane world and the numinous, Sylvie opened her eyes.

Only a foot from her face was a hopeful smile underneath a ridiculous handlebar moustache. Her brows twitched together.

"I was hoping you'd wake up soon," said the smile. "I'd love to buy you a drink."

She looked back at him, eyes as flat as a snake's. "No."

The smile faltered. Sylvie got up without a word and walked to the dance floor.

The bass line throbbed under a skirl of bright strings and woodwinds. The lights spun crazily. Barely registering the other dancers, Sylvie slid into the song and began to move. Her head rolled back. Arms snaking, hips rolling, she grapevined around the floor, easing in and out of the gyrating bodies, alone with the music. Time passed and she sank deeper and deeper, the music like liquid color in her veins, flowing through and around her, waving her like a water fern.

She came to herself after a while, still dancing, in a moving sea of bodies, but now there was someone in front of her. He was facing her directly, eyes boring into hers. She broke the connection and whirled away, but he whirled with her, effortlessly synched to her steps. She scowled at him. He held her gaze, expressionless, an ordinary man of nondescript appearance, and kept dancing right along with her.

Annoyed, she left the dance floor and returned to her bar stool. The ice cubes in her drink had melted but it was still cool. She sucked it down greedily and ordered another.

When it arrived a hand reached across the bar and waved a twenty at the bartender.

"I've got it," said the man who had been dancing in front of her. The bartender glanced at her, and when she didn't demur, shrugged and took the bill to the cash register. When the change was returned, the man slid a five back to the bartender without taking his eyes from Sylvie's.

"I'll take your drink but I'm not looking for company," she said, her voice cool.

The man looked back at her. His face was pleasant, clean-shaven and ageless. She would have forgotten it quickly except for the eyes. They were bright in the pulsing bar lights, and in constant yet barely perceptible motion. They were looking at her, but jumping ever so slightly, a tiny disconcerting movement.

"You were doing the LBRP."

Her eyes flew wide. For the first time she focused in on him intently.

"What?" Her voice was sharp.

"The Lesser Banishing Ritual of the Pentagram. You were—"

"I know what the LBRP is. Why do you think I was doing it on the dance floor?"

He smiled slightly. "I recognized your arm and hand movements. Plus you were saying it."

"What, you read lips? You couldn't have heard me out there even if I was speaking aloud."

"No, but once I realized what you were doing it was easy to tell what you were murmuring." He leaned closer to her, and his smile widened, showing very white teeth. "I'll tell you something else. I don't think you even realized you were doing it. You were deep in trance."

Sylvie drew in a deep breath. "Who are you?"

"My name is Mord." He paused a moment. "93."

Her gaze sharpened. "I'm not a Thelemite. Not a huge Aleister Crowley fan."

He shrugged. "I'm not interested in your religion, just your practice. No labels, baby." His feral grin flashed out again. "And, like, wow, what's your sign?"

This drew a reluctant smile from her. "Manticore, with Bitch rising. So, Mord the Thelemite, why are you watching me on the dance floor? And what do you mean by 'my practice'?"

His jitterbugging gaze held hers. "I need some help with a Goetic invocation. I think you might just be the perfect partner."

~~~

Sylvie threw her handbag onto the couch, and indicated to Mord that he should follow it. "Do you want water or wine?" she asked over her shoulder as she headed into the small kitchen.

"Water," he replied, taking in the sparse furnishings which consisted of a couch, a small table, and a variety of shrines set up around the perimeter of the room. Living grapevine, twined with ivy and a purple strand of Wandering Jew, was wreathed around the crown molding. There was a sophisticated sound system in one corner next to a rolled up yoga mat.

Sylvie poured them each a glass of water from a jug in the fridge in which strawberries and cut lemon floated. She handed him one, put hers on the table in front of the couch, and folded herself neatly onto a huge furry pink cushion on the floor. A big tawny cat with seal points and brilliant blue eyes oozed from behind the couch and settled into her lap.

"Why do you need to summon a Goetic entity, and why do you need anyone to help you do it?"

Mord took a sip of the cold water. "You get right to the point, don't you? I like that. It's one of the reasons I think you're the one I need."

"You didn't know that about me when you accosted me on the dance floor," she pointed out. "I don't do demons, I don't get involved with strangers and their esoteric bullshit problems, and I don't like my dancing getting interrupted. You don't have long to convince me you're worth one more minute of my time."

Mord smiled at her, baring his white teeth. "You're intrigued. And you don't scare easily or you wouldn't bring an odd stranger into your home. But don't worry, I'm not going to ease you into it. Time is of the essence, and I need us both to move quickly."

His smile faded, and the jumpy light in his eyes intensified.

"My lover has been stolen by a demon. I need to summon a stronger one to get him back. I need help to do it. Help from someone with balls and brains and know-how. And I need it fast."

Sylvie's eyes widened but she kept her expression carefully neutral. "How do you know your lover didn't take off with the busboy?"

"I saw it happen," said Mord, not smiling at all now. "We were at a rave, and some idiots decided to open a portal. I don't think they knew their way around a pentagram let alone a portal, but as it happened the rave was taking place on a ley line." His mouth twisted ironically. "They knew not what they wrought. They were dancing and chanting a bunch of bullshit Goddess names, getting all garbled up between Drawing Down the Moon and summoning Earth Magick to heal the planet and spreading Love and Light and rubbing their bits together when someone must have stumbled upon an actual incantation. Lars and I were off to the side, dancing with each other, just grooving on the music when we saw the flash in the middle of a bunch of tie-dyed hippies, and she appeared."

Mord paused and drank the rest of his water, his hand shaking slightly.

"I'm not even sure if they noticed her entrance. Some of them, maybe. She looked like a woman, but we saw her materialize. White skin that glowed like pearl, and long wild blue hair, built like a Frazetta painting and dressed to show it all."

His head drooped for a minute. Then he took a deep breath, lifted his eyes to Sylvie's and continued.

"We were startled and intrigued, but not scared. Not at first. Lars grabbed my hand and pulled me toward them to get a closer look at her, and that's when she took notice of us. She didn't look at me for more than a second, but she zeroed right in on Lars."

Sylvie leaned forward. "Why? What about Lars made her go for him?"

Mord's mouth twitched. "Lars is beautiful. Startlingly beautiful. And he was so alight as he looked at her, so excited that this event was happening right in front of our eyes. He's—well, he's hard not to look at, especially when he's like that. He's beautiful, she wanted him, she took him. Just like that. She came undulating out of the crowd toward us, never taking her eyes off him. We stood there like idiots, staring at her with our mouths open. She flowed right up to him and took him by the hand. There was another flash of light, and they were both gone."

They both sat in silence for a few moments. Then Sylvie got to her feet and began to prowl around the room.

"No one else noticed?" she demanded. "Flashes of light, a cartoon-busty woman with blue hair appears and snatches a gay man, and you're the only one to see it?"

"I know how it sounds," he replied. "But yes. Some of the ravers looked confused, but most of them were drunk, or spaced out on X. There was a lot of writhing and moaning, but they seemed to forget they'd seen her. Or maybe just assumed she'd gone somewhere else."

"And how much Ecstasy had you two taken?" asked Sylvie, looking at him levelly.

"None. We don't ever indulge in alcohol or drugs, no more than a ritual sip of wine if it's called for." He smiled briefly. "Like you, perhaps, we prefer to achieve our altered states through movement and ritual."

"You don't know what I do," said Sylvie, almost absently, as she continued to circle the room. She paused in front of a shrine with the statue of an ivy-clad God with a panther wound around his legs. "So, what's the rest of it? How do you know what actually happened to him? What if he's dead?"

Mord didn't flinch. "I've seen them in my scrying mirror. She's a succubus, and her name is Nahemah. She's fucking him to death, and she's laughing at me while she does it." He looked up at her, naked pleading on his face. "Please help me."

~~~

Moondark at the corner of Church and Market. Now it was time to summon the demon they had selected. Now it was time to find out what that help would cost them.

Mord took an ornate silver flask from his pocket, opened it, and set it inside the triangle. "Cognac," he said to Sylvie's raised eyebrow. "I hear Foras likes the good stuff." He moved the cauldron of water to just outside the triangle, set a black votive candle in front of it, lit the candle.

He checked his watch again. "It's go time. Are you ready?"

Sylvie grinned at him. "Let's summon a demon."

They faced each other, inside the circle, in front of the triangle, hands raised with palms facing each other but not touching. Mord opened his mouth and began to vibrate a single tone, steady and even. It bounced back from the shield and began to fill the circle. As his breath began to fade Sylvie picked it up and vibrated in the same key. They repeated this two more times, until the sphere in which they Worked was resonating.

They moved apart and stood on either side of the triangle. Sylvie pulled the built-up energy from between their palms and began to draw the sigil in the air with her right forefinger, over and over. Mord, suddenly seeming much taller, began to vibrate the name of the demon. For several minutes nothing happened.

Mord's eyes met Sylvie's over the triangle, despair blooming.

She scowled. Her forefinger stabbed the air. She drew the sigil larger, then larger yet. Suddenly she punched into the center of it, the silver ring glinting, and shouted over Mord's vibration.

"I invoke and move thee, O Foras, and being exalted in power above ye, I say unto thee, Obey!"

A faint mist began to coalesce over the crystal. It swirled, faded, then grew more solid until the form of a man hovered inside the triangle, only slightly translucent. He was tall, with strong shoulders and big biceps emerging from a sleeveless tunic. His hair was long and straight, black silk in the starlight, his face a mask of darkness.

Sylvie continued with the invocation, her voice growing stronger as she spoke. By the end her words rang like chimes in the night, high and pure. She raised a clenched fist, showing the silver ring. Foras lifted his head slightly at this, revealing a face of sharp contours and cold beauty.

~~~

Mord and Sylvie fell silent and utterly still. The cauldron of water on the ground rippled, catching the starlight, then quieted. The demon too remained motionless, a red glint of eyes visible in the darkness under the black hair.

Sylvie tried to speak, but her voice croaked and died away. The thing inside the triangle did not move, but a whisper of laughter shivered inside the enchanted circle.

Sylvie's brows drew together.

The demon took a step closer to her, careful to remain within the triangle.

"You've tweaked the invocation, girl. Risky. What is it you want badly enough that you're willing to chance the Lesser Key of Solomon, yet not adhere slavishly to it? Perhaps I could be persuaded to aid you in spite of your little attempt at coercion."

A shiver of fear ran up Sylvie's spine at the undertone of menace. She steadied as she felt Mord's strong warm support flow from him and wrap around her. Foras felt it too. He continued to ignore Mord, but a chiseled shoulder twitched in irritation.

Sylvie indicated the cauldron of water. "Look into this, O Foras. We want the human back, and we want to prevent the succubus Nahemah from returning for him."

The demon remained still, not looking at the cauldron. His red eyes remained fixed on her. "What do you offer?"

Sylvie's voice was sharp. "The usual. Alcohol. Incense. Good chocolate. The opportunity to affect the material world in a limited fashion."

The demon smiled slightly, revealing sharp white teeth that reminded Sylvie suddenly, unsettlingly, of Mord.

"I'm disinclined to accept your offer."

Sylvie's gimlet gaze bored into him. "Because?"

Foras's smile widened. "Those are nice trinkets if you need help finding your child's lost woobie, or your missing stash of cannabis. You expect me to battle a succubus for these, and the dubious pleasure of your company on a drab side street near the Candy Kitchen in Frederick, Maryland?" The smile disappeared abruptly. The expression visible on the shadowed face sent a thrill of fear through Sylvie. "Go play your summoning games with a Ouija board and your Wicca Meetup group. You are in over your head, little mage."

Mord spoke up from the far side of the triangle. "What do you want? Whatever it is, I'll do it."

At Sylvie's quelling glance he fell into dismayed silence.

Foras did not look back at Mord, but his eyes gleamed like a satisfied cat's. He continued to regard Sylvie from the very edge of the triangle, a sharp black boot fitted right into the corner.

"I want to roam your world for a time. Just a little. And I want to drink of mortal experience." At Sylvie's instinctive jerk he added, "Not to kill, or even injure. I am a Mighty President and capable of much subtlety. If you cooperate I can sip the shimmer of mortality as you would a fine wine, without so much as a squeak from the bleating herd from which it will be harvested." The red eyes bored into hers. "And you will enjoy it, girl. You like power. I can taste it in you. We can Work together, and I can teach you many things."

Sylvie's eyes narrowed.

"Look into the cauldron, demon. It may be that Nahemah is too much for you. Let's see first if you are of any use to us before we make bargains."

She heard Mord expel his breath in a huff as Foras removed his ruby stare from her and directed it into the cauldron. What he saw there caused him to make a small exclamation, and bend over to the very edge of the triangle and peer into it. Sylvie noticed with a thrill of satisfaction that Foras took care not to allow any part of himself to touch the barrier created by the triangle. She glanced down into the cauldron, but could see nothing but reflected starlight on water.

Foras straightened. "Toothsome. I can see why you want him back. Why not offer this pet of yours to the succubus? It's not a great trade, I admit, but succubi aren't discriminating. Since she's got that one practically used up, she might be willing to take a fresh mount, even if it's of lesser quality."

Sylvie was pleased that Mord remained still, not rising to the bait. "You bind her, you return the man to us alive and unharmed. Nothing else is on the table."

Foras rose to his full height, towering over the humans standing outside his triangle enclosure. "This is no great matter. I could do it tonight, but that would not afford you the time you need to give me what I require in exchange. Do as I ask, and at the full of the moon you can return here and I will free your human male and banish the succubus so thoroughly that she will not trouble you again, at least not in this incarnation. Do you agree?"

Mord spoke again, this time his voice firm and level. "Two more weeks with that creature and he will be dead. It has to be tonight."

Finally the demon turned his head and looked at Mord. "Time passes differently in the realm where he now exists. He will be more drained, surely, but no permanent damage will ensue. I can ensure this. But I will not unless my own demands are met." He moved back and included both Sylvie and Mord in his red stare. "Your summoning was successful, and you could perhaps do it again even against my will, but beyond that you are less effective than you think. You cannot compel me to help you. You can, however, persuade me."

Sylvie kept her eyes on his face. "Tell me what you want. Specifically."

"I want you to collect energy, from the mortal activities that generate it. Sex, birth, ritual, warfare, grief, ecstasy, despair. I will tell you what to look for. You will simply put yourself in situations where you will encounter or create the necessary emotions. A small piece of me shall accompany you and collect it, storing it until the full moon when it will be delivered unto me. The collection process will not harm the donors, nor will they be aware of the process. Do you agree?"

"What do you mean, a piece of you will accompany me?"

The demon's lambent eyes rested on her. "Do you have a pet?"

"Oh—yes," she replied, surprised. "My cat, Pooka. Why?"

Foras smiled. "Pooka will have a companion for a time."

~~~

Foras lifted his hands and contemplated them. They were beautiful, elegant, long-fingered. He waggled his fingers as if playing an invisible piano. Then he grasped his left index finger in his right hand and pulled it off.

Black blood fountained, splashed on the inside of the triangle barrier, and ran down in inky streams. The demon held his hand over the corner of the triangle, near the cauldron. The blood formed a viscous pool. He set the white finger with its ragged root into the center of the pool. Then he looked up into Sylvie's shocked face and smiled.

"Enjoy your new pet. Don't be too frightened. It's not enough of me to be a real danger to you. But it will help you find what I require, and serve as a repository for the energies I wish to absorb. Most of the cattle with whom you mingle won't even realize it's there."

Sylvie swallowed hard as she looked at the curled digit, lying inert in the black splatter. It twitched.

She pulled her gaze away and looked up at the demon who towered above her. "I am not going to carry that thing around with me."

Foras touched the torn place on his left hand, and it smoothed. Sylvie almost expected to see the finger grow back, but it did not.

"The servitor will travel on its own, and will not inconvenience you. It is only partially self-willed, and only insofar as it needs to be in order to fulfill its directive, which is to aid you in collecting what I require. It is also imbued with my power of invisibility, at least to the casual gaze. If you request it, it can extend this protection to you while you're in close proximity.

"Banish it if you choose. I care not. You are capable of that much. But then you have no hope of acquiring my help in your quest.

"Do as thou Wilt. That shall be the whole of the Law, no?"

The grin which Foras directed at Mord was ripe with malice. With a slight bow in Sylvie's direction, the demon began to dissolve into wisps of vapor. In moments the only things in the triangle were the pool of blood, the finger, the sigil, and the now-inert crystal.

Sylvie took a deep breath and started to reach into the triangle. Mord grabbed her arm. They both stared.

The curled white finger began to move. It rolled around in the clotting blood, until it was entirely coated in the thick dark fluid, only the nail glinting at them like an eye.

The eye blinked. When it opened, it had a pupil, a vertical slit.

A second eye opened next to it. The finger began to pull the gelatinous ooze into itself. For a moment it heaved and roiled, the eyes darting wildly, then resolved itself into the shape of a small inky cat. It shook itself, prowled around the perimeter of the triangle, then sat on the sheet of moleskin and began to wash itself.

~~~

Back at Sylvie's apartment Mord began to unpack the ritual items. Sylvie sat on the couch where he had pushed her, drinking a glass of wine so deeply crimson it was almost black. The demon cat imp thing, almost the same color, prowled around the apartment, ruby eyes bright.

Pooka glared from a windowsill, fur spiky, emanating a continuous growl.

"I'll need to bury that crystal in soil for a while to cleanse it," she told Mord as he unwrapped it. "Put it in a bowl of salt for now."

As Mord moved into the kitchen to follow her instructions, the imp slid behind him. He eyed it warily. It stared back at him with Foras's eyes. He squared his shoulders, turned his back on it, and searched for what he needed in Sylvie's cupboards. Sylvie made no effort to help, just leaned back on the couch twirling the wineglass stem in her fingers.

When everything was put away Mord poured himself a glass of fruited water and joined Sylvie on the couch.

"Are you OK?" he asked her.

She sat up and drained her wine. "Yes. We succeeded, right? The first phase is complete. We summoned him, and he has agreed to help us. Now we need to collect energy like crazy for the next couple of weeks, and then . . ."

Her voice trailed off. Mord picked up the thread.

"Then we face the real test. Did we summon the right demon and can he really get Lars back from that bitch. We won't know until it happens, but so far we're on the right track." He glanced at the imp, now curled up on Sylvie's furry pink pillow, ignoring Pooka's unrelenting snarls. "But can you live with that thing for the next two weeks?"

Sylvie looked at it. It gazed back, eyes slitted in contentment.

"I'll be fine. Not so sure about Pooka." Hearing her name, Pooka raised her snarl to a scream, then abruptly leapt from the windowsill and stalked over to the couch. She jumped up onto Sylvie's lap and settled in, tense and watchful and proprietary. The imp closed its disconcerting eyes and began to purr loudly.

"Mord, why did you insist that we do the summoning at the 'Earthbound' mural? What about that spot is so important? It's super impractical. There are a million places more private, including right here."

Mord laughed shortly. "Well, as to the last, summoning a demon in your home seems unnecessarily risky. But yeah, there are plenty of quiet places we could have gone and not had to bother with the Nothing-To-See-Here shield." He stood and began to pace. "I'm not sure if this will seem too out there, but I have a sense for places of power. I've been finding them, by accident at first, ever since I was a teenager. That's how I knew what happened when Nahemah appeared, why the portal was so easy for amateurs to open. It's kind of my specialty. I've known about the ancient power on the corner of Church and Market for years. I've even done some minor Work there—elemental balancing, grounding, your old friend the LBRP." He stopped and turned to face her. "I just knew it was the right place, where we could tap into the ley line and amplify our Work. I know it sounds wacky."

Sylvie gave a yelp of laughter. "Buddy, we just summoned a Goetic entity, we have a demon imp companion for the next couple of weeks, and we've made a pact to banish a succubus and retrieve a tormented mortal. You being able to sense power spots isn't going to faze me."

She stood and stretched. "I'm wiped out. I'm going to bed. I think you should move in here for a little while, until we get Lars back. I don't know what this thing"—she pointed at the seemingly slumbering imp—"requires in a practical sense, and we need to be ready for anything." She went into her bedroom and returned with a pillow and extra blanket. "Pooka sleeps with me. You can snuggle up with the hell-spawn."

Mord lifted an eyebrow but did not protest as she picked up her cat and disappeared into the bedroom.

~~~

Music pounded in Sylvie's ears as her feet pounded past the bell tower in Baker Park.

She waved a greeting to the line of sugar maples along the path on Carroll Parkway. As she and the imp ran by them, each dryad nodded its crown toward them in turn, then rustled their branches at each other in excitement.

It was a busy afternoon at the park, lots of parents with children, tennis players on the public courts, besotted lovers, and other runners. None of them seemed to notice the small dark shape that flowed at Sylvie's heels. None except for the dogs they passed who barked, then retreated to the length of their leashes, whining anxiously. She could hear the owners scolding or comforting, their tones puzzled.

"Don't scare the damn dogs," she panted, shooting a quelling glance at the imp effortlessly pacing her.

To her surprise she heard, for the first time, the imp's bell-like voice in her head. "Dogs are stupid," it said. "I like to scare them."

Sylvie was running too hard to laugh, but she sputtered as they approached the band shell. The park's carillon rang out, and a group of rugby players began to assemble on the wide lawn. The imp surged ahead of her, angling toward them. Sylvie knew what it wanted.

"Give them a chance to get going while I finish my run," she told it. "Once more around the perimeter, then you can suck up their scrimmaging, OK?"

As they circled the park again the imp enjoyed a shrill lovers' quarrel, other runners' exertions, and a noisy toddler meltdown near the lake. By the time they returned to the rugby practice its eyes were dreamy with satisfaction.

"Enough?" asked Sylvie after she had cooled down and stretched. The imp sauntered back to her from among the struggling rugby players.

It blinked at her sweetly and sent an image of her at work.

189

Sylvie sighed. "OK, you can come to work with me tonight. But be discreet, please."

The imp licked a paw, ignoring such an obvious non-issue.

~~~

The imp leapt onto the bar and surveyed the crowd at Bushwaller's with pleased interest. The bartender working with Sylvie did a double take, then rubbed her eyes and turned back to the blender.

"Only a couple of days until the full moon," she commented sourly to Sylvie. "The crazies are already out, and I'm starting to see things."

"I'm thinking this one will be a doozy," agreed Sylvie as she popped the tops off four bottles of Flying Dog beer and handed them over the bar to eager hands. Her elbow jostled the imp, who hissed at her. She grinned at it. It flattened its ears and disappeared into the crowd.

There was no dance floor at the Market Street bar but the tables and booths were overflowing and bodies moved in syncopation as the band rocked it out. Sylvie was far too busy to trancedance, but she unconsciously moved in the music's rhythm as she worked. She could see the imp sliding between the patrons, sometimes winding itself around one it found appealing.

"You're going to get stepped on," she murmured when it appeared in her ice bin, watching her grate fresh nutmeg onto a cocktail. It narrowed its eyes at her, and in her mind she heard, "Fat chance."

It was almost three in the morning when Sylvie finished her shift. She was exhausted, but the night was cool and fresh, and she didn't want to go straight home to her apartment in a beautiful old house on Rockwell Terrace, near Baker Park. She walked slowly up Market, enjoying the rare silence and stillness. The imp shadowed her, its feet almost but not quite touching the ground. When they reached Third Street it began to move away from her.

"Hey!" she called after it. "Where are you going? It's late. I'm going home now."

It paid no attention to her. It continued to waft its way up Third toward the Saint John's Cemetery. As she watched it go, Sylvie noticed some of the city night-cats, the skinny fierce ones, materialize in its wake. They followed it silently. She watched them until they were out of sight, then shrugged and turned back along the quiet main street.

In two blocks she was at the 'Earthbound' mural, and she paused to look up at the pensive face of the old angel, leaning out of his window. Nothing on the empty sidewalk in front of it showed any signs of the ritual that had taken place there only a week before.

"I wonder what you thought of a demon materializing right here under your nose?" she breathed to the angel.

The angel did not reply.

190

After a few minutes Sylvie walked slowly back up to Third Street, turned away from the direction the imp had taken, and went home alone.

~~~

"Hey! Your cat is freaking me out."

Sylvie was standing naked by the window. She glanced back at the man lying in her bed. Pooka was nowhere to be seen, but the demon imp was lying on the man's stomach, eyes slitted, purring loudly.

"It's a freaky cat," she replied. "Ignore it."

The man rolled over, displacing the imp and exposing a well-muscled derriere.

"I don't think I can sleep with it in the bed," he said. "It doesn't weigh anything at all, and I don't like the way it looks at me. Like I'm an appetizer or something. Can we shut it out of your room?"

Sylvie pulled an over-sized Thing One t-shirt over her head.

"No, but don't worry about it. It's time for you to go."

The man sat up, his handlebar moustache quivering.

"Dude, seriously? What did I do wrong?"

Sylvie walked over to the bed and drew a delicate fingernail over his spent penis. It twitched and lifted. The imp stirred and raised its back as if it had been stroked.

"Nothing," Sylvie replied. "You were exactly what we—I—needed."

"Then why can't I stay the night? Jesus, I thought you liked me. Is your roommate really your boyfriend? Is that the problem?"

"Oh, I like you," said Sylvie. "And no, he's not." The imp looked from her to the penis and back again. "Well, you can stay a little longer if you like."

A smile bloomed under the moustache.

"But then you have to go," she added, pulling the shirt off and straddling him. "I sleep better alone."

~~~

Sylvie's phone dinged with a text from her landlord. "I'm outta here, go ahead and crank it up," it read.

Sylvie stepped out onto the tiny balcony off her second story bedroom and looked over the parking area beside the house. Her landlord lived in the main part of the house below her little apartment. He came out carrying his briefcase and waved to her as he got in his car. She waved back, ignoring his wistful look, then went inside and walked over to her sound system. In seconds the room reverberated to drums and bagpipes.

"Cu Dubh!" she wailed, then howled like a wolf.

For the next hour she worked out hard to the driving music. Jogging in place gave way to strenuous calisthenics interspersed with free weights. Pooka retreated to the bedroom but the imp came in close. As sweat spattered the yoga mat it closed its eyes and inhaled deeply. It rubbed hard against Sylvie as she lifted into a side plank. She shoved it away but it returned with a red glint in its eyes.

"You're intrusive," she told it. "Don't touch me when I'm sweating like a racehorse, even if you don't feel like much."

The imp padded over to the kettlebell, touched it with a delicate paw and looked at her expectantly.

~~~

The dead girls under the bridge by the library lolled in the water. There were three that evening, bobbing among the water lilies. Sylvie had seen as many as seven at a time. The other dead whom Sylvie regularly encountered in downtown Frederick often tried to communicate, but the floating girls kept their silence. She ignored them, but Mord did a startled double-take before shaking his head and walking on. The imp froze on the edge of the canal, staring. It put out a tentative paw as a white naked foot floated past, then withdrew it without trying to touch. No one else on the busy walkway seemed to notice the girls.

Mord and Sylvie strolled along Canal Creek. To the casual observer they were just a couple enjoying the early evening, but both were deep in trance, letting the labyrinthine undercurrents of the city direct their steps. The imp flitted along not far from them, ducking in and out of shops and restaurants, weaving between pedestrians, peering into the lily-strewn water of the canal and batting at the koi.

Strains of music filtered into Sylvie's consciousness. Street buskers sometimes set up near Market Street. Without speaking they moved toward the music. A small crowd had gathered around a trio, two skinny boys in shorts and tank tops playing a guitar and a hand drum, and a zaftig girl in a gypsy skirt, who sang in a voice as rich and lush as her figure. There was a smattering of applause at the end of the song. A few bills and coins pattered into the bowl on the sidewalk.

Sylvie started to walk away, but Mord paused as he tossed a five into the bowl. "Where did the bugle player go?" he asked the singer. She tucked a lock of wavy auburn hair behind her ear and looked at him in confusion.

"Bugle? We don't have any brass. Just us," and she indicated the boys who stood behind her.

Mord looked confused too. "Oh. Sorry. I could have sworn I heard a bugle."

She smiled at him and shrugged. "Just us. But thanks, man."

As they resumed their walking meditation Sylvie glanced at him curiously.

"What was that about?"

"Didn't you hear a bugle? Before we saw them, when we could only hear the music?"

She shook her head. "Not that I remember." She eyed him. "Is it important?"

He was silent for a moment, then he too shook his head. "I guess not. Weird."

She touched his arm. "Look at that heron. He's about to get some dinner."

A night heron stood motionless on a rock in the canal, its long beak angled downward. A small dark shape was crouched at the edge of the water. At first Sylvie thought it was the imp, but the imp materialized between her feet, watching the heron with interest. After a moment Sylvie walked on. Mord fell in beside her, and they both narrowed their focus to the ground immediately before them, moving back into trance. The imp did not follow them right away, but remained by the canal, watching.

~~~

On the afternoon of the full moon Mord wrapped items and placed them carefully in Sylvie's knapsack as she read off their list of ritual requirements. Pooka and the imp, who had finally reached a truce, sat on opposite sides of the couch and watched with interest.

"That's it," she said as he carefully slid a sickle-bladed athame into a front pocket. She looked out at the warm, sunny afternoon. "Doesn't look like the day for a demon battle, does it?"

Mord moved to the couch, his face its usual bland mask, only the jittering eyes betraying his stress. "I know Foras was just being a dick, but he made a good point. If something goes wrong, and Nahemah wins, I want you to try and make her take me and release Lars."

Sylvie started to protest, then stopped. "OK," she said. "But we're getting Lars back."

Mord smiled slightly. "Yes." Pooka strolled over to him and demanded chin skritches, her sapphire eyes half-closed. Mord obliged, then looked up at Sylvie who stood, pensive, at the window. "Sylvie? Why did you agree to help me?"

She shrugged. "I'm not really sure. The whole thing interested me, I guess. I've never encountered anything like this—or you—before." She turned to him, narrowing her eyes. "I've never asked why you didn't just go to your Order. You're a Thelemite. You hang with ceremonial magicians. Seems like that's the obvious place to get help."

Mord buried his fingers in Pooka's tawny belly. Her purr started low and grew to a roar.

"They would. But I haven't told anyone there what happened." He sighed. "The sordid truth is that Lars got into it with the head of the Order. She felt he was dismissive and rude about some of the Outer

Court material. She had a point. Lars can be a bitch." He lay back on the couch, and Pooka moved onto his chest. "They would still help, don't get me wrong. They're my brothers and sisters. But—" his mouth twitched. "This is uncharted territory. I was—I am—terrified that the drama would affect the Working. I'm too close to it. Even a lower level demon would know that I'm emotionally tied to the Work and would take advantage, so I had to get someone else to take point." He met her eyes squarely. "I have confidence in you. Now. I was taking a chance before, and yes, going off instinct. I've seen you around the occult community. And I'm a good judge of character."

Sylvie didn't blink. "And?"

Mord met her gaze squarely. "I know you know. I didn't have a connection to you. If things went wrong, I would be very sorry, but it would have been bearable."

Sylvie's face relaxed. "Thank you for the honesty." The imp was staring at them intently, its crimson eyes moving from one face to the other. "How do you feel now?"

Mord's gaze did not waver. "If something were to happen to you now, it would break me. Almost as badly as losing Lars."

The only sound in the apartment was Pooka's purring.

After a while there was a mutter of thunder. Sylvie turned back to the window.

"Clouding up," she commented. "Looks like a storm is coming."

Mord stood and joined her. Dark thunderheads heaped on the horizon.

"Let's get downtown before it breaks," he said.

~~~

Lightning lit the late afternoon sky over the city as they parked in the garage on Church Street. The air felt electric. Black clouds roiled overhead, but no rain fell as they made their way toward Market Street.

The imp was moving in front of them with its liquid pace when suddenly it froze. Its head snapped around. With a great leap it turned back the way they had come and in less than two seconds turned left onto Maxwell Avenue and disappeared.

"Hey!" Sylvie shouted after it. "Get back here!"

She started to go after it, but the first raindrops hurled down upon them like tiny bombshells.

Mord opened an umbrella.

"Let it go," he said. "It seems to know what it's doing."

Setting up went quickly. There were indeed a few curious glances directed their way as they busied themselves under the 'Earthbound' mural, but whether due to the deflection shield or the rising wind and rain, their little patch of sidewalk was not invaded by any casual passers-by.

Thunder muttered. Lightning stabbed the thick air over the city. A shriek of metal and rubber followed by car horns tore the air from the direction of East Street. Out of the clamor walked the imp. Sylvie gasped with relief and stepped outside the circle. She picked up the imp, holding it close to her chest.

"Where did you go? What the fuck do you mean, taking off right when we're getting ready to begin?"

"You have not showed me 'death'," it put into her mind.

She stared at it. "I hope I don't have to. Did you see something die?"

"No," it replied sadly. It closed its eyes. Sylvie got a confused image of a cat huddled next to a gravestone and a snake slithering away with a little plant in its mouth, its skin slipping off and lying in a jeweled heap. She was about to ask more, but it wriggled out of her arms.

Mord finished pouring the triangle within the circle. The crystal was in place, as was the cauldron of water. Sylvie placed a snifter of liquor, a Zoe's chocolate truffle on an exquisite Wedgewood dish, and a single blood red rose into the triangle. Mord raised an eyebrow at the rose.

"It just felt right," she snapped. "Sometimes you go with UPG."

"Unverified Personal Gnosis has its place," he agreed. "Even with Goetic demons. If it helps get Lars back, I'll give the fucker an entire flower shop." For a second his bland mask slipped, and the depth of his anguish showed in his face.

Sylvie touched his arm. She turned to the imp, sitting on the pavement, its tail coiled neatly around it. She took the curved athame and cut a doorway into the circle. The imp stepped easily inside then halted outside the triangle. It emitted a short, sharp cry.

"It's time," said Sylvie. "Ground yourself."

Mord straightened his shoulders. He closed his eyes. Sylvie did likewise. Earth energy flowed into them, up through the soles of their feet.

Sylvie lit a stick of dragon's blood incense. She looked down at the imp. It looked back at her, red eyes alight. She picked it up, stroked it briefly, and set it down inside the triangle.

They began the invocation.

Foras appeared more quickly this time. The mist swirled over the crystal and coalesced into a man-shaped form mere seconds after the sigil was drawn and name vibrated. He was dressed in leather greaves and a bronze breastplate with a Gorgon engraved on it. A short sword hung from his belt. His crimson eyes gleamed, but his smile was cold as he regarded them.

"I am prepared to uphold my end of the bargain, if you have done so as well."

Sylvie stared back at him. She said nothing, only indicated the imp, sitting motionless at the demon's feet.

His eyes flicked over the imp, the offerings, then settled on the cauldron of water just outside the triangle. The gleam in his eyes intensified.

He picked up the imp and ate it.

Sylvie's instinctive cry of protest died away as the demon swelled. He became taller, broader, the leather armor stretching over his muscles. He threw back his head, black hair flowing over his shoulder blades, and laughed aloud, causing the enchanted circle to quiver.

His brilliant gaze swung back to Sylvie.

"Set me free."

When she didn't move, he flexed his shoulders with impatience. "Your only portal to the succubus is through the cauldron. Give me access, or creep away and cower in your little maidenly bed. You may choose to squander the power I now carry, but I shall not. There are other dimensions in which I can move and exert my influence, and I lose patience with you."

Sylvie and Mord locked eyes. She could see that his shock equaled hers. How could they have overlooked such an important detail?

She picked up her sickle athame. After a brief, appalled glance at the figure looming inside the triangle, she cut a doorway.

The demon stepped through. He took hold of Sylvie's arms and smiled down into her face from his great height. "Did you think all the power was stored in my servitor? No. Some of it is also in you." He stooped and fastened his mouth on hers.

Under other circumstances, Mord would have thought Sylvie had gone weak with lust. Her knees buckled, and her head fell back as the thing gripped her chin to gain better access to her mouth. Her arms beat a futile tattoo against the massive chest then fell to her sides.

With a cry Mord leapt across the triangle and seized the demon's arm. Foras shook him off with a brief flex of his bicep, sending him flying to the periphery of the circle. Then the demon released Sylvie. She slid limply to the ground, and lay still. Mord scrambled to her, gathered her in his arms, pushed himself back against the brick wall, away from the demon, cradling her head in his lap. She did not move for several seconds. He fumbled for her wrist, groping for a pulse, eyes frantically searching her still, white face. Then her eyelids fluttered. She stirred in his arms, and moaned faintly.

Sobbing with relief, Mord hugged her, then slid gentle hands over her face, her lips.

Her eyes focused on him, but a loud crack like thunder erupted just feet from them, and their eyes snapped back across the circle.

Foras had plunged a hand into the cauldron, and was pulling something through. A screech of rage shattered the air inside the circle. Foras was jerked forward. He set his jaw, planted his feet more firmly on either side of the cauldron, and began to haul with all his strength.

196

His hand began to emerge slowly from the wildly rocking cauldron, gripping a tangle of ocean-blue hair. More waves of hair began to spill over the sides of the cauldron, writhing like snakes. For a moment the demon seemed stymied, his face set in a hard grimace. He buried his other hand in the thick locks of hair and pulled until his breastplate creaked, stretched almost to the breaking point.

A long strand of ectoplasm spurted out of the cauldron. It resolved into the form of a woman, facing the demon in a fighter's crouch. She was clad only in a cat suit that gleamed like water on her pearly skin. With a banshee scream she launched herself at the gigantic warrior form, clawed fingers going for the eyes. Foras raised a forearm to deflect her. Then he punched her, full in the face.

She flew backward and bounced off the invisible wall of the circle. Almost too fast for the eye to follow, she somersaulted back and kicked high, aiming for the demon's face. He moved his head slightly, grabbed her foot and flipped her onto her back. She spun and went for his groin with stiffened fingers. The sword swept out and backed her off. Hissing, she crouched and circled. Mord and Sylvie flattened themselves against the wall as she crept past them, but she never took her eyes from Foras.

The demon kept his sword between him and the succubus. Nahemah spat and snarled. She slapped her hands together. A flaming ball appeared between them, and she flung it. Foras batted it back with his sword. His beautiful face was quiet, without expression. Nahemah screamed and leapt for the demon's throat. Her lips pulled back, revealing sharply pointed teeth. He swatted her aside. She knocked the cauldron as she fell, spilling some of its water. A faint cry emanated from within. Mord gasped, reached forward, and pulled it out of the way.

"Open the circle," roared Foras.

Sylvie's eyes flew wide. "Turn you loose on Frederick?" she gasped.

Foras did not look at her. His eyes were fixed on Nahemah as she slithered upright, hissing at him.

"Free me to defeat her, or perish in this enclosed space. Decide NOW!"

Mord did not hesitate. Cradling the cauldron with one arm, he reached for the athame lying on the ground, and cut a portal into the circle.

With a scream of triumph Nahemah leapt onto the roof of the building. A flash of lightning illuminated her against the sky. She grinned down at them. She spun and leapt across Market Street, disappearing over the roof of the Candy Kitchen, headed east. Foras swept out his sword and followed.

A roll of thunder cracked through the night. The streetlights flickered. Car brakes screamed. A group of teenagers fled past in the now pelting rain, something close behind them. Mord groped for the umbrella and held it over them as they huddled against the wall in the rain. He kept the cauldron with its remaining water close to his side. His eyes met Sylvie's.

"What now?" he whispered.

"I don't know," she replied. She pushed herself into a sitting position. "Uncharted territory for me too."

They both stared into the storm. "His invisibility will extend to her, I think," said Mord. "But beyond that it's anybody's guess what they're doing to the city."

The noise of car horns increased, interrupting the rolls of thunder. Shouts rang up and down Market Street.

"Come on," said Sylvie, and got up on shaky legs. "We've got to find out what's going on."

Mord took a moment to slide the cauldron under the backpack next to the wall, and followed her.

But before they could get further than the corner of Market Street, a violent wind stopped them in their tracks. Across the roofs of the city a struggling pair of great figures came into view. They leveled blows at each other, staggering, falling, rising again. The storm raged around them.

Foras reared high against the wind-wracked clouds, limned by lightning. He brought his sword down at Nahemah's head. She watched it descend. Her snaky locks writhed then leapt up, grappling with the sword. Foras held on grimly. Nahemah leveled a deadly kick at his groin, knocking him off balance. The tendrils wrenched the sword from his grip.

Nahemah shrieked in triumph. Lightning played up and down her straining cat suit. She gripped the sword, shimmied into the air, and drove it down toward Foras's throat with all her might.

He fell back before her, stumbling to one knee. He righted himself briefly, but the sword came down on his shoulder. Black blood spurted high. Foras fell onto Third Street, narrowly missing a bus.

Sylvie and Mord watched in horror. The demon lay dazed in the street. Nahemah screamed aloud and somersaulted off the roof, landing in a crouch in the street. She lifted the sword, licked it. She advanced on the great form lying huddled on the ground. The sword rose.

The blade flashed down. At the last possible instant, Foras rolled away. Sparks flew as the metal hit the rain-washed pavement. The demon staggered to his feet. He backed across Market, keeping his eyes on the succubus who stalked him like a jaguar.

Foras listed to and fro. He moved past the pair of mages, frozen on the corner. Back he went, under the eyes of the angel. Back into the doorway cut into the circle.

Nahemah followed him.

"What is he doing?" gasped Sylvie.

Mord's jaw dropped open.

"He's luring her," he whispered.

Foras fell to his knees. He raised an arm as if to protect his face. Nahemah leapt into the circle, swinging the sword back over her head. Foras's eyes flicked to Sylvie.

"Your ring," he said.

Without a single thought, Sylvie pulled the silver ring off her middle finger and flung it straight at him.

Foras gestured with his upraised arm.

The ring expanded, gaped. The descending sword was swallowed in its circle. Both sword and ring disappeared.

Nahemah blinked, but recovered. She leapt forward and grappled with Foras. They wrapped their arms around each other, a parody of passion. Foras got a hand under her chin and shoved her away from him.

Nahemah opened her jaws, unhinging them like a snake. She spat a gob of virulent green at Foras. It landed on his breastplate and began to sizzle, eating through the bronze. In a single movement he unfastened it and flung it aside. She screamed with joy and spat again, ejecting a ball of blue fire right at his heart. There was an explosion of light, then the smell of burning flesh. The demon roared. He sunk his fingers into his own chest, and ripped out the blue projectile, tearing away flesh with it. He flung the burning blue ball into Nahemah's snaky locks. She shrieked and began batting it into embers, as the smell of burning hair joined the meat stink in the circle. Fast as a snake she turned to the cauldron and slithered inside, causing a hiss of sulphuric steam.

The hole in the demon's chest gaped, ragged. His eyes narrowed. Then they flew wide.

The imp crawled out of his chest. It leapt through the air, landing on the lip of the cauldron. It disappeared inside.

For a long moment, the two humans and the demon stared at each other.

"What the fuck?" said Sylvie.

Foras shook his head. But before he could answer, the imp's rear end appeared at the rim of the cauldron. It backed out with agonizing slowness. Its head emerged, a hank of sizzling blue hair clamped in its jaws.

It dragged Nahemah out, a long string of matter that formed itself into the succubus as it emerged. In a matter of moments she was back in the circle, screaming and stinking.

As she scuttled on the ground, slapping out her burning hair, Foras leaned over her. He lifted a foot, and stepped on her.

~~~

She looked up, eyes wide, no longer beautiful. Her unhinged jaw sagged onto her chest. Terrible sounds emerged from it. Plasma began to extrude from her wide mouth. Her enormous breasts swelled even larger, then exploded into globules of wet fat. The noises began to fade.

Foras reached down and took her face between his hands. He began to knead. Her skull popped and deflated. The demon continued to pull her limp body into the wet ball of matter, working the inert flesh almost tenderly. Soon the succubus was an amorphous blob, becoming smaller and more dense as Foras pushed and squeezed.

As Mord and Sylvie stared, wide-eyed, Foras formed the ball into the figure of a pigeon. He held it up. It spread its wings wide.

"Nefarious!" it screamed. "Blasphemious!"

He reached up and placed it on the windowsill of the mural next to the angel. It flattened into the wall. It looked as if it had been there since the window was painted.

Foras stood back and cocked his head. "That should hold her. She might work her way free in a few hundred years, but even then she won't be able to make herself a nuisance, not for a very, very long time. Nothing you will have to concern yourselves with." He looked down at his tattered chest and scowled. His injured shoulder was dark and wet. "Physical bodies are so vulnerable. Not sure they're worth the bother."

Mord staggered to his feet. "What about Lars?"

~~~

Foras looked blank. Then he nodded.

"Oh, the mortal." He stepped over to the cauldron, now holding only a small puddle of water in the bottom, and peered within. He frowned. "I may have miscalculated. It's almost expired. Are you sure you still want it?"

Mord's hands clenched into fists.

"Fulfill the rest of your bargain, demon," said Sylvie.

Foras shrugged. "As you wish." He reached into the cauldron and began to pull.

An ankle formed itself first, gripped in the demon's hand. The rest of the body followed. In a moment a naked man lay within the circle, utterly inert.

Mord cried out and flung himself at the motionless form. Sylvie scrambled over to them, taking the limp wrist.

"He's got a pulse," she told Mord after a moment. "He's alive."

Mord's hands were running over the long blond hair of the man on the ground. He bent and kissed him tenderly on the mouth.

"Baby," he whispered. "Come back to me."

The man stirred. He whimpered, and opened his eyes. Mord began to weep.

The man's arms lifted slowly. His hands slid up Mord's back and held. For several moments they held each other, silent except for Mord's muffled sobs.

Finally Mord looked up. He wiped his face on his sleeve. He reached down and helped the other man to a sitting position, one arm encircling him. He smiled at Sylvie through his tears.

"Sylvie, meet Lars," he said.

Sylvie stared. Even without the unusual circumstances, Lars would have provoked staring. He was a small man, probably not much taller than her, with the lithe taut body of a dancer. His long hair was the color of the moonlight, even dirty and tangled, tumbling over his shoulders. His skin was mahogany with golden undertones. Vivid green eyes met Sylvie's. He smiled.

Haggard, filthy, near death with exhaustion, that smile still caused her breath to catch.

A crowd was gathering not fifty feet away on Market near a fender bender between a bus and a car. The sound distracted Sylvie from the scene before her. She ran a hand through her drenched hair and staggered to her feet.

Foras stood just outside the tattered circle, observing the aftermath of the storm dispassionately. The imp sat next to him, its tail coiled neatly around its feet. The hole in the demon's chest glistened.

Sylvie stepped beside him. They watched the crowd mill and sway. Sirens shrilled nearby.

"They're going to notice us soon," she said. "We need to end this. We both got what we wanted." She studied his profile. "Thank you, Foras."

He glanced down at her. "Did we? You got your mortal. I got battered. Stimulating, yes, but enough? Hm."

Her eyes narrowed. "What do you have in mind?"

He turned to her. His eyes were molten ruby. "To taste more of this corrupt, decaying, violent world. To submerge myself for a time in the carnal pleasures it offers. To wield my might in this realm, so different from my own."

He took a step toward her. His voice dropped an octave, became velvet. "I could share such things with you, little mage. Power and pleasure beyond your dreams."

He moved in closer. Sylvie retreated. The brick wall met her back. He loomed over her.

"Imagine seeing the hanging gardens of Ishtar's palace," he murmured, dark music. "Time itself is no barrier. We could explore Humbaba's cedar forest, and pluck jeweled fruit from the gardens beyond the mountain of the Twin Scorpions. Watch the fabled walls of Troy rise under the toiling hands of Poseidon, and ride the Horse to oversee their fall."

His voice fell to a whisper. "Dance with the maenads in long-forgotten rites, around apple-green fires on the plain of Nysos. Learn the ancient Mysteries of the true Bacchanal. Participate in the omphagos. Feel milk and honey spurt up from the earth under your feet." A hand slid up her arm. "I can give you all this and more. Be my apprentice. My paramour. My Lady."

His mouth was almost touching hers.

Sylvie's head swam. Her life, her job, her home and Work paled in the face of the visions unfurling before her. A fierce longing sparked deep within her, for power, for beauty, for mastery of time and space and the elements, to break free of the mundane cloying morass of dull mortality. Something in her struggled to soar.

"Sylvie!"

Mord stood a few paces away. Lars lay on the ground beyond him, his face turned toward them. Mord's eyes no longer jittered. They bore straight into Sylvie's. He held her athame, and its curved point was aimed at the hole in Foras's chest.

"Sylvie," he said, more quietly, but eyes and athame did not waver.

From behind him came Lars' voice, weak but steady. "Don't listen to him. Demons lie."

Foras straightened, but his gaze too never left Sylvie's face. "I lie, when it suits me. You have a rudimentary Truthsense, which I can enhance. What does it tell you?"

She searched herself. Her eyes met his. "You're not lying."

The red eyes flared with triumph.

"But you're not telling me all of the truth either," she continued. She pushed herself away from the wall, and took a step toward him. "I'm more maenad than mage, demon. And for a maenad, nothing is more important than freedom. To receive your gifts, I would have to become your thrall." She shook her head. "No."

The furry warmth drained from the demon's voice. "So. You would continue to dwell among cattle, serving cocktails and doing Tarot readings? I underestimated you."

She smiled a little. "Maybe."

She took another step forward. Foras took a step back.

"But sometimes I dance with demons."

She reached up and took him by the back of the neck, pulling him down to her. This time when their mouths met, it was she who pulled the energy into herself, drinking deep of the fires within. She did not break the contact until she brimmed with it.

Eyes blazing, she smiled into the demon's eyes. For the first time he looked disconcerted, just for a moment. Then he smiled back.

"You fascinate me, mortal girl. I've never met one like you." He glanced down at the imp, who was staring at Sylvie. "I find this servitor is more self-willed than I bargained for. It wants to stay with you. I'm inclined to let it. Will you accept it?"

The imp rose, stretched daintily and twined around Sylvie's ankles. She reached down to it, feeling warm fur for an instant before her fingers sank into nothingness. She smiled.

"Does it mean you get to spy on me?"

Foras shrugged. "Maybe, if I wish. Perhaps you could devise ways to foil me. It will, if nothing else, make your dull little life more interesting." He turned from her, surveyed the chaos on Market Street, and rolled his big shoulders back. "Regardless, I am going to stay here for a while. My own realms and provinces will recall me presently, but I'm enjoying this little vacation. I'd forgotten what a delicious fetid cesspool this world is. And what you spurn, girl, others may appreciate."

Mord advanced, wielding the curved athame. "O Foras, I banish—"

"Pffftttt," said the demon, and made a careless gesture. The athame clattered onto the sidewalk. "Don't bother me, boy."

He looked up at the angel, leaning on his windowsill above him. "I think my friend here will give me a perfect vantage from which to observe for a day, or perhaps a century. And I'll have the pleasure of tormenting my nemesis over there."

The pigeon's black eye sparked furiously, then went flat again.

Foras grinned at the trio of humans who gaped at him. "Yes. This will do nicely. Drop by and visit from time to time." He turned his gaze on Sylvie again. "If you change your mind, the summoning will be very easy the next time."

The great form wavered, turned to mist. It hovered in front of the 'Earthbound' angel for a moment, then disappeared inside the painting. The angel's eyes gleamed red, then returned to their calm painted gaze.

The pigeon's head shoved forward out of the wall and shrieked "Viscosity!" then went flat.

A woman ran toward them from the crowd by the bus. "Are you hurt?" she called out, angling toward Lars who was struggling to rise and cover his nakedness. "I'm a nurse!"

Mord went to meet her. "Thank you. We may need an ambulance."

In moments there was a crowd around Lars, who was sitting up wearing someone's raincoat. Mord looked around for Sylvie. She stood under the angel, the imp beside her, looking up at the impervious mural. When she felt Mord's eyes on her she blew him a kiss.

"Call me," she mouthed, and began to gather the ritual implements lying scattered on the sidewalk.

~~~

The sun was setting as Sylvie left Frederick Memorial Hospital the following day and began to walk toward her home, a few blocks south. The harried staff at the hospital had accepted unquestioningly that Lars had been just another victim of the freak storm on First Saturday. He had been treated for contusions, shock and exhaustion, given IV fluids, and was about to be released with instructions to rest for at least a week, instructions Mord vowed to see obeyed to the letter.

The imp materialized as she strolled down Bentz Street. It leapt lightly onto her backpack and rode, gazing out over her head, front paws amid the purple spikes of her hair. Sylvie couldn't feel it but she knew it was there. She smiled to herself.

She paused at Church Street. Part of her wanted to turn left, to walk to the mural. The imp sat motionless, waiting.

But she went straight, not to her apartment, but into the gathering shadows of Baker Park. As she crossed the creek the imp leapt from her head and peered under the bridge. A koi surfaced and submerged again. The water lilies breathed. A huddle of rats glanced at the imp and froze. One bared its long teeth. They all backed away, then ran.

As the imp caught up to Sylvie, shapes seeped from the walls and trees. The girl and the demon-thing slipped into the park and lost themselves in the dusk. A train of Others flowed in their wake.

CONTRIBUTOR NOTES

D. M. Domosea is a certified adult for eight hours of the day and a universe creator for the rest. She is working diligently to bring the stunning worlds and characters of her debut novel series to the masses. She lives in Maryland with her husband, youngest daughter, and the writer's required minimum of two cats. You can find her on the web at www.dmdomosea.com or follow her on Twitter @DMDomosea.

Dr. Dale A. Grove is a product developer by day and a writer by night. Possessing a vivid imagination, Dr. Grove has created a variety of stories, new products, and over ten U.S. patents when he has worked at Owens Corning, Johns Manville, LNP Engineering Plastics, Tekni-Plex, and US Silica. In his spare time, Dr. Grove has written five books in the science fiction genre: *Gray Maneuvers*, *Gray Extraction*, *ELIZA*, *Loose Strings*, and soon to be released *Outlier Revolutions*. His next novelette will be entitled *Furniture for Sale*, and it's the story of an elderly patron of an assisted living facility whose reality is not what it seems. For further information on these and other short stories check out http://www.newdrofscifi.com or go to Amazon.com or Goodreads.com and search for books by Dr. Dale A. Grove.

Tisdale Flannery is not a cat, but she loves to imagine the experience of anyone not herself, perhaps not human, perhaps not of this world – and then write it.

Amanda Linehan is a fiction writer, indie author, and INFP. She has published four novels and a couple handfuls of short stories. Her short fiction has been featured on Every Day Fiction and in the *Beach Life* anthology published by Cat & Mouse Press. She lives in Maryland, likes to be outside, and writes with her cat sleeping on the floor beside her desk. Check out more of her fiction at her website: amandalinehan.com.

A. Francis Raymond is a physicist/astronomer, software engineer, and long-time science fiction geek. Ray is inspired by many of the classic sci-fi authors, especially Isaac Asimov. She loves to write about robots and at least 75% of the unfinished pieces sitting on her hard drive have a robotic or android main character. She also likes statistics 93% of the time. Ray primarily writes "fantastical science fiction." That's fiction with some basis in science but meant to be thought experiments that result in fantasy rather than something she believes could really happen. Read more at afrancisraymond.com.

Charmaine Weston is an English professor, specializing in technical writing and academic research. In her free time, she explores her thoughts about sci-fi, fantasy, and romance for the speculative fiction journal *Luna Station Quarterly* or shares her fantasies in explicit detail. Most often, Charmaine's time is spent chasing her dogs and submitting to her cat overlords.

Edwin Stanfield has spent over ten years on active duty with the Air National Guard. This is his second published work.

J. J. Maxwell is a graduate of Emerson College in Boston with a degree in Professional Writing. He woke up one morning and realized that if he could produce just one good story, he might be able to deduct the tuition as a "business expense." The IRS did not agree nor found it funny. The IRS is like that. Nevertheless, he continues to write across multiple genres. When not writing, he enjoys working out, cooking, bad B-movies, eclectic music, and volunteering at the Frederick County Literacy Council.

James Allnutt is a farmer and writer in rural Maryland. This is his first published work.

Anna O'Keefe has been writing her whole life. Her first book titled, "Our Trip to the Zoo" was self published before it was cool to do so. It received three gold stars from her third grade teacher. Anna loves anything that makes her stop and think. She is currently working on short stories, poems, and finding a perfect latte.

Anna O'Brien is a writer and veterinarian living in Frederick, Maryland. She is a contributing editor for the magazine *Horse Illustrated* and managing blog editor for the speculative fiction journal *Luna Station Quarterly*. Her fiction has most recently appeared in *Cheap Pop*, *Cold Creek Review*, and *Blue Fifth Review*. She was a 2017 Pushcart nominee. She loves bicycles and dogs and bicycling dogs.

Suz Thackston absentmindedly turned a corner, walked through a mirror and found herself in a land of myth and magic. Please don't send help.

Kirby Evans [cover artist] is an accountant who lives in Frederick, Maryland. After accomplishing long sought-after career goals, he took up painting as a hobby. He is self-taught in this endeavor. In his spare time one will also find him enjoying other activities such as reading, watching television and movies, and attending trivia night at local venues.

Claudia Tisdale [chapter artist] is pursuing a degree in sociology and studio art at Hood College in Frederick. She loves the city of Frederick in all its brick and water particulars, she loves a good story, and she loves most of all the opportunity to set her imagination free with line and shadow.

The Frederick Writers' Salon is composed of a diverse group of novelists and short story writers, some who have been writing for decades and others who are just beginning their journey. We meet regularly to share and critique our work, to encourage one another, and to discuss all aspects of writing and publishing.

Made in the USA
Middletown, DE
02 September 2020

16667885R00116